BEFORE SHE FELL

NATALIE SAMMONS

To my boys

Susan Grey had been gone from the party for a while now, she needed to get back to her guests but she also needed to collect herself, and rest her throbbing feet. With her cocktail glass, half empty, carefully placed on the vanity table, Susan slumped into the chair beside it.

She wasn't sure what the hell had just happened but she knew without any shadow of a doubt that the consequences of this evening were going to ripple into every aspect of her life, like throwing a stone into a still pool. There would be no way to reverse what had been said, not that she wanted to, she realised with something that felt akin to relief.

No matter that it had been said off the cuff, she knew that her words were true, that they felt right. Only, before tonight she had been too afraid, too aware of the ramifications to acknowledge them, let alone say them.

Gently, she eased off her ridiculously high-heeled shoes and wiggled her toes. They had been in the sale, a bargain she couldn't possibly pass up, she had told herself when she'd purchased them a week ago specifically for tonight. She rarely wore heels these days and these ones were practically skyscrapers.

All of her family and friends, not to mention a few important acquaintances, had joined her in celebrating her fiftieth birthday. A milestone she felt too young to have reached already, although right now, at this very moment, she felt aged and tired, the weight of the evening pressing down on her shoulders.

She purposely sat up a little straighter.

In what she knew was an attempt to smother her mixed feelings about the day, Susan had decided to go all out, throwing a party to rival all parties, she'd even hired an events company to manage the whole affair.

Her only stipulation for the evening was that it was to be extravagant. And it certainly was. Her garden had been utterly transformed. A huge marquee bedecked in swathes of gold and white had taken centre stage, with a DJ booth at one end and an ostentatious cocktail bar at the other. In its centre was a large square dance floor illuminated with colour-changing lights.

The remaining space was occupied by tables and chairs draped in shimmering fabric and cleverly decorated with candles and crystals. Perhaps it was too much, perhaps she had gone overboard, but it was her birthday after all and it was her money, so why not?

A particularly loud laugh from outside drew a wry smile to Susan's lips. She hoped everyone was still having a good time, that their fun hadn't been dampened by the earlier episode, an episode which everyone had seemingly been aware of.

So far, the night had been something of a rollercoaster for her. It had all started so well before it had taken a turn for the worse.

Susan wasn't sure what to make of it all, the hateful words that had been thrown around, the secrets that had been spilt.

But then, perhaps now was not the time to try to unpick it, perhaps it was best to leave it until tomorrow, to sleep on it and to look at it again with fresh eyes.

Yes, that was what she would do. And besides, she had a garden full of guests she didn't want to disappoint.

Placing her still throbbing feet back on the carpeted floor, Susan leant forward to examine herself in the vanity table mirror. Her shoulder-length blonde hair had been pinned up by the hairdresser earlier in the day, and thankfully it still remained in place. Her make-up, however, hadn't fared as well.

A streak of black mascara was smeared under each eye from the angry tears she had shed. Licking her index finger, she expertly eliminated the smudges. If only it was that easy to do in life, she thought.

With a resolved shake of her head, Susan shoved away the remaining sadness, the annoyance, which still lingered. She didn't want the entire night to be completely soured by what happened earlier, it was still salvageable, she hoped.

Today, her birthday had become something of a turning point, a precipice for Susan. She had felt an increasing pressure as the day had neared. It was as though time itself was closing in on her, not just for her birthday but for her life. And she wasn't prepared to start her fiftieth year like this, sad and hurt.

Fifty was officially middle-aged, Susan thought. She could no longer pretend to be thirty, to ignore the signs of ageing which were unavoidably creeping up on her. She wasn't a slim size ten anymore. The menopause, which had reared its ugly head a couple of years ago, had added a good few inches to her waist and a good few pounds to the scales. The once cute laughter lines framing her eyes were now unattractively deep-set and she felt that they often made her look as though she were scowling. Then there were the grey hairs, hairs which appeared overnight and seemed to have a mind of their own, shooting up and out of her scalp as though they had been electrified, these she had to have professionally dyed blonde every six weeks.

It was the tightening rope of age that had led to Susan re-evaluating her life. And it was during this re-evaluation that Susan had decided she wanted a change, to do something spectacular, and tonight she was planning on making a big announcement, to tell everyone of her plans; she just hadn't found the right moment yet.

But she would. In fact, she was going to do it now, this very moment, that would certainly rejuvenate the party and distract the guests from the earlier hiccup.

With a renewed sense of purpose, Susan seized her glass and downed some of its contents.

Dutch courage, she told herself.

With a wince, she slid her feet back into her shoes and rose. Clasping her glass, she exited her bedroom.

At the top of the stairs, Susan paused. From the relative darkness inside the house, she had a perfect view of the party below through the arched floor-to-ceiling window. Several guests were clustered together outside the marquee, cigarettes in hand, whilst waiting staff dashed about with trays of canapés and empty glasses. Music, upbeat and loud, drifted up to greet her.

It was this window, Susan recalled, with its unhindered view across the garden and beyond that to the South Downs, along with its very grand central staircase, which had enticed Susan away from London. They had moved to the outskirts of Storrington, a West Sussex village almost five years ago now, and she had never looked back.

Not until tonight, that was. But it was no good living in the past.

She turned away from the window to descend the stairs.

Holding up the trailing skirt of her silver dress in one hand

and her glass in the other, a little of the orange cocktail remaining, Susan tentatively took the first step.

A quick yet even noise coming from somewhere behind her, one which was almost indiscernible over the din of the party, had Susan turning her head in curiosity.

The house had been declared as out of bounds for the guests, apart from the use of the kitchen and downstairs bathroom for the catering staff.

Perhaps it was him, perhaps there was more he wanted to say. She almost stopped herself from turning around, aware that nothing good would come from a further encounter this evening.

Only, before she could find any words to deter him, to delay whatever it was he wanted to add, she screamed as something firm and unyielding was thrust into her back.

She was knocked off balance.

Susan was falling.

Her hands flew out, unsuccessfully, in a desperate bid to find purchase.

The cocktail glass she had been holding moments ago hit the wooden stairs, shattering. The fragments cascaded to the ground like orange-coloured raindrops on a winter's day.

The skirt of Susan's dress caught and ripped on the heel of one of her ridiculously expensive shoes. The shoe became dislodged, abandoned on a higher step as she continued to fall.

Susan's full weight crashed down on her arm.

With a resounding snap, it broke.

Her scream of terror turned into one of agony.

Her ribs cracked as they hit the edge of a step.

Her ankle twisted as she fiercely tried to right herself, to no avail.

Her shouts of pain were drowned out by the lively music and loud conversation of the party outside.

Susan tumbled down each and every step of the sweeping grand staircase, her body ravaged by the unforgiving hardness of the stairs, until she eventually stopped at its base.

For the briefest of seconds Susan thought she saw a figure silhouetted in front of the large floor-to-ceiling window, before her head hit the flagstone floor.

Before everything went black.

2

GRACE

Detective Inspector Grace Roth was sat at her desk in the corner of the quiet room, half hidden behind a stack of papers.

She was diligently working her way through the case file in front of her, reviewing the phone records in a stalker case.

Grace, the newest recruit to Brighton's Criminal Investigations Department, had been promoted, much to her own astonishment, a few months early after a very rigorous interview process.

Only, before she could embrace her new role, a long dreamed of position, an internal investigation had been ordered, positioning her on desk duty. Despite that having been concluded two weeks previously, Grace had yet to find herself assigned her own case. Instead, she continued to support her colleagues as best she could from her desk chair.

Her confidence and perhaps even her reputation had been eroded before she'd had the opportunity to cement them in place.

She swallowed down the bad taste the experience had left

in her mouth and returned her attention back to the phone records.

Despite there being hundreds, if not thousands of calls, texts and other messages from the perpetrator to the victim, Grace wouldn't want to be so cocky as to presume that this was an open-and-shut case. After all, you never could tell. Occasionally an offender would get lucky, employing some clever-dick barrister with knowledge of a loophole to get the case thrown out, who didn't care that they were releasing a dangerous individual back into the world, only that they'd won. Or more disturbingly because of an error on the police department's part.

Something that Grace understood better than anyone.

Shit, Grace shook her head in the hope of dislodging her thoughts, *you're already beginning to form a twisted view of the system.*

'Roth, I'm doing a tea run, you want one?'

Grace looked up to find DI Harry Amberidge making the universal hand gesture for tea at her from across the other side of the office. With a half-smile, she gave a thumbs up.

Before Grace, Harry had been the newest recruit. And yet, he worked with such conviction, such confidence, that you could be forgiven for thinking he had been in the job much longer.

Grace suspected that some of it was bravado, he had even hinted as much when Grace had started, when she had been keen for all the advice and support on offer. Still, she wished that some of his self-belief, faked or otherwise, would rub off on her. Especially now.

She had started to worry over every minute detail, sometimes even waking in the middle of the night, concerned she'd forgotten to file some request or highlight some shred of information which could prove to be crucial to solving a case.

She'd tried to tell herself in those moments that she was being irrational, that she had done everything according to the book. But she had messed up once before, what was to stop it happening again?

'Strong with one sugar,' Harry said a few minutes later, placing a cup of tea in front of her.

She looked down at it; a white mug with the Everton football team's logo emblazoned on the side, then looked up at him, her eyebrows raised as if to say, '*Really?*'

Harry was a large man, easily measuring over six foot. He was well-groomed with a short beard and despite the suit he was wearing Grace knew that he had several tattoos covering his left arm. It was fair to say he didn't look like your typical copper.

Harry laughed out loud. 'You'll come to see that Everton are the only acceptable team to support. Brighton will be lucky if they even finish in the top half this year.'

'The men's team perhaps, but the women's team could end up finishing top of the league,' she corrected.

Grace delighted in the fact that she knew more about football than Harry. He pretended to be an avid fan but she knew he only really followed the sport to fit in. That didn't stop him from goading her though.

Grace, on the other hand, loved it, particularly the women's football. She was a season ticket holder and attended as many games as she could, off-duty permitting.

'The Chief wants to see you in her office,' Harry said before Grace had even sipped her tea. He was wiggling his eyebrows conspiratorially, before adding, 'I think she's got a case for you.'

The entire team were well aware of the investigation against Grace and the resulting outcome which identified that she wasn't at fault. Still, Harry was the only one she had openly talked to about it.

He understood her desire to put the past behind her, to wipe the slate clean, but the only way to do that, to demonstrate her worth in the team, was to lead her own case. Though for reasons unbeknownst to her, DCI Potter still hadn't pulled her from desk duty.

'Seriously?'

'Yep,' Harry responded, a hint of a smile pulling at the edge of his lips.

Grace stood and ran her fingers through her perpetually wavy brown hair, tucked a loose strand behind one ear and then straightened out her navy-blue suit. 'Wish me luck,' she said, moving out from behind her desk and striding purposefully towards the corridor.

'Good luck,' Harry called from behind her.

Grace couldn't help it, but her heart began hammering with anticipation as she strode to the DCI's door at the far end of the building. Yet, her prevailing thought was one of scepticism. She could have been summoned for any number of reasons.

With a firm knock, Grace waited to be admitted.

After a moment, DCI Potter's distinct voice called out, 'Enter.'

Grace squared her shoulders before pushing through the door. 'You wanted to see me, ma'am?'

DCI Potter was sitting behind her large desk, files and paperwork spread out before her. Clearly that didn't change the higher up you got, Grace thought to herself, thinking of her own desk.

'Yes, take a seat. I'll just be a moment,' she responded, indicating the empty chair in front of her desk, before averting her gaze back to her laptop.

Grace sat down.

Covertly, she eyed her superior whilst she waited. DCI Kate Potter was in her mid-to late-fifties, Grace knew, but she could probably pass for late forties. She was athletic-looking, with soft features and kind eyes. Her hair, currently pulled back in a neat bun, was fashionably grey. Grace knew that Kate had worked her arse off to get to where she was, fighting not only the stiff opposition but also the doubters who still believed this role was a man's role.

Despite not having been in the team for very long, Grace had come to understand that Kate was well-respected and well-liked. However, Grace was reserving judgement, her only real experience of the DCI's authority not having been overly positive thus far. But then that wasn't either of their doing.

'Right, sorry about that,' DCI Potter offered, turning her attention back to Grace. Linking her fingers, she rested her hands on top of the desk. 'How are you?'

Caught off guard by the question, Grace took a second to respond. 'Good, thank you, ma'am. Keen to get out from behind my desk,' she said honestly.

'I thought that may be the case.' She smiled lightly. 'I have a bit of an unusual case that could do with some attention...'

Grace knew there was more to come so waited for the DCI to finish.

'It's an attempted murder. Possibly. We got an anonymous tip-off. The victim, a woman, is currently in the county hospital with a skull fracture and brain bleed. Could end up a murder investigation.' Potter dug around the files on her desk. Finding the one she wanted, she pushed it across the desk to Grace who was attempting to school her features into neutrality despite her building excitement.

Grace took it and flipped the cover open. She scanned the sparse report sheet. 'There isn't a lot to go on,' she mumbled, more to herself than to DCI Potter.

'No. Unfortunately the scene was never deemed a crime scene so no evidence was collected.' Potter left the implication lingering between them. Grace didn't need to be a genius to understand.

Was this some sort of test? A clueless crime Grace had to solve to redeem her reputation, a reputation which had been marred by someone else's actions, actions which seemed to cling to her like a shadow she couldn't shake.

Fine. I'll take the bait and I'll rise to the challenge.

She knew she didn't need to remind the DCI that she had been cleared of any wrongdoing, so instead Grace said, 'I am only interested in doing honest police work. If there is any evidence to find, I'll find it, and if not, I'll use all our other resources to put together an ironclad case.'

'If you're not ready though...' DCI Potter said.

She wasn't being patronising, Grace realised. Still, she couldn't help the tartness of her reply. 'Of course I'm ready. I can handle this.'

'I don't expect you to manage this on your own.' Potter thankfully stopped short of saying *'There is no i in team'*, instead, she riffled through a few pieces of paper on her desk. Locating the one she wanted, her eyes skimmed over the handwritten notes before she added, 'DI Amberidge has almost wrapped up his investigation, he can support you. You'll just need to keep him in the loop until then. And DS Cartwright can assist.'

'Yes, ma'am.' Grace's calm composure was undermined by the slight quiver of excitement in her voice. She finally had her first case.

Leaving DCI Potter's office with the case file in her hand, Grace strode purposely back to the office. As she entered she could feel Harry's gaze on her. She met his stare.

His eyebrows were raised in a silent question.

She lifted the case file up; his eyes drifted from her to it. He smiled.

And Grace smiled in return.

She was going to solve this crime, she was going to prove to all of them that she deserved to be in this team, that she could do it and finally shake off that fucking dark shadow lurking over her head.

3

—————

MARTIN

Martin Grey stepped into the small, cluttered room which had become all too familiar over the course of the last few days. His gaze drifted across the numerous pieces of equipment; ventilator, pumps and monitors, tubes and wires, noting that nothing new appeared to have been added and similarly nothing had been removed, before he took a seat in the worn leather high-back chair beside Susan.

Susan was in an induced coma, an attempt, he had been informed by the hospital staff, to protect her brain whilst she recovered from surgery.

She had a significant skull fracture and a brain bleed, along with three broken ribs, a broken arm and a fractured ankle. Not to mention an array of nasty bruises and cuts.

One of the doctors, Martin couldn't remember exactly who now, those early hours and days had all blurred into one, had gone so far as to suggest that Susan was lucky to be alive. Had she been found any later, had the ambulance not arrived so promptly...

It had been a member of the catering company, a young girl sneaking off to call her boyfriend, who had practically stumbled over Susan's unconscious body at the foot of the stairs.

No one claimed to have seen or heard anything. No one knew what had happened. But her shoe, one of those fucking expensive ones, had been found on a higher step. Everyone had made the same assumption: she had tripped.

Martin sat rigidly, with his weathered hands gripping the armrests of the chair. He hated hospitals. No, it was more intense than that, he absolutely loathed them.

They were full of sick people, of dying people, of germs and infections. He detested coming here, abhorred walking past the hordes of ill people, the patients who might infect him with their illnesses.

He refused to touch anything, instead kicking open doors with his foot and pressing the lift button with his elbow. To help him get over the hospital threshold, Martin had found that a shot of whisky or brandy or even vodka helped. And for that exact purpose he had a small hip flask tucked safely in his jacket pocket.

He resisted the increasing urge to swig from it now, aware that someone might see him. Martin knew he was consuming copious amounts of alcohol to help him function, because without it, well, he would surely fall apart.

At least Susan was in her own room, he reassured himself frequently. He wasn't sure he could have visited her if she was on a ward, surrounded by other dying people. *Was that what was happening to Susan? Was she dying?*

He shook his head to dispel the bleak truth.

Martin had come to feel as though he was in a tank, a terrarium to be more specific. One wall was half glass, looking out, or more precisely, looking in from the nurses' station. It was like being on display, with nowhere to hide from prying eyes and overly sympathetic smiles.

But as Susan's husband, Martin knew that he was expected to keep everyone updated, to offer glimmers of hope to her family and friends in what was an otherwise dire situation. He knew it would appear peculiar if he didn't visit daily, and so he had to continue visiting, to fulfil that role, to portray the dutiful husband.

Martin looked at his wife.

Her face was slack, giving the impression of sleep but it was her lips which Martin focused on, which he found most distracting. They were pulled awkwardly, uncomfortably, to one side against the unforgiving plastic of the breathing tube. They looked dry and chapped. For a moment, his grip on the chair eased. Fleetingly, he considered leaning forward, dipping his finger into the untouched water on the table beside him and wetting her lips with it. But he didn't, afraid he might somehow dislodge the tube or a random wire. Besides, he thought solemnly, touching her lips felt like an intimate gesture, one which he wasn't sure Susan would approve of. He refastened his grip on the chair. The solid wood of the armrests keeping him grounded. At least for the moment.

His gaze drifted to Susan's hair, or at least the few strands visible around the extensive bandages encompassing her head. It was matted and tinted red in places. Blood, Martin realised with a shudder.

This didn't look like his wife. This wasn't his wife.

He leant back in the chair, pressed his back against the firm leather, taking slow and steady breaths. *Just another thirty minutes,* he reassured himself, *and then you can leave.*

Martin was considering whether to stop by the pub, or whether to pick up a bottle of whisky to take home, to drink in solitude. He knew he drank too much; he had been drinking too much for months now, and this incident, this accident, had only compounded that need in him. Subconsciously, his hand found its way to his jacket pocket, he tapped against the small silver bottle stowed there.

Of course, he had been drinking the night of Susan's fall, it was fair to say that he had been drunk before the evening had commenced, much to Susan's annoyance.

His jaw tightened at the memory of the party, the completely over-the-top and unnecessary party. Susan hadn't consulted him on it, hadn't asked him about it. She had simply announced that it was happening and that he could attend if he wanted. 'If you want to,' had been her exact words. They hadn't been said with malice, she hadn't thrown them at him in some argument, but it wasn't an invitation. She had just offered it up in passing as though she didn't care either way.

It was no wonder he'd been pissed so early that day. He'd been made to feel like an outsider in his own home. There had been caterers, waiters, the marquee company. Martin had watched as they took over his home, his garden, each one of them striding around with such purpose as he drifted, fluttering from room to room, feeling increasingly displaced, increasingly unwanted.

'Mr Grey?'

Martin blinked away the memories and looked towards the door expecting to find one of the nurses. They often came in, wanting to check Susan's observations, or to change one of the many infusions or drips.

He hadn't expected to find a serious-looking young woman in a navy suit hovering at the threshold.

'Yes?'

'I am Detective Inspector Roth,' she said, holding up her badge.

4

———

GRACE

DI Roth had made the snap decision to attend the hospital on her way home. She felt that she had gotten to grips with the investigation details and following a discussion with Andy Rivers, the attending officer following the fall, Grace was now more than certain there was a case to be built.

She had managed to track Andy down only an hour earlier, finding him in the staff room, a coffee in one hand and a car magazine in the other. He was about to commence a night shift.

She had slid casually into the seat next to him, laying the case file on the table.

Grace had worked with Andy for a time during her own police training. He had been patient and enthusiastic and thorough. All the elements of a great teacher.

He was one of those individuals, however, who clearly loved what he did and therefore held no desire to do anything else, to get his foot further up on the career ladder, despite Grace's encouragement at the time.

'DI Grace Roth,' he'd said, a smile on his lips. 'To what do I owe the pleasure?'

Grace had skimmed over the initial pleasantries before indicating the file with a slight tilt of her head.

He raised his eyebrow a fraction, letting Grace know that his interest was piqued, before laying down his magazine.

Flipping open the file's cover, Grace had watched as Andy scanned the initial page.

Interestingly, he hadn't seemed at all surprised to be faced with it again, in fact, Grace was sure he had nodded. It was the slightest movement, barely noticeable, the sort of nod that said, *'Yep, I knew this one would pop up again.'*

'Tell me your thoughts,' Grace had asked then without giving anything away. She hadn't wanted to influence Andy's recall in any way, hadn't wanted to affect what he believed was pertinent.

Andy had paused for a moment, perhaps to consider how best to answer, before he said, 'The whole scene felt like an act, like I'd stepped into the middle of a performance.' He'd wrinkled his nose slightly as though he suspected he wasn't making much sense. 'Although everyone was upset, I got the impression that for a few, it wasn't real. That they were just playing along.'

Grace nodded. Andy's intuition had told him that something was amiss and for Grace that held a lot of weight.

She'd asked him if he could be more specific though, to which he'd replied, 'I'm not the least bit surprised to see this file again, or that you obviously have some intel which is investigation-worthy. Her fall, Susan Grey's, looked like an accident but when I left that house, I said to myself, "If that woman fell, it was because someone pushed her". But it was just a feeling, there was no evidence to indicate a guilty party.'

Grace had offered Andy a smile, satisfied and perhaps reassured that this was definitely a case worth delving into.

Grace silently took in the scene before her, allowing the weight, the importance of her role, to settle over her. Opposite the door was Susan Grey, her motionless body hidden beneath a taut white sheet, leaving only her shoulders, arms and head visible. Bandages encircled the crown of her head whilst her face was largely obscured by the breathing tube taped securely into place.

Grace's heartbeat quickened at the sight, at the intrusive and inappropriate memories which unexpectedly attempted to force their way into her mind. She pushed them out.

It was clear to see that this woman, engulfed by endless machines, was in a critical condition. At first glance Mrs Grey looked as though she might very well be dead already, it was only the rhythmic rise and fall of her chest which suggested otherwise.

Having spent more than her fair share of time in hospitals, Grace typically found them to be a comforting place, one that offered people hope and relief, even if for just a few hours or a few days. Yet there was little about this room, this situation, which allowed for even a modicum of hope to blossom.

To Susan's left, was a man. Grace regarded him for a moment, his posture rigid and his knuckles white from the grip he held on the chair. He was staring, unblinking, at something that Grace couldn't see. Obviously consumed by his own thoughts.

Grace presumed that this must be Susan's husband, Martin.

Martin was a slight man both in size and stature with thinning grey hair, a long pointy nose and red cheeks. He wore glasses which, at that precise moment, worked to amplify the dark circles framing his eyes.

Understandably, Mr Grey appeared dishevelled. His navy

shirt, visible beneath his jacket, was noticeably wrinkled, as though he hadn't bothered to change out of it before going to bed last night. His jeans looked as though they were in need of a wash and his hair, which was presently sticking out in all directions, needed a good brush.

With an inhale, Grace took a small step forward, moving into the confines of the room.

'Mr Grey?'

It took a moment for him to acknowledge Grace, but his expression when he did was one of confusion.

'Yes?'

Grace made a brief introduction, flashing her badge in his direction. As she did, she didn't fail to notice the flickering of fear which crossed Mr Grey's expression before it was gone, replaced with a look of unease or was it simply tiredness?

Without awaiting a response she proceeded into the room, coming to stand on the opposite side of the bed, of Susan. She tucked her badge back into her pocket.

Grace knew she'd need to handle this situation sensitively, the victim was, after all, still alive, but were that to no longer be the case, were Susan Grey's injuries too extreme to recover from, then she would have a murder investigation on her hands. And a murderer. So she still needed answers.

'What is this about?' Martin asked, uncertainty dancing in his voice. He began to rise.

'Please, don't get up.' Grace smiled, holding out her hands as though it would keep him in place. It didn't. 'I wanted to talk to you about your wife's accident.'

Grace watched Martin intently as she spoke, looking for any signs of guilt, or even understanding, but what she got was something that looked like suspicion. His eyes narrowed and his thin lips pulled tightly together. *Unusual, but not enough to make him a suspect. Yet.*

'What about it?'

'I have reason to believe that your wife may not have fallen.'

His gaze automatically dropped to Susan, as though he needed to confirm she was in fact still in the bed beside him, that she had suffered a significant injury. 'I don't understand what you mean.'

'Mr Grey, can you think of any reason why someone would want to harm your wife?' Grace was purposefully holding her cards close to her chest. If she revealed there had been a tip-off and more specifically an anonymous tip-off, Mr Grey and all those who could prove to be pertinent to the case, people Mr Grey associated with, would likely write this off as a hoax. They would claim that it was someone making trouble and not take it seriously or give a second thought to something that was said; it could also stop them from coming forward with information that might prove to be vital. Better to allow him to believe that Grace had more to go on. At least for now.

'You can't be serious?' He laughed without humour. When Grace didn't respond, didn't revoke her question, Martin frowned before slumping back in his chair. In what appeared to be a subconscious tic, he ran the palms of his hands over his knees. The gesture made him appear nervous. *What does he have to be nervous about, I wonder?*

'Mr Grey?' Detective Roth pressed. She was trying not to be alarmist at this point, but unless she figured out who was responsible, an individual capable of attempting murder was on the loose, free to strike again.

'No. No, of course not,' he insisted, shaking his head at the same time, yet his voice lacked the sort of conviction Grace had expected to hear. There was something he wasn't saying, Grace was positive.

'Are you sure? Has she had a dispute or a grievance with anyone, any issues at work or at home?'

Martin didn't miss the implication.

His eyes widened, his face became hard and his tone defensive. 'What is this? What is happening here? Am *I* under suspicion?'

'No,' Grace replied, she didn't need to add the '*not yet*', her tone suggested as much. 'I am simply trying to establish if anyone had a reason or motive to harm your wife.'

Before he could respond, a middle-aged nurse in a tunic rapped on the already open door. 'I need to check Mrs Grey's observation,' she said unapologetically before she entered the room.

Detective Roth and Mr Grey lapsed into an awkward silence, punctuated only by the measured beeps of a machine and the scratching of the nurse's pen on paper.

When she finally left, Grace cleared her throat before continuing with her questioning. 'Can you talk me through the night of the fall? What do you remember?'

Martin's brow crinkled as he said, 'Not much really, everything's been a blur since it happened.'

Grace nodded in understanding. She really did understand, not that she was about to share that with Martin Grey. Instead, she shut off her emotions, boxed them up and buried them in the back of her mind, preferring to remain professional, detached.

Despite her empathy, Grace still needed more to go on. 'There was a party, wasn't there?' she nudged, hoping to give Martin a starting point.

'Yes.' Grace watched as he closed his eyes. Was he attempting to recall the memory, to visualise that party? She waited patiently. 'It was Susan's fiftieth,' he eventually offered. 'She arranged the whole thing herself, a garden party with a giant marquee, a buffet and cocktails. She'd invited the entire world and his wife. There must have been over a hundred guests.'

It wasn't unusual to organise your own birthday party, but something was off in the way Martin said it, an unhappiness or perhaps even annoyance leaking in. Had he not approved? Despite a growing list of questions forming in her mind Grace chose not to interrupt. She wanted Martin to talk, to feel comfortable talking to her before she scrutinised and unpicked his memory.

'I think she was trying to impress everyone.' He smiled dryly. 'God knows how much it cost, but when Susan decides she's going to do something, she always does it. Cost be damned.'

'What time did the party begin?'

After only a moment's pause, Martin said, 'People started arriving about half past six.'

Grace jotted it down. Her records showed that the 999 call had been made at 21.28pm. *The evening had barely gotten underway.*

One of the machines surrounding Susan beeped then. Both Detective Roth and Mr Grey stared at it, waiting for another sound. When it didn't arrive, Grace proceeded. 'Can you tell me about Susan's movements? Who did she talk to, that sort of thing?'

'She talked to everyone,' he responded, sounding exasperated. 'It was her night and she was playing hostess. I'm not sure there was anyone she didn't talk to.'

Grace could feel her frustration bubbling. Although Mr Grey appeared to be cooperating, his responses were vague at best. Grace couldn't help but be suspicious. *Was he purposely being evasive? Was he trying to hide something through being equivocal?* Grace knew she was going to have to push a little harder, or this case, if there even was one to build, would fall apart.

'I see. I am going to need a list of all the guests that you can remember.' Before Martin could object she continued. 'Can you tell me about *your* movements between six thirty and nine thirty that night?'

Grace watched as Martin's jaw tightened and his nostrils flared.

There it was again, that defensiveness. *What was he hiding?* Everyone had secrets, things that they would rather not admit but here it was precisely Grace's job to work out what that was and if it had anything to do with Susan's fall.

'I spent the majority of the night propping up the bar.' He gave an almost cocky smile, one which didn't suit him.

So that was going to be his alibi. Grace made a note of it, but she also didn't miss his choice of words. 'So when you weren't propping up the bar, where were you?'

'What?' Martin asked, taken aback.

Grace looked down at her notepad. 'You just said that you spent the majority of the night by the bar, that would suggest that there were times when you were somewhere else?'

Mr Grey audibly swallowed, then he waved his hand dismissively. 'I just had a business meeting. It didn't take very long.'

'And where did that take place?'

'In the house,' Martin identified, and guessing Grace would want more information, he added, 'In my study.'

'Who did you have a meeting with?' she pressed.

'Joshua Maddison.'

Grace nodded, writing the name down. 'What time did the meeting take place?'

Mr Grey's eyebrows pull together. *He is either trying to remember or trying to find another way to be vague.*

'He was a guest at the party so I can't be exact but at a guess I would say eight thirty, perhaps nine o'clock.'

Potentially right before Susan's fall.

Call it a hunch or a gut instinct but Grace couldn't shake the feeling that Mr Grey was definitely hiding something. He wasn't being forthcoming at all.

'I see. How long do you think this business meeting lasted for?'

'No longer than thirty minutes, forty at most.'

So Mr Grey, by his own admission, was in the house only minutes before Susan fell. Is that a coincidence? And who holds a business meeting at a party?

Unsatisfied, Grace pressed for more information. 'What was your meeting about?'

Martin frowned. 'Why is that of any importance?'

Grace inhaled deeply. 'You informed me that you spent most of the party at the bar, I was simply curious as to the nature of the meeting. If it was one which might have required you to have a clear head?'

Martin offered a tight smile. 'It wasn't anything formal,' he responded, 'I was simply giving Joshua some sound advice.'

'I see,' Grace said, then added, 'I am going to need his details, so he can corroborate your story.'

'Of course,' Martin Grey replied, his hands now buried inside his jacket pockets.

5

JENNIFER

Jennifer, elbows propped on the counter and chin cupped in her hands, stared out of the storefront. She was distracted. Understandably so. There were so many things up in the air, hanging in the balance, that Jennifer didn't know what she should be doing, and had found herself doing nothing.

She hadn't been to visit Susan. Jennifer couldn't face seeing her younger sister. She knew she should, knew she was being a coward, but she also knew that someone needed to keep the business going. So that was what she'd done. She had opened the shop promptly every day since the fall and manned the fort. Susan would have wanted her to do this, Jennifer had repeatedly told herself.

She was adept at burying her head in the sand; she was doing it now. Rather than visiting her sister, she repeated the same pathetic excuse over and over and instead relied on sporadic calls to the unit for updates.

The small bell above the door chimed delicately, announcing the arrival of a customer. A couple, perhaps in their early thirties, entered, dragging Jennifer from her reverie.

Jennifer straightened and fixed her features into a friendly smile. 'Good morning,' she offered casually without making eye contact.

The shop, Grey's Books, was Susan's business, but it had always been Jennifer's dream. A dream Susan had seized in the wake of her relocation, her financial fortune allowing it to come to fruition.

Susan had thrown a substantial amount of money at the project, purchasing a large premises on the high street and bedecking the interior with modern fittings, creating a light and airy shop. Admittedly it worked, it was inviting and fresh, but it wasn't how Jennifer would have done it, it wasn't how she had always imagined it. Jennifer would have adopted a more traditional approach, opting for dark wood shelves, worn leather chairs, and secluded nooks to hide in with a good book. But Susan hadn't asked for her opinion, hadn't included her in the decision making.

Still, the shop had been well-received in the village and business had been consistent to say the least.

The couple had separated. Perhaps not sure what he was looking for, the man browsed the new releases which were displayed at the front of the shop, whilst his partner had wandered off with more purpose towards the back of the store, towards the fiction and romance sections.

Jennifer smiled lightly to herself. That was where she would also be found in a bookshop, in the romance section. Her smile faltered then.

Jennifer's life had been devoid of romance, of companionship, which was perhaps the reason she chose to submerge herself in stories, to fill the hole that would have otherwise remained empty. She knew she had never put herself out there, not in any meaningful way. She was afraid of getting hurt, of being rejected.

A memory, cruel and humiliating, jumped into her mind.

Her cheeks flared red before she quickly dispelled it. No, she didn't want to think about that again, didn't want to relive that moment, to acknowledge that it had ever happened.

In an attempt to keep herself busy, Jennifer turned to the laptop positioned behind her and hit the refresh button. One new sale. Jennifer jotted down the title.

She had been the one to suggest the website, or at least to recognise the online potential for selling more books. That was another idea that Susan had taken, employing a web designer and social media team to set it all up. Jennifer had offered to do it, had wanted to do it but...

Someone behind Jennifer cleared their throat, purposefully. Looking over her shoulder she found the couple, standing shoulder to shoulder, staring back at her.

'Did you find what you were looking for?' Jennifer asked customarily as she took the books they had placed on the counter.

'Yes. Thank you.' It was the woman who responded. She was attractive, Jennifer decided, surreptitiously taking her in. She was petite, with a full face and wide brown eyes, and dressed casually in jeans and a fitted top that showed off her svelte frame. The man beside her, who was absorbed in his phone, was handsome, his dark hair lightly peppered with its first few grey hairs, his nose straight and his shoulders broad. He looked as though he could have just stepped out of one of Jennifer's romance novels.

'Cash or card?' Jennifer asked, scanning both books before placing them into a paper bag.

'Card.' It was the man. He'd responded without bothering to lift his gaze from his phone. His hand, with a card poised in his fingers, was simply extended, waiting to be presented to the appropriate machine.

Annoyance bubbled below Jennifer's skin, but she didn't

react, didn't let it show. She was an expert at smothering her emotions. Wordlessly she pushed the card reader in his direction but ensured that it was just a fraction out of his reach. It was the least she could do, she thought aggressively.

Unaware of Jennifer's slight, he tapped the square of plastic against it before pocketing the card.

People can be so oblivious, so self-absorbed. At least that was what she told herself to help quell the constant anger that simmered within her, to stop the words of fury which frequently threatened to burst out of her.

With the receipt printed, the woman picked up the bag, offered a brief smile and turned, her partner following.

Jennifer knew that she would be instantly forgotten about. She was, after all, unremarkable.

Catching a glimpse of her reflection in the glass pane of the door, she frowned.

Jennifer was overweight; she had always been overweight and it had only got worse as she had got older. But what did she expect, she didn't enjoy exercising nor did she have the determination to diet. Still, it didn't mean she was happy about it. She had never been one to embrace her size, instead, she had learnt to hide it as best she could, opting to wear oversized jumpers and dresses. Although she rarely wore dresses these days, too self-conscious about her arms, her calves, about drawing attention to herself.

Jennifer moved out from behind the counter, piece of paper in hand. She headed to the biography section and with fingers tracing lightly over the spines, she quickly located the book which had been ordered.

With it tucked securely under her arm, she retraced her steps back to the front of the store, only to be interrupted by the chiming of the door once more.

Glancing up, Jennifer halted. The woman who now stood in

the entrance wore a serious expression, one so grave it sent a shiver shooting down her spine.

'Can I help you?' she questioned cautiously.

'I am looking for Miss Russell?'

'That's me,' Jennifer confirmed nervously, moving back behind the counter. She felt safe there, as though the wooden structure might provide her with some protection, or at least some distance.

The woman, who was tall, perhaps five foot eight or nine, pushed the door closed behind her and moved towards the counter. Her hair was pulled back in a ponytail and her dark, fitted suit made her look severe, dangerous even. Jennifer found herself taking a small step backwards. The emptiness of the shop suddenly became deafening as Jennifer realised they were alone.

'Miss Russell, I am Detective Inspector Roth, do you have somewhere we can talk in private?'

The cold fear which had already been wrapping itself around Jennifer's insides, now grabbed hold with an iron fist. Her mind whirled uncontrollably. What was this about? Was she in trouble? What did this woman, this detective, want with *her*?

Jennifer couldn't restrain the panic which was rising to the surface. She had never been in trouble before, had never even had a parking ticket.

'Um...' Jennifer looked at the detective and then around the store. She didn't know what to say, didn't know how to act, she was suddenly acutely aware of every facial expression she made, every slight movement of her hands. Was the detective also aware?

Jennifer's instincts told her that she didn't want to move to the office, to be confined in an even smaller space with

Detective Inspector Roth. 'I'm the only one working today,' she muttered, as if that answered the question.

'All right,' the detective replied, her voice firm, unyielding. 'An allegation has been made regarding your sister's fall. Do you happen to know anything about that?'

6

GRACE

When the shop assistant had confirmed she was Susan's sister, Jennifer Russell, Grace had been surprised but she'd hidden it well.

It was hard to find a resemblance between the two. From Susan's social media account, Grace had put together a profile of the victim, of a lively, bubbly, attractive woman who was clearly attempting to squeeze the most out of her life. In comparison, the woman standing before Grace now looked as though she had given up on living, as if she was doing her utmost to fade into the background, swamped in drab, ill-fitting clothes, her hairstyle outdated and in need of a colour. Then there was her expression. Despite the expected concern which went with having a detective show up at your place of work, this woman looked as though she rarely smiled, rarely laughed. She looked utterly unhappy.

Detective Roth didn't like having private, personal conversations in public spaces, but she could see from Jennifer's eyes, from the fear shining there, that this was what needed to happen.

Despite the stillness of the shop, Grace cast a sweeping

glance around. Empty. Even so, she stepped right up to the counter, so she could talk quietly. You could never be too careful, for all Grace knew a customer was secreted in a corner, or hiding behind some shelving that she hadn't noticed.

'Have you spoken with Mr Grey recently?' Grace pressed at Jennifer's fervent denial to her previous question. She needed to know what she was up against. If Jennifer had already got wind of the allegation, if Martin had suggested that she disregard it as nonsense, Grace would have some work to do to convince her otherwise.

'No, I haven't,' Jennifer responded with a note of defiance, the fear in her expression abating.

That struck Grace as very odd. Surely you would want to be kept updated, wouldn't you? Talking daily to find out how your sibling was, if there was any improvement or even deterioration?

Detective Roth audibly inhaled, then said, 'We received a report claiming that your sister's fall was not an accident.'

Jennifer's eyes widened in what might have been surprise. 'Well, that is,' she paused as though searching for the right word, 'preposterous,' Miss Russell finally scoffed. 'And what, did Martin suggest it was me, that I had something to do with it?' Anger permeated Jennifer's voice now and Grace could see that her hands had balled into fists.

Without missing a beat, Grace asked, 'Did you?'

Jennifer blustered, her cheeks reddening as she blew out her breath, her denial loud and aggressive. 'Of course not. Why would I do that? She's my sister. If it was going to be anyone it would be Martin himself, or Christopher.'

It was as if saying the names had pulled Jennifer out of her rant, the realisation of her accusations sinking in. She looked as though she wanted to physically slap a hand over her own mouth to keep any more words from flying out. 'I didn't mean that, I'm not actually blaming them. Sorry.' She shook her head for emphasis. 'I think I must be in shock or something. I need to sit down.'

Jennifer pulled out a stool which was tucked into the counter corner and perched on it, allowing Grace to quickly pull out her notebook. She turned to a fresh page and jotted down a couple of thoughts, not wanting to overlook anything. There was so much to unpick in what Jennifer had said that Grace wasn't sure which avenue of questions to follow first.

'That's all right, I imagine this has been a very stressful time for you,' she offered, keen to keep Jennifer talking.

Jennifer nodded, her shoulders which had been hunched, visibly relaxed.

'Yes it has. I've had to keep the shop open, fulfil all the orders, buy in new stock, sort out the staff rota. It hasn't exactly been easy.' Then almost as an afterthought, she added, 'Not that I mind, of course.'

The normalcy of this woman's problems struck Grace as peculiar. Her sister was hanging on to her life by a thread and she was talking about staffing and sales.

Everyone dealt with grief and trauma in different ways, Grace understood, keen not to become too blinkered.

'Mr Grey provided a list of guests, I don't recall seeing a Christopher listed.' Detective Roth left the sentence unfinished, the question unasked, hoping Jennifer would pick up on it, that she would start to cooperate.

'Christopher Maddison, Susan's ex-husband,' she confirmed.

'Why do you suppose he wasn't on the list?' Grace was attempting to be clever, knowing that Miss Russell would likely clam up if Grace asked her why she suspected either of these men. But asking probing questions, ones which would gradually reveal the truth often seemed easier to answer, easier to accept. They came with less guilt.

'Martin and Christopher have never gotten on. I guess Martin just didn't want to accept that Christopher was there. That Susan had invited him.'

'I see.'

A thought, a memory danced in Grace's periphery, something she had been told or something that she had read. Then, before she had even had time to realise she was asking another question, she said, 'Maddison, any relation to Joshua Maddison?'

'Joshua is Susan and Christopher's son,' Jennifer confirmed.

Interesting. Why didn't Martin tell me that?

'Mr Grey and Joshua, do they work together?'

Jennifer practically snorted. 'Those two working together, I think they would both say when hell freezes over. They don't get on, they've never gotten on really. Besides, Martin hasn't worked for years, not since his redundancy.'

Grace struggled to maintain a neutral expression. *Mr Grey wasn't exactly being transparent then. Why were they meeting if not to talk about business and why lie?*

Detective Roth made a mental note to look more closely into Mr Grey. She already knew that Susan had profited from selling her company in London, she had enough money in the bank to live comfortably for the rest of her life. However, Grace had not looked into Mr Grey's financial affairs, yet. *Was that the motive, money?*

Grace's pulse quickened as she grasped onto the first break in her case, the first possible lead.

Despite being sure she now had something to work with, Grace still wanted to know why Miss Russell felt that Christopher was also likely to cause Susan harm. Having a second lead to follow wouldn't hurt, after all.

'Why do you suppose Susan invited Christopher if she knew her husband wouldn't be pleased?'

A look passed across Jennifer's face, one which Grace couldn't read. 'Susan and Christopher's relationship has always been complicated.'

'How so?'

Jennifer looked up towards the ceiling and inhaled deeply before letting her eyes come to rest on Grace. 'They were childhood sweethearts who met too young.' She shrugged. 'They could never seem to make it work, although they tried for Joshua's sake. Susan moved on, I think, but Christopher struggled, especially when she married Martin. Susan wanted to be amicable but Christopher always turned any opportunity he could into an argument. Still, Susan continued to have him around.'

'Did they argue on the night of the party?'

Jennifer pursed her lips for a moment. 'I don't know. It wouldn't surprise me if they did.'

And there is my other lead. Jealous ex-partner. A crime of passion perhaps?

Jennifer appeared to have relaxed fully now, her body no longer showing signs of tension, her expression calm, the fear having all but dissipated. Grace knew she may not get this opportunity again so continued with her inquiries. 'You were obviously at the party, weren't you?' Grace asked for clarity.

'Of course. All of the staff were.'

What an unusual response, Grace considered. *Why hadn't Jennifer said, 'Of course, I'm her sister'?*

'Can you tell me what you remember from that night, what you remember of Susan's movements?'

The calmness Grace had only moments ago witnessed, disappeared instantly. Miss Russell had thrown up a barrier, her eyes becoming shuttered. She swallowed in what appeared to be a nervous gesture. *Surely this was an easy question, one of the easiest ones?*

Jennifer opened her mouth to answer, when a small bell rang from behind her, stopping her. Detective Roth turned to see two elderly women entering the shop.

Whilst Jennifer stood up and welcomed the customers, pointing them in the direction of the requested travel section, Grace took a moment to review her notes. Her suspect list, now consisting of two names, Martin Grey and Christopher Maddison, was a promising start.

With the customers out of earshot, Jennifer moved forward, closing the gap which she had initially instigated between herself and Grace. In a low voice she said, 'I spent the evening at the table reserved for bookshop staff. I barely spoke to Susan, I'm afraid to say. She was very busy, entertaining her guests. I saw her fleetingly but the marquee was packed. From what I saw, she looked as though she was having a great time.'

'Is there anything else that sticks out in your mind, anything unusual?'

Jennifer paused for a moment before finally saying, 'No. Well, maybe. Susan had hinted that she had a surprise, something she'd planned on announcing at the party but she obviously never got the opportunity. Or she simply changed her mind. Beyond that, I can't offer you anything more specific.'

'An announcement?' Grace's interest piqued.

'Yes, she mentioned something about it the day before, here at work, but as I said she might have changed her mind. Susan could be spontaneous like that, but she was also prone to changing her mind.' Jennifer shrugged as though attempting to brush away the idea. 'Now if you don't mind, I need to go and help my customers.'

'Of course,' Grace offered, watching as Jennifer moved out from behind the counter. 'Miss Russell,' she called out before Jennifer disappeared from sight. Jennifer looked back over her shoulder. 'I may have more questions for you as my investigation proceeds.'

Grace didn't wait for a response, instead she turned and left. Once outside, she looked down at her suspect list. Then without hesitation she found herself adding Jennifer Russell to the bottom of the page, punctuated by three question marks.

7

SUSAN

TWO WEEKS BEFORE SHE FELL

Susan bustled into the shop. She was late.

Anticipating the look; the disapproving, I-was-here-on-time look which Jennifer was undoubtedly going to throw in her direction, she dipped her head purposefully and darted straight to her office, shutting the door behind her.

She didn't have time for Jennifer's tantrums today, she had some important and exciting meetings to prepare for, the first of which was in only a few short minutes.

Susan had barely logged in to the computer when a forceful rapping at the door interrupted her.

She sighed, knowing it would be Jennifer. 'Come in.' Susan did her best to keep the bite from her voice.

Jennifer opened the door fully. Susan didn't know why that bothered her but it did. She couldn't just poke her head around, opening the door just a fraction. No, she had to throw it open all the way, exposing Susan to anyone and everyone in the shop. It was a power thing, one that had always rumbled in the background of their relationship. *Sisters*.

With raised eyebrows, Jennifer said, 'We have a big stock delivery arriving shortly.' It was a question disguised as a statement, what she really meant to say was: '*We have a big stock delivery arriving shortly, are you planning on helping seeing as how you're late and appear to be hiding in here?*' Jennifer never went as far as to actually say what she wanted, but Susan had years of training and experience to work out the undertone, the unsaid words.

Inhaling deeply, Susan nodded. *Shit.*

She had forgotten, of course, as Jennifer probably suspected, but Susan wasn't going to admit as much. 'I have a business call shortly,' she said, nodding towards the computer, 'I will come and help with the delivery after that.' Then for good measure she added, 'If it's arrived.'

Jennifer's interest noticeably piqued at the mention of a business meeting. 'What's the meeting?' she asked curiously. 'Do I need to be involved?'

Susan barely resisted the urge to roll her eyes. Despite this being Susan's business, Jennifer had always displayed a sense of ownership for the place.

Susan had known it was Jennifer's dream to own a bookshop, but in reality she would never achieve it. She lacked the drive and determination to find a way to get what she wanted. So Susan had used some of the money from the sale of her company to buy the store.

She had wanted to give Jennifer a purpose, to give her back a spark of happiness in her otherwise miserable life. Only, Susan had needed to ensure that the business was viable, that it turned a profit month on month, which meant that she had needed to do it her way. If she had left it to Jennifer, the shop would have likely been dark and dusty and something akin to a money pit. As it was, the shop was working, in fact it was doing surprisingly well.

Still, despite having provided Jennifer with her dream, she was frequently a pain in the arse, often over-inflating her role and clashing with Susan on every and any aspect of its daily running.

Instead of answering straight away, Susan looked past Jennifer into the shop in an obvious attempt to highlight the customers who were browsing and within earshot of their conversation. 'No, it's just the bank,' she responded vaguely.

Jennifer followed her gaze, registered the shoppers, then returned her attention back to Susan. 'Fine. I'll let you know when the delivery arrives.' Before Susan could respond, could tell her that she didn't want to be disturbed, Jennifer had grabbed hold of the door-handle and pulled it shut with more force than was necessary.

Susan exhaled sharply and shook her head.

Unbelievable.

There were so many retorts, so many comments which Susan could throw Jennifer's way, but as always she bit her tongue, aware that it wouldn't help, nor would it make a difference. Jennifer was just Jennifer.

She turned back to the computer and opened the file titled *Future.*

Being on the precipice of fifty seemed to have had a profound impact on her, making her feel as though she needed to make changes in her life, whilst she could. This meeting with the bank was the first step in making those changes.

8

GRACE

'Good morning.' Grace smiled at DI Harry Amberidge and DS Amy Cartwright. As briefings went, this was definitely an informal one. Having met with Jennifer Russell that morning, Grace had stopped off and brought some pastries before heading into the office.

Her small and select team were now sitting around a table, in one of the incident rooms, with coffees, pastries and the case summary before them.

'As you will see, there really is very little to go on at this point. However, having visited both Mrs Grey's husband and her sister, I get the distinct impression they are both hiding something. My first inclination is that there is a case to be built, we are just going to need to dig deep to find our suspect.'

Both Harry and Amy were nodding in response. Grace had barely slept the previous night, considering how to play this, where to focus her attention first. She couldn't afford to fuck this up, couldn't afford to make any mistakes.

'I have already been to see our victim, Susan, as well. She remains in a very critical condition. The hospital has all my details and are going to keep me updated if anything changes.

But we need to bear in mind that if Mrs Grey succumbs to her injuries, this could quickly become a murder investigation.

Mr Grey reported having a business meeting on the evening of the accident with one Joshua Maddison, Mrs Grey's son from her previous marriage. I plan to follow this up as a priority. It was also reported that Mrs Grey may have had a disagreement of sorts with her ex-husband that evening which I will look into further.'

Grace paused to take a sip of her coffee and to enjoy the moment. It felt exciting to finally be leading a case. So many times before she had sat in one of these meetings, her orders provided by someone else. This time she was making the decisions, deciding what was a priority. It really was a wonderful feeling.

'Amy, I'd like you to start interviewing all the catering staff, the details of the company's owner are in the file,' Grace said with a nod of her head towards the file in Amy's hand. 'You should be able to ascertain who was working that night from her. They were using the house kitchen for food preparations, which in turn gave them access to the property, whereas the party guests should have been outside. Cross-reference any details with our database. Despite the unusual behaviour of the family, this could simply have been a robbery gone wrong.'

Grace made a mental note to ask Mr Grey if anything obvious was missing, devices, jewellery, that sort of thing.

Amy nodded her head enthusiastically, her brunette ponytail swishing with the movement. 'I can also make a start on the guest list. Start eliminating a few names at least.'

'That would be great, thank you. Jennifer Russell did mention a possible announcement which never happened, I am sure it is nothing but might be worth enquiring about, see if anyone else knew anything about it.'

Grace suspected that like her, Amy felt she had something

to prove. DS Cartwright had recently returned from maternity leave and appeared to be as keen as Grace to get stuck in once more, to demonstrate that she hadn't lost her touch.

'I should be wrapped up with my case in a day or two, just waiting on some transcripts so that I can get the paperwork completed, so let me know what you want me to do,' Harry offered lightly before taking a bite of a croissant. He was wearing a fitted grey suit over a crisp white shirt, Grace noted, which showed off his impressive physique.

He wasn't what you might call typically attractive. His hooded green eyes seemed as though they were constantly assessing you and a nasty-looking scar ran through his left eyebrow, but he had a smile which transformed his face and he had a terrible sense of humour.

Grace could see why so many of the females in the department found Harry attractive. She saw the appeal too, only right now she wanted to focus on her career, on solving this case, then maybe she would allow herself some fun, she thought fleetingly.

Grace considered Harry's role for a moment. 'Can you look into the tip-off. Get in touch with the call handler, see if there's anything about our informant that might give us a clue as to who he is. I want to banish any suggestions that this was a hoax as quickly as we can.'

DI Amberidge nodded. 'Will do. What about the girl who found our victim? Shall I follow that up, see if there is anything else she can remember?'

'Good idea.'

'What about the crime scene?' DS Cartwright enquired. 'Are there any forensics?'

Grace took another sip of her coffee before she shook her head. 'Unfortunately not. Susan's fall was initially deemed as an accident from the get-go although uniform did attend. We can revisit the scene in due course but I am not convinced we'll find anything at this late stage.'

'That's going to make this more tricky,' Amy commented.

'Yep,' Grace agreed. 'Without any evidence, a confession or something equally concrete, the CPS will just throw it out, so we need to find that proverbial needle in a haystack for this one. But we will,' she added with conviction.

And she would because Grace knew that solving this case was the only way to move on, the only way to rebuild her reputation.

Back at her desk, Detective Roth returned her attention to the information in front of her. She had decided to take another look into Susan Grey before she headed out to speak with Joshua Maddison. There had to be a motive for the attack and Grace had an inkling that if she brushed away the façade that Martin Grey had attempted to paint, she would find a lead to follow.

Harry slammed his phone down with such force, Grace found herself peering up. He looked pissed off.

'Whoa, you all good?' Grace asked.

'Control room.' He sighed. 'They haven't been able to give me anything useful on the anonymous caller apart from that it was a male, I'm afraid. The number used was withheld. They're going to email over a copy of the recording but still, I can't believe that in this day we can't trace that number.'

'Shit.' Grace sighed in understanding. There were always going to be hurdles, she had just hoped to get a little further along before hitting one. This potential witness could be the difference between securing a conviction or not. 'We still have a lot of leads to follow. Perhaps the waitress will be able to shed some more light on things for us.'

She wasn't prepared to feel derailed at this point.

'Oh, on the brighter side,' Harry interrupted, a smirk on his lips. 'I forgot to tell you, I have thought of the perfect name for our investigation.' Grace raised her eyebrows in a silent question. 'The stair case.' He laughed loudly. 'Do you get it? Stair case, staircase.'

Grace rolled her eyes. 'That is not funny,' she responded dryly but she couldn't hide the small smile which had found its way to her lips.

9

———————

JOSHUA

'I can have it ready for you in an hour,' he said, leaning back in his chair, feet propped up on the desk. Arrogance rolled off of him in waves.

He listened to the voice on the other end of the phone for a moment, a half-smile tugging at the edge of his lips. 'Mate, what can I say? It's good shit and if you want it, you'll wait.' Hearing the person on the other end relent with a sigh, Joshua quickly added, 'Same place as usual. See you shortly.' Then he hung up, pocketing his phone.

Joshua saw himself as an entrepreneur, running several small businesses out of his one-bedroom Brighton flat. Nearly all of them made him decent money and most of them were legal. Just not this one.

Dropping his feet back on the floor, he stood up and made his way to the coffee table in the middle of the lounge. Pulling open the central drawer, he plucked up a small clear bag of weed and pocketed it, shutting the drawer with his toe.

He wasn't always going to have to do this, he reminded himself. Very soon, this week in fact, he would begin putting the wheels in motion for his next venture. He was just waiting on a call, a very important call.

He was moving on to bigger and better things.

It wasn't that he felt guilty about selling drugs, no. If they were stupid enough to buy them then someone was going to sell them. So why shouldn't it be him? Joshua simply had his sights set higher than being a low-level drug dealer.

It wasn't happening exactly the way he'd planned but he would prove to them, to the doubters, that he could do it, that he had what it took to run a real business. He would get his next project, a whisky bar, off the ground, he would make it a success and then they'd see. See that he wasn't a fuck-up, wasn't a failure.

From the corner of his eye, he could see the discarded folder, containing his proposal and presentation. He had done his research this time, had looked into every possible variable he could think of but that hadn't been enough. They hadn't given him a chance to prove himself but that was all in the past now, he didn't need their backing, didn't need her approval.

Slumping down on the sofa, Joshua knew he could be at the drop-off in under ten minutes, but he didn't want it to seem as though he wasn't busy, that he didn't have other important things to attend to first.

At that thought, he pulled his phone from his pocket once more and logged in to the selling site. He checked his online store, no sales.

Joshua, alongside selling drugs, also bought and sold expensive and limited edition trainers, scouring the internet for the best ones, often importing them from America, before selling them on, for a reasonable profit, of course, to the British market. This had been his first business.

He usually sold a couple of pairs a week.

Originally, he'd had high hopes for this idea, he'd planned to cut himself a nice slice of the trainer market. He had dreamed big. He'd proposed setting up his own website, shortly followed by the opening of his own store.

Only the trade had not lived up to his expectations, one to two pairs a week didn't warrant such an outlay of money. But it continued to be a nice little earner nevertheless.

Before he chucked his phone down on the coffee table, it beeped.

His dad. Again.

As always the message was brief.

Any news on your mum?

Guilt twisted in his stomach.

His dad wasn't allowed to visit as he wasn't classed as immediate family, yet Joshua, who was and who could, had only been to see his mum once and that was only for a few minutes. He had basically stood at the door before fleeing.

Firstly, he knew that her arsehole of a husband was going to be there, presiding over her, and Joshua didn't want to be in the same room as that prick. He never wanted to see him again.

But mainly it was because Joshua felt stupid. He didn't know what to say. He had never been very good with words, was never able to express his feelings calmly which was perhaps why he'd been in so many fights over the years and why he had been in trouble with the law a few times too. And besides, she probably wouldn't want him there anyway.

The last time they had seen each other, well he didn't want to think about that. But his guilt extended beyond his lack of visiting.

He shoved the thoughts from his mind, he was not prepared

to revisit them now or ever. When his mum woke up he knew she would be angry, but he would deal with that, he would apologise, he would grovel if he had to but she would forgive him eventually.

She always did.

10

GRACE

Joshua Maddison's block of flats on Brighton seafront was impressive to say the least. A double-fronted, period building carved up into six small units. It was clear from the well-presented façade that these properties were expensive.

Grace couldn't help but wonder if Susan had bought this for her son.

As expected, Grace had done some digging on Joshua and it was fair to say that his past was rather chequered. He had been arrested on four separate occasions in the past six years alone; once for a breach of the peace, twice for drug-related incidents and once for harassment. He had been fined and required to undertake community service, which he had. Somehow Grace couldn't imagine him as a nine to five kind of guy with a steady pay cheque.

Using the trade button to gain access, Detective Roth entered the lobby before locating Mr Maddison's door on the first floor. She pressed the bell and waited.

Eventually, footsteps approached before there was a pause. Grace knew he was looking through the door viewer. She had purposely stood to the side, out of sight.

'Yeah?'

'Joshua Maddison?'

'Yeah? Who's asking?'

'Detective Inspector Roth.' Grace didn't have time to add, '*I would like to talk to you about your mother,*' when she heard Joshua cursing.

He didn't respond, instead Grace listened to rushed steps moving away from the door, further into the property followed by the distinct sound of doors, perhaps a cupboard, being slammed.

Grace sighed. This was not normal behaviour. His rap sheet had indicated two counts of drug-related offences, best guess was that he was currently in possession and stashing what he had.

'Just coming,' Joshua called breathlessly from the depths of his home.

She shook her head. She wasn't looking for an extra bust, not today. If it was obvious, she wouldn't be able to ignore it, she realised. If not, she would ask her questions, clarify the meeting that Joshua had with Martin and ascertain whether either of them had reason or motive to harm Susan.

Perhaps she would offer him some words of caution on her way out if she suspected drugs, let him know that it would only take one small phone call to the right department to have his home raided, and then advise him to consider making different choices with his life.

Eventually, the door was unlocked and opened.

Joshua's resemblance to his mother was striking. His hair, most noticeably, was the same shade of blond, his nose was straight with a slight slope at the end like hers and his eyes were an identical blue. But that was where the similarities stopped.

Joshua was six feet tall with broad shoulders and a smug look locked into place.

'What can I do for you, Detective?' Joshua practically drawled as he leaned against the door-frame.

Grace offered Mr Maddison a small smile before she said, 'Do you mind if we go inside?'

Without hesitation, he grinned and said, 'Of course.' Joshua moved to the side, making a sweeping arm gesture.

Prick.

He was going to be one of those, smarmy and annoying, Grace realised, striding into the lounge.

The sun was streaming into the room through the large bay windows, rays of light dancing across the sparse furniture. Grace found herself squinting against it momentarily.

Joshua, clearly accustomed to the brightness, given that there were no curtains at the windows, followed her in and flopped down on the sofa.

She watched as he leant back and spread his arms wide along its back.

He was making a show of being relaxed, Grace understood, only she could see straight through it, and besides, he didn't yet know why she was there.

'Do you know why I am here?' Grace asked.

Still grinning, Joshua turned his hands, palms up towards the ceiling, in a shrug. 'Why don't you sit down and then you can enlighten me?'

'Thank you, but I prefer to stand,' Grace responded curtly. 'I am here to discuss your mother's accident. I presume you've heard that an investigation into the incident has been opened?'

His smile faltered at that.

He doesn't know. No one has told him. How is that possible?

Joshua pushed himself off of the sofa in one swift motion, moving to stand in front of the bay window, his back to Grace, his hands now shoved deep into his pockets.

'No, I hadn't heard.' There was anger in his voice. 'I'm not particularly close to anyone on that side of my family.'

'What about your mother?'

Joshua turned to face Grace. His expression was hidden as he was silhouetted against the brightness of the day. 'What?'

'Your mother? Are you close to her?' Grace was careful when she chose her words. Despite Susan remaining in a critical condition, she was still fighting, she was still here.

He laughed without humour. 'Are you close to your mother?' he countered.

Two years ago that question would have floored Grace, would have had her breaking down in tears. She had been exceedingly close to her mother, who had devastatingly lost her battle to breast cancer. Although it no longer hurt to talk about her, she rarely did.

So when she answered, aware that Joshua may soon be in the same boat, she was cautious. 'I was. Yes. But I am here to talk about your mother, not mine.'

Joshua seemed to understand, but didn't go as far as to offer an apology. He moved back to the sofa, but rather than sitting down, he perched on the armrest. 'What's going on?'

'We have received information suggesting that your mother's fall wasn't an accident.' *God, how many times am I going to have to repeat that statement?*

Joshua screwed his face up. 'You can't be serious?'

'I wouldn't be here if I wasn't,' Grace responded.

Joshua blew his cheeks out then raked his fingers through his hair. 'Wow, okay. So what do you think happened?'

Grace rolled her shoulders, she didn't like to admit that all she had at the moment were theories and speculations, so she said, 'I was informed that whilst attending your mother's birthday party, you and Martin Grey had a meeting, is that correct?'

Joshua laughed once, making a comical 'ha' noise. 'That definitely wasn't a meeting.'

'What was it then?'

'A telling off at best, a warning at worst.' Perhaps noticing the confusion which passed across Grace's features, Joshua continued. 'I have never really liked him. I couldn't see what it was that Mum saw in him, I mean he is nothing like my dad. Martin seemed to take offence any time she offered to help me out.'

So this was about money. 'I see, so had she recently offered to help you out?'

'Not exactly, no. But she knew I was working on a new project.' Grace noticed his eyes flick towards the desk, to a folder there, likely a business plan of sorts. 'Martin obviously got wind of this and didn't want Mum to get involved. He told me that, under no circumstances was I to ask her for financial backing.'

Grace smothered her smugness, Joshua Maddison was talking, and freely, giving her all the information she needed. No coaxing of any description required here.

'Did she know, do you think, that Martin had spoken to you?'

Joshua stood up again. 'She found out. Walked in on us, said that half the party had heard us arguing.'

That's interesting, Grace thought. She would have to ask Amy to enquire about an argument when she contacted the other guests.

'Then what happened?'

'I said some things, she said some things in retaliation. I stormed out and left them to it. That's it. Then Dad texted me later to say there had been an accident.'

Grace was watching Joshua exceedingly closely, looking for

any flicker of a lie. She didn't see it but there was something else, something he wasn't saying.

What was it?

'What time did you leave?'

Joshua appeared to think for a moment, then shrugged his shoulders. 'Perhaps nine, maybe a little after that. I didn't look at my watch but I know I was home by ten.'

That pretty much matches up with what Martin had said, only why overlook something as crucial as Susan being present? Surely he knew that Joshua would say as much?

That might mean Martin was the last person to see her before the fall. Or he might be the one responsible for it.

Martin Grey was looking more and more culpable as Grace's investigation continued, but she was still lacking motive and evidence. She needed more.

'Where did this conversation take place?' Grace asked, extracting her notebook. She wasn't sure Martin had divulged that information. She quickly flipped back through a couple of pages.

'In the study, at the top of the stairs.'

Perfect positioning, Grace realised.

Detective Roth managed to restrict her excitement to a simple nod of the head despite her heart thumping wildly in her chest. Although she didn't get the impression that Joshua would be reporting back to Mr Grey, she still wanted to keep her cards close to her chest at this point.

Despite having a very promising lead, Grace was diligent and there was one more suspect still to discuss. 'Am I correct that your dad also attended the party?'

Grace watched as Joshua became shuttered, it was as though a switch had just been thrown. 'Yes. He was.'

'Do you happen to know if he spoke to your mum?'

'I wouldn't know. You'll have to ask him.' Joshua's response was clipped, his tone defensive. It was clear he wasn't prepared to talk about his dad at all. *That's fine,* Grace thought to herself, *he is next on my list to interview.*

'Thank you very much for your cooperation today,' Grace offered, deciding it was time for her to leave.

She made her way back to the door aware that Joshua was following her. As she opened the door and stepped out into the hall, she turned back. 'One more thing. Were you aware of an announcement that your mother had planned on making at the party?'

From the obvious confusion on Mr Maddison's face, Grace knew even before he spoke that he had no clue what she was talking about.

'No. What was it about?'

'Thank you for your time,' Grace said, purposely ignoring Mr Maddison's question. Perhaps the announcement would prove to be a red herring, Grace considered. Still, it was worth asking about.

Grace strode out of the building and back to her car.

She had one more lead to chase up.

11

____

CHRISTOPHER

Christopher hoped that doing something physical would take his mind off of Susan. It hadn't. She was still in hospital, he was still here and now he had completely fucked up the original windscreen of his Triumph Spitfire.

'You fucking twat,' he growled in the garage and threw his gloves onto the floor. He wanted to throw something else, wanted to trash the entire room, but he didn't, aware that when he lost his temper he seemed to damage things which were important to him.

Instead, he turned to the punching bag hanging neglected in the corner and took his anger and aggression out there, punching with a ferocity he hadn't experienced for years. Since Susan had told him she was getting married to that douchebag, he realised. Thinking of Martin, or Susan and Martin together, spiked his fury. A low growl left his lips as he continued to pummel the worn leather.

His knuckles throbbed and his wrists protested, but he kept hitting the bag, throwing jab after punch after jab until sweat was dripping down his neck and back.

Eventually, his energy spent, Christopher stopped, his

shoulders and chest heaving as he breathed. His hands, aching, hung limply at his sides.

His temper had always been an issue, something he also recognised in his son. Christopher did his best to keep it under control, to set an example but he felt too passionately, loved too hard, hurt too painfully.

Susan had always known that, had always loved him and hated him for it.

He couldn't keep his damn mind from drifting back to her, no matter what he was doing, no matter how hard he was trying not to think of her.

With a sigh, Christopher turned around slowly to survey the classic car once more. A giant spider web of a crack now weaved its way from the bottom left-hand corner to the top right-hand corner of the glass, practically splitting it in two. Christopher had to clench his teeth together to stop the tirade of curses spilling out.

Everything you touch you manage to fucking break.

He'd been restoring the car for the past two years, working on it whenever he had a spare few hours.

He hadn't known what he was doing when he'd taken on this project, he'd only known that he had always wanted one, had promised himself growing up that one day he would have enough money to own this very car. He had learnt how to fix engine parts, how to touch up the body work, how to deal with small patches of rust and finally, how to remove the windscreen so that he could replace all the seals.

And then you go and undo all your hard work.

He was tempted to walk away, to forget what he'd just done, ignore it until he was in a more stable frame of mind. But he couldn't because this was something he could fix, something that was within his gift to correct. Or at least he hoped. What he couldn't fix was Susan.

With Susan at the forefront of his thoughts once more, he had the compulsion to call again. *Just in case*, he told himself. Then, he would remove the windscreen once more.

Grabbing his phone from the side, Christopher hit redial. After a few rings, the receptionist answered. 'Brighton hospital, how can I help?'

He cleared his throat. 'ICU please.'

'Connecting you now.'

As Christopher wasn't deemed to be immediate family, even though they had a kid together, he wasn't allowed to visit and the nurses weren't allowed to discuss Susan's condition with him, or at least that's what he'd been told when he'd rung, and he'd called several times now. Still, he continued to try.

It is a fucking stupid rule.

'ICU,' a young voice finally responded.

'Hi, I was hoping to get an update on Susan Grey?' Christopher found himself holding his breath, in anticipation, in hope.

There was a pause on the line. Perhaps the woman, a nurse he presumed, was looking at Susan's chart, considering what to tell him, when she finally spoke again. 'Is that Mr Maddison?'

Christopher's shoulders sagged and he exhaled. He'd been blacklisted, he quickly understood. They all knew not to talk to him, probably at that dickhead's request. Christopher's free hand balled into a tight fist, his already raw knuckles protesting against the movement.

'Yes. I just want to know how she is, that's all.' He knew his voice was pleading but he didn't care. He may never get to talk to Susan again, to see her again. The thought was too overwhelming, too real, so he forced it out of his mind. The very least he could do was keep calling, even if he was repeatedly told the same thing.

The nurse sighed. 'You know I am not supposed to tell you anything?'

'I know,' he responded honestly, a bud of hope unfurling as she hadn't given him a flat refusal.

'I can't give you specifics,' she eventually offered, 'but Susan is critical. Each hour that we get through is positive. She is in a coma to protect her brain. What I can tell you is that her condition hasn't worsened so far. She is a strong woman, Mr Maddison, I imagine that if anyone can pull through this then it is her.'

A lump had risen in Christopher's throat. He exhaled, blowing out his cheeks. 'Thank you. Thank you very much.'

'You're welcome,' she responded before hanging up.

Christopher continued to hold the phone to his ear for a minute as a modicum of relief washed over him. Susan was fighting, that was all he'd needed to know. She hadn't given up and so neither would he. He could right the wrongs he had done to her. When she was better, when he could visit, he would apologise for hurting her, for how messy and fucked up he'd let things get.

The image of Susan lying on the floor flashed into his mind. He had to physically shake his head to expel it. He never wanted to see that again, didn't ever want to remember it.

'So, what'd they tell you?'

The voice made him jump. Standing at the garage door was Rachel, Susan's best friend. She was wearing one of his T-shirts and nothing else.

She shouldn't be here, he should have had the balls to tell her it was over, that it was a mistake, one which they'd repeatedly made, had been making even before Susan's fall. He didn't know why exactly but it felt as though they were having an affair, as if he were cheating on Susan. Ridiculous he knew, she was married to someone else after all. And yet when he was alone, when he'd drunk more than he should have, Rachel was the only one there offering him some comfort.

'She's still critical,' he answered, pocketing the phone, 'but she's fighting.'

'Good. That's really good.'

Christopher wasn't convinced Rachel felt the same level of guilt about what they'd been doing as he did. Well, she sure as hell wasn't trying to put the brakes on things, he'd reasoned. But this wasn't her fault, this was all on him. Another burden to shoulder.

'Breakfast?' she asked, disrupting his thoughts.

'Sure,' Christopher responded, not wanting to be a dick, not right at this minute. She offered a quick smile before disappearing back into his house.

But he was going to end it, he told himself, he had to, and before Susan woke up.

12

GRACE

Christopher lived in what appeared to be a modest end of terrace house with a small garage attached at its side, in a cul-de-sac tucked away from the main road.

Climbing out of her car, Grace got the distinct feeling she was being watched. Looking around at the other homes she couldn't see anyone. *Although, did that curtain just twitch?*

Grace imagined that everyone knew everyone with their houses butted up tightly against one another and that as an outsider in this impasse, Grace would probably have sparked some interest.

Let them talk, she thought as she approached Mr Maddison's property.

Christopher Maddison's house had a low iron fence, painted black, surrounding its edges, with a small gate and path leading to the front door. Another larger gate, in front of the garage, was open and the garage door stood at half-mast.

Following her instincts, Grace took that entrance.

As she neared, she could hear noises coming from inside, the shuffling of feet, the low hum of a radio.

Grace crouched down peering into the garage.

Her gaze immediately flicked to the car taking up most of the floor space. Despite little interest in cars, as long as it drove without issue Grace was happy, she could appreciate that this vehicle was something of a classic and obviously well maintained.

At the far end, partially concealed under the hood of the racing-green car was a large man. He was clearly concentrating, she thought, as he hadn't heard her approaching steps on the gravel drive.

Purposefully, Grace cleared her throat.

The guy jumped, his head clashing loudly against the open bonnet. 'Shit.'

Grace internally winced, although chose not to apologise, Maddison was high up on her suspect list after all and she didn't want to show any signs of weakness.

As the man peered around from behind the hood, his hand now rubbing at his head, Grace knew that this was Christopher Maddison. Joshua's resemblance to him was noticeable.

In his overalls, Grace could see that Christopher, like Joshua, was well-built, his tall broad frame made him look as though he would be at home on a rugby pitch. His dark-brown hair which was greying at the edges was cut short and his eyes, also brown, were so dark they could have been black.

He obviously took pride in his appearance, Grace decided. But it was his expression that sent a shiver skittering down her back. His narrowed eyes, which were fixed on Grace, were like steel.

Adopting her game face, serious but not frightening, Grace introduced herself. 'Mr Maddison, I am Detective Roth.' Without invitation she ducked under the metal door and stood up within the confines of the garage.

Something flickered in Christopher's expression but it was

gone too quickly for Grace to know exactly what it was. Understanding perhaps.

Then just for a moment, she watched as he looked past her to the partially opened garage door, before glancing over his shoulder to the door leading inside the house. His exits, his ways out, Grace realised. He was feeling cornered, trapped even. *But why?*

Just like Joshua, Christopher had had several previous run-ins with the law, all of them violence-related. GBH, common assault and battery. Interestingly, they were against men. Still, that didn't mean he hadn't hit a woman, maybe they just hadn't come forward, that he hadn't been caught.

Grace knew she had to keep her guard up.

In an attempt to defuse what she felt was becoming an increasingly hostile environment, she nodded towards the Triumph Spitfire. 'Nice car,' she offered conversationally.

'It's a bit of a project,' Christopher grunted in response, perhaps feeling judged.

Okay, enough with the niceties, you have a job to do.

'Do you know why I'm here?' Again, she tried to keep her tone neutral, non-threatening. She was hyper aware that she had put herself in a confined space with a man prone to violence.

'Joshua called, said you're looking into Susan's fall.' His hand fell to his side as he moved around to stand beside the car.

Finally, Grace thought. She didn't exactly want them all talking about the case, inventing stories she'd have to unpick, but she had been finding the whole situation odd. They hadn't been communicating at all, they weren't giving each other a heads-up.

'That's correct. We are interviewing everyone close to Susan and those who also attended the party.'

Christopher nodded.

'Can you tell me about your movements that night?'

He shrugged. 'I went to the party for a bit. I had a couple of beers, and I was just about to leave when there was a commotion, when Susan was found.'

Now it was Grace's turn to nod. 'So you were there, in the house, when Susan was found?'

'Yes, I mean no.' Grace raised her eyebrows and Christopher took a breath. 'I was just leaving when I heard that young lass scream, so I ran back in.' He paused, then added, 'I saw Susan on the floor.' His face darkened with his words, his memories.

So he was one of the first on the scene. Grace couldn't help her mind from whirling. *Christopher could have been in the house all along, he could be trying to cover his tracks. It would make sense.*

'Why were you in the house if the party was outside?'

Mr Maddison pressed his lips into a thin line and shuffled from foot to foot. 'I'd needed a piss. There was a queue outside.'

Liar.

Grace could practically smell the dishonesty on him. He really needed to work on his poker face.

'I see. Is there anyone who can corroborate this?' She held his stare, challenging him, willing him to slip up.

'I can.' In the doorway behind Christopher, a woman was now leaning casually against the frame, her arms crossed. Grace couldn't help but notice that she was only partially dressed in an oversized T-shirt, her bare legs and feet on display. Her stance was indifferent, uninterested even, as though it was normal to find the police in your home.

'And you are?' Grace questioned without missing a beat, even though the arrival of this individual had caught her off track.

'Rachel. Christopher's girlfriend.' As she responded, she smiled widely, smugness emanating from her like warmth from a fire. Only, from Grace's vantage point, she could see that

Christopher's expression didn't reflect Rachel's, if anything he suddenly looked sheepish, guilty even.

'Sorry, Rachel, your last name is?'

'Burstow.'

Grace nodded and made a note of this. She couldn't recall seeing that name on the list Martin had provided, but then there were a lot of names, it would have been easy to overlook one. She would obviously check when she was back in the office.

Rachel moved casually into the garage, squeezing her curvy frame into the small space afforded to her at Christopher's side.

She looked so out of place, Grace thought. Not that the garage was filthy, if anything it was relatively tidy, with most things seeming to have a place, including Christopher. The only thing that didn't have a place here was Rachel. She, however, didn't appear to feel the same, apparently unbothered as she stood barefoot on the concrete floor.

'So you were also at Susan Grey's party?'

'Yes.'

'How is it that you know Susan?'

Rachel's bravado, the unembarrassed, I-don't-give-a-shit-if-you're-police attitude faltered momentarily as she said, 'I'm Susan's best friend.'

Ah. Grace paused to let this new twist settle in, as she considered all the ways the threads of this case were overlapping and knotting together.

So Susan's ex-partner, father to her son, was dating her best friend. *Jennifer had suggested that Christopher dating would cause friction, but had she known who he was seeing or was she just guessing?*

Also, did Susan know?

Did they argue about this on the night of the accident?

'Was Susan aware of your relationship?' Grace eventually asked, deciding that this was the most pertinent of questions.

'No,' Christopher responded instantly, at exactly the same moment Rachel said yes. Grace's eyebrows rose high at the disparity but remained silent, aware that one of them would likely start talking or backtracking. She'd soon know who was lying.

With a subtle nudge from Rachel that Grace just caught in her peripheral vision, Christopher sighed into the awkwardness. 'She knew,' he admitted.

'I had felt that telling Susan was the right thing to do,' Rachel continued. 'We are all adults after all,' she offered as vindication.

Grace wasn't sure how she would feel if she learnt that her ex and her friend had been sneaking around behind her back, but then she would hope that her best friend was more of a friend than Rachel appeared to be at this present moment.

'I see. How long have you two been dating?'

'Not that long,' Christopher replied quickly. The vagueness of his response spoke volumes, the undertone suggesting that it had perhaps been longer than he wanted to admit.

'And when exactly was Mrs Grey made aware of your relationship?'

Grace watched as Rachel and Christopher looked at one another, some silent conversation occurring between them. It was Rachel who then turned and met Grace's waiting stare. 'At the party.'

When Grace deigned to respond, her disbelief evident, Rachel rushed to say more. 'She was fine about it really. Shocked, which is understandable, but then she was fine. Besides, she had more pressing matters to attend to.'

'More pressing matters?'

'Yeah, well Martin and Joshua were having a full-blown screaming match, so she went to break that up.'

Christopher had turned to his girlfriend, a look of loathing burning in his eyes as he said in a low but audible voice, 'I think you've said enough now.'

'I see.' *So Joshua had been telling the truth, his mum had joined them in the study. That also meant Christopher was looking less like her prime suspect, although she didn't want to rule him out entirely.*

He does have a history of violence. Perhaps he'd accosted Susan after she'd left Martin in the study, perhaps they'd argued about who Christopher had chosen to date. He could have easily lashed out.

Grace had a lot to consider. So finally, she said, 'I have everything I need from you both, for now. I'm sure I will have more questions so don't plan on going anywhere.' She offered a smile which didn't meet her eyes.

Grace was just about to duck back under the garage door, desperate to return to the office and pull together a timeline when she looked back over her shoulder. 'My card. Call me if either of you remember anything else.' She laid her business card carefully on the rear of the car before she bent low and exited the garage.

Fucking hell, there were so many twists and turns in this case to navigate already that Grace's head was spinning.

13

SUSAN

TEN DAYS BEFORE SHE FELL

Susan studied the latest sales report, scrutinised it. She was completing her proposal and it was vital that every detail was accurate; she didn't want to find that she had overlooked anything or made a mistake that would put all her plans in jeopardy.

She had chosen to work from home, at the large oak kitchen table. Beside her was a steaming mug of coffee carefully positioned in between her work.

Jennifer had prying eyes, she would have been too curious, or more likely too nosy, to have left Susan to it. She would have seen the spreadsheets, the graphs, the premises details and would have wanted to know more. Only Susan wasn't ready to share this. Not yet. Not before it was more official. Not until she had been granted approval.

So she had set up camp at home.

It reminded her of those lockdown months, when Covid had swept through the country like a tsunami rendering everyone except for the key workers, sedentary, until the disease was in retreat, or at least more manageable.

Both her and Martin had been working from this table,

wanting to remain in one another's company, despite having a perfectly good study upstairs. They had sat at opposite ends. Occasionally they would look up and grin at each other, sometimes Martin would pull a face during Susan's business calls just to lighten the mood, to make her giggle. She smiled sadly at the memory. That was before Martin lost his job, before he'd lost his purpose and before they'd fallen into a loveless coexistence.

If Susan was being honest, she couldn't even recall what the catalyst had been, probably something insignificant, something unimportant. And yet it had been allowed to spiral, *they* had allowed it to spiral, a small crack in an otherwise happy marriage turning into an insurmountable chasm.

She brushed the thoughts away.

She was on a deadline and didn't have time to wander down that road now.

Turning her attention to the sales report once more, Susan felt a swell of pride. She hadn't been sure that the business was going to turn a profit, she had been confident that it would break even, but the figures had been, well, unexpected. Once they had tapped into the online social media channels and platforms and started running multiple book clubs, both of which had been rudimental ideas offered up by Jennifer, the shop's profit margins had boomed.

And that had been the push that Susan needed, the foundation on which she planned to move forward.

What Susan really wanted, what she secretly aspired to, was to be able to look in the mirror in another ten years, another twenty years and know that the woman staring back at her had given everything to this life, had grasped every opportunity and had dared to dream big.

Just because she was turning fifty didn't mean she was past her best, that she should simply stop and be grateful for what she had already. No, she had so much more to achieve, to do. *If the bank approves*, she reminded herself, resisting the inevitable excitement which came with a new project.

Susan's phone chimed, piercing its way through her thoughts.

With clumsy hands, she patted the many pieces of paper scattered all around her like snowflakes until she located the telltale lump of the mobile.

A small sigh slipped from her lips as she grasped the phone and saw who was calling. She answered nevertheless.

'Good morning.'

'Did you get my email?' Joshua asked.

No niceties, no polite conversation. No, *'Hi, Mum. How are you?'* or *'How's the shop?'* Joshua could be infuriatingly selfish at times, typically when he wanted something and Susan had learnt that any attempt to sway him from his plan was fruitless, regardless of how flawed it may be.

Joshua had to do it, convinced that whatever the idea was, it was going to be a big success. He would throw everything at it for a month or two, maybe a little more and when it didn't live up to his expectations, when it began to fail because he hadn't done his research, hadn't considered any sort of contingency plan, he would let it, before moving on to the next thing with an air of indifference. He would simply brush it off with a shrug of his shoulders.

Susan had allowed herself to become incensed in the past, inciting arguments which fell on deaf ears. Her exasperation doing little more than annoying him, he would just wave off her frustration, her attempts to press and push him, as though he were batting away a fly. Once he had given up, it was finished.

'Yes I did.'

'And?'

Susan needed to handle this with care or more precisely,

handle him with care. The truth was that she had glanced at his email briefly, but noting that he hadn't put any time or effort into it, she had decided not to waste any more of her own precious time reading it properly.

'And,' she began, dragging the word out, 'as I have said before, I think that your idea has potential.'

'But?' Joshua interrupted with obvious aggression, reading her hesitation.

Just like his father. Quick to burn hot.

'But, what I asked you for was a proper proposal. I wanted to see what the expected expenditure is going to be; rent, staffing, stock, that sort of thing. I wanted to know what you anticipate your profit margins to be, what your turnover is going to be. I wanted a business plan, Joshua.'

What Susan didn't add, knowing that it would only cause an unwanted argument, was that she wanted to see him put in the legwork this time, to demonstrate that he fully comprehended what it would take to set something like this up properly. A whisky bar wasn't some online shop, there would be employees who would be depending on a monthly salary to survive, there would be wholesalers who would expect bills to be satisfied on time, there would be rent to be paid, on time.

'So what are you saying? That you don't want to invest?'

Susan didn't have the energy nor the headspace to get into this any further, she had her own business plan to finalise and currently she wasn't getting it done.

'What I am saying is that the information you sent me is not enough, it's lacking any real detail.' A movement from the corner of Susan's eye distracted her, her trail of thought faltering. Martin was standing in the kitchen doorway. Listening. How long had he been standing there, she wondered?

Having been seen, Susan watched as Martin strode in and

turned the kettle on before diverting her gaze, instead choosing to look out to the garden through the large folding doors.

'Mum?' Joshua nudged her back to their conversation.

'Sorry, Joshua. Give me what I've asked you for and I promise to give it some serious consideration.'

'Fine.' Joshua didn't even say goodbye before hanging up, an air of toddler tantrum about his final word.

Despite tingling with anger, Susan managed to gently replace the phone amongst the mess surrounding her, a small shake of her head the only outward sign of her annoyance.

Perhaps she had been too easy on Joshua in the past, she considered. Too keen to support his endeavours no matter how poorly thought out they were. Perhaps he was this way because of her, because she had always jumped in to help him, never leaving him to figure it out on his own.

She knew Martin was hovering, probably wanting to comment on what he'd heard, his presence having charged the room, but like a coward she now trained her attention on the computer in front of her. But as expected, she couldn't focus, not with him there, not when she could feel his gaze burning into her.

She looked up.

'Did you have something you would like to say?' Her tone was neutral, her words absent of any emotions.

Martin took a sip of his coffee before he spoke. 'Whatever it is he's come up with, it will be a waste of money and time.'

Susan bobbed her head slowly then replied, 'Perhaps.'

Martin looked absolutely affronted by her response, his eyes widening. 'He is one of life's cock-ups, Susan,' he all but shouted this time. 'None of his bloody schemes ever amount to anything. He is too reckless, too impulsive and you facilitate his behaviour by supporting him.'

If they had been on better terms, Susan knew that she

would have been the one saying exactly what Martin had just offered up. After all, was she not just thinking the very same bloody thing? But right now, today, they weren't and so she felt her defences rising. Childish as it may be, she did not want to admit that Martin was right.

'Thank you for your opinion, Martin. Joshua is compiling a business plan which I fully intend to scrutinise before making any decisions.'

'Unbelievable. You're not stupid, Susan, so don't act like it. Investing in one of Joshua's ideas is no better than throwing our money down the toilet.' And with those parting words, Martin stormed out of the kitchen.

Susan could have reminded him that it was actually her money, that he hadn't contributed to their finances for several years, and yet she didn't. That would have been a low and unfair blow to strike. Instead, she remained mute, the unexpected hurt she felt keeping her rooted to the spot.

14

GRACE

Grace was back in the incident room. It was the perfect space to think and besides, it had a large whiteboard which she was presently using to map out her investigation.

She had been struggling to concentrate in the busy, shared office, feeling as though all eyes were on her, her colleagues waiting to see how she fared leading her first investigation. Perhaps she was being paranoid, she thought absently.

Utilising the whiteboard Grace had sketched out the possible avenues of the case. She had started by writing, *Susan Grey; Victim*, in bold letters at its centre. She'd then drawn three lines tracking away, each one labelled with a name; *Martin Grey, Christopher Maddison, Joshua Maddison*.

These were her prime suspects. The individuals who had given her the most cause for concern, the people who had something to potentially gain from Susan's death. Although Grace truly hoped it wouldn't end that way.

For the moment, she was following her gut and discounting Jennifer Russell and Rachel Burstow.

Martin was the most likely, she recognised, pacing backwards and forwards in front of the board.

'What do you know about him?' she said aloud to herself, encouraging her tired brain to pull the pieces of this puzzle together into something resembling a case.

Most crucially, it appeared as though Martin was the last person to have seen Susan before she fell. They had been arguing, in the study, which was positioned at the top of the stairs, only minutes before she fell.

Plus, from what Grace had ascertained, there was a significant imbalance in Susan and Martin's financial assets. Despite the house being jointly owned, Grace believed that Martin had been unemployed for some time, leaving a question mark over his monetary worth, whereas Susan, by all accounts, was wealthy and maintained a steady income.

Did they argue about money often? If there was a disparity, did Martin feel jealous or perhaps out of control of the situation?

That could be the motive right there.

The fight, according to Joshua, had been about Susan investing in Joshua's business, Grace reminded herself as she paused her pacing, her gaze fixed on the whiteboard. It would be a reasonable leap to suspect that their disagreement escalated, perhaps Susan walked out. Martin could have easily followed, they could have argued at the top of the stairs. Martin might have lashed out either purposefully or in the heat of the moment, causing Susan to fall.

Grace thought it through again for a moment, acknowledging that this was definitely a workable theory. All she lacked was any sort of proof.

Thankfully Amy was making a few enquiries into Martin's finances.

If her suspicions were correct, Martin could be brought in for questioning, although it would help if there was an eyewitness, someone who saw them outside of the study.

Grace grabbed the whiteboard pen and next to Martin's name wrote: *Motive; Money?*

'Okay, Christopher Maddison,' she said into the silence again. 'What did he have to gain by harming Susan?'

She was frowning even as she said it. He was clearly prone to violence, his previous offences were testament to his temper.

Susan had found out about Christopher's relationship with Rachel Burstow. Did they have an altercation, a verbal confrontation resulting in Christopher striking Susan, causing her to fall?

Again, that was a plausible conjecture from what little Grace had to work on. And yet, something was niggling in the back of her mind, a thorn which was scratching at her, wanting her attention. She followed the thread of her thoughts.

Christopher was one of the first on the scene, which he had already admitted. *Why admit that, why willingly put yourself at the scene?*

She pondered over this for a moment before concluding that he'd had little choice but to admit to being there. There was a witness after all, the waitress who had found Susan.

Rachel had also verified his alibi, that he had nipped inside to use the loo, putting Christopher outside the house up until two or three minutes before Susan's fall.

'Meaning?' the word slipped from her lips. *Meaning he wouldn't have had enough time to get inside, find Susan, start an argument resulting in the assault before getting back downstairs again and out of sight.*

She sighed loudly.

Grace suspected that Rachel was lying about being with Christopher before he entered the house, call it hunch, a gut feeling but something felt off. She had been too quick to offer an alibi, too keen to jump to his aid. Regardless, if Christopher was responsible, it left Grace uncertain as to how he could have got out of the way before Susan was found by the waitress.

Perhaps she would have to put a pin in that particular conundrum for a moment. Still, she wrote next to Christopher's name: *Motive; Impetuous passion?*

Finally, there was Joshua.

He too had argued with Susan right before her accident, only he claimed to have left the party after their disagreement, leaving his mother alive and well with Martin. What Joshua had failed to provide, however, was an alibi for his whereabouts at the time of the incident. *Could he prove that he had left the premises as he said? Did anyone see him leave?*

Grace believed that Joshua was the least likely of the suspects and yet, aside from Martin, he potentially had the most to gain from her death. Presumably he would be one of the beneficiaries of Susan's substantial estate were she to succumb to her injuries, solving his investment issues. With the pen in hand once more, Grace scribbled next to Joshua's name on the whiteboard: *Motive; Inheritance?*

Before Grace could get any further, a tap at the door had her turning on her heels. Amy had opened the door just wide enough to poke her head in.

'Got a minute?'

'Yes, of course. Come in.'

Amy slipped into the room, allowing the door to click shut behind her.

Although there was almost ten years between them, Amy was possibly the closest in age to Grace, apart from Harry, of course.

'So,' Amy began, as she plopped down into one of the chairs around the conference table, 'as requested, I have done some digging into both Susan and Martin Grey.' Her eyebrows rose, an indication that she had found out something crucial or at least a little bit juicy. Either way Grace found herself sitting down opposite Amy.

'And?'

'And, you were right. Serious inequity in finances. That's not to say that Martin doesn't have any funds,' she added quickly. 'It looks like Martin was made redundant during the pandemic, he received a substantial pay-off which appears to have remained largely untouched in his bank account. There is also some money trickling in from stocks and shares. They have a joint account, which is where most of the expenditure occurs. All what you would expect to see really, although Martin is only contributing a very nominal amount. It would seem that Susan covers most of the outgoings, at least for the house. But it is Susan's personal account which is the most interesting. She made a substantial payment the day before her accident.'

'How substantial are we talking?' Grace was leaning forward in her seat.

'Quarter of a million substantial.'

Grace whistled, then asked, 'Do we know who to?'

'Not yet,' Amy offered an apologetic smile, 'I'm working on it though.'

Grace's mind whirled frantically. *Who did she pay and why? Could that have been the reason behind her attack or the catalyst for it?*

Was Martin aware of this payout?

'Okay,' Grace said, 'that is great work but if you could find out who that payment went to it would be extremely helpful.'

'I'll get on with it now,' Amy offered. 'Oh, and I have ticked a few more off the guest list. Sounds like this party was quite the night for fall-outs, apparently one guest witnessed a couple, tall, well-built guy with a beard, and a blonde woman, both fortyish having a right to-do.'

Christopher and Rachel, Grace knew instantly. She knew it

was a long shot but she had to ask, 'Did they happen to mention roughly what time that was?'

'Nine or thereabouts. Apparently it was rather heated, the woman was seen to slap the guy, hard, across the face before storming off.' Seeing Grace's obvious excitement, Amy then said, 'That was important, wasn't it?'

'Yep, it just busted someone's alibi. And any news on the caterers yet.'

'Still waiting for the owner to send across the staff list for that evening. She has been away and isn't back until tomorrow. Obviously we already had the details of the girl who found Mrs Grey but that's it until the owner sends me the names.' She offered another apologetic smile.

'Let's hope that when she does send it across it opens up a couple of new avenues to explore. Great work though.'

'No problems.' Amy smiled as she rose from her seat and exited the room.

At least for now, Grace knew what her next moves were going to be. Shuffling together all her papers, she headed into the office with purpose.

15

CHRISTOPHER

Christopher was holed up in the corner of his local, away from the hustle and bustle, or more precisely, away from the people.

His mood was dark. Not only was Susan still lying critical in hospital, but the police were sniffing around, claiming it was attempted murder, of all things.

It wouldn't help that Rachel had lied, told that detective that she was with him when she wasn't. There had been too many people around and their fight had been too public to go unnoticed. Someone was going to blab and when the truth came out, which it inevitably would, they would turn their attention to him, would start to delve into his past. If they hadn't already, that was.

Shit.

Why the fuck did she lie? We would have been better off saying nothing.

He took a deep swig of his Guinness, the fingers of his free hand tapping rhythmically on the table.

God, he missed being able to smoke in the pub. Hated

having to venture away from his warm, comfortable spot, the one that made this feel like an old-man pub with its worn carpet, scratched table and dark pictures, to stand out in the cold or rain to have a smoke.

He resisted the urge, telling himself he would at least finish his pint first.

'Chris.' His name drew his attention. Christopher looked up to see Adam, his neighbour, peering around the edge of the bar. Feeling less than sociable right now, he simply nodded his head in acknowledgement. Under normal circumstances he would have offered something more in return, he would have probably even grasped his pint and joined Adam at the bar. But not today. Today he wanted to be alone, to wallow.

'Can I get you one?' Adam asked, indicating the glass still in Christopher's hand.

He was just about to decline the offer, aware that with that drink would likely be the expectation of company, when Joshua breezed in, coming to stand beside Adam.

'Hey, long time no see,' Adam offered, slapping Joshua on the back. 'God, you're the spitting image of your dad, ain't ya?'

Christopher watched as Joshua rolled his eyes. He knew that his son heard that a lot, although he struggled to see the resemblance himself. If anything, Christopher thought Joshua looked just like his mother.

The thought of Susan had him clenching his jaw tightly.

'So I've been told.' Joshua laughed good-naturedly. 'Buy you a drink?'

'Oh yeah, sure,' Adam replied.

Five minutes later, with Adam deep in conversation with the barman, Joshua sat opposite Christopher, placing two pints on the sticky, scuffed table. He slid one across to Christopher's waiting hand.

'Cheers, son.'

For a few minutes they didn't talk about Susan, the investigation, the potential murderer amongst them. Instead, Christopher decided to ask his son about his day, hoping for a distraction.

Thankfully Joshua obliged, even if they both knew they were avoiding the inevitable. Still, Christopher found himself relaxing a fraction at the normalcy of the conversation, his jaw going slack, his taut shoulders softening.

Christopher had never felt like he was a good dad, not when Joshua was younger. He had always loved his son, but had lacked patience. He couldn't soothe Joshua when he cried, and struggled to understand what he had wanted when he didn't have the words. It changed only as Joshua matured, moving out of the toddler phase and becoming a real character, someone who could communicate and laugh and demand that Christopher found his feet as a parent.

That had been around the same time Susan had ended things, having had enough of his shit. She had packed up all of hers and Joshua's things and moved out, leaving him profoundly alone.

And yet, she had never let him forget his responsibilities.

So here they were, father and son, Joshua's company feeling like a comfortable pair of slippers, which was just what Christopher needed.

Only as the conversation dried up, having skirted around the edges of what they really should talk about, Christopher finally sighed and said, 'That woman, Detective Roth, came to see me earlier.'

'I told you she would,' Joshua responded, downing the dregs of his pint.

He wasn't fazed at all by this turn of events, Christopher realised, a knot of unease coiling in his stomach.

In truth, he wasn't sure that Joshua had been affected by

Susan's accident at all. He had only been to see his mother once, from what Christopher understood, and he sure as hell didn't look as though he was struggling to deal with it.

But then Joshua dealt with things in his own way, Christopher reminded himself, often avoiding or pretending that unpleasant, difficult issues weren't important. Essentially ignoring them until they went away or he was left with no choice but to face them. Christopher didn't want to acknowledge what that would mean in this situation.

'What did she ask you?' Christopher said, ignoring his more morose, more sinister thoughts. He had lowered his voice to avoid being overheard, not that anyone else was close enough, not that anyone else cared.

Joshua shrugged, then said, 'She wanted to know about my argument with the douchebag. What time I left. Did I see anything weird. That sort of thing. Oh, and if I knew anything about an announcement Mum had been planning on making.'

Christopher frowned. 'What announcement?'

'That's what I said, I've got no clue. She hadn't mentioned anything to me. I had asked her to invest in my new business but then we had that fight,' Joshua offered as though that may have somehow been the answer.

Christopher was sure that, if Joshua had asked Susan for money, she would have gifted it to him in one fashion or another, she had always doted on their son. Perhaps she had decided to share the news at the party. The business venture Joshua had already told his father about sounded like a big deal, like it was announcement-worthy.

But he still wanted to know more about the investigation. 'And, did the detective seem...' What was the word he was looking for? Finally he settled on, 'Suspicious?'

Joshua frowned. 'Why would she be suspicious?' Then as

understanding dawned on him his eyes widened. 'Do you think I did it?'

'I never said that,' Christopher answered immediately, his hands instantly raised in an attempt to placate his son, because he hadn't meant that. He knew Joshua wouldn't hurt his mother but his lack of empathy, lack of emotion, certainly might raise concerns if not eyebrows.

After all, if anyone should be feeling guilty, should be under suspicion, it should be him. Christopher knew he'd hurt Susan, time and time again, and the night of her birthday was no exception.

'You really are a piece of work you know,' Joshua growled at him, interrupting his spiralling mind. 'I didn't do it. When I left she was with Martin.' Then just to be spiteful he added, 'What about you though, did you do it? Did you hurt Mum?'

More than you know.

'Look, I'm sorry,' Christopher offered, 'I am just trying to see it from the copper's perspective. You have only been to the hospital once and it's been a week now.'

Joshua's expression altered, the anger dissolving into something resembling guilt. 'He's always there.' Joshua sounded like a petulant child and yet Christopher understood.

Neither of them had ever understood what it was that Susan saw in Martin, he was the polar opposite of them both.

Perhaps that was the appeal, he was nothing like Christopher, the man who had let Susan down repeatedly, who hadn't been able to change even when she'd begged him, even when she'd threatened to walk away.

'You have as much right to be there as he does, more if anything. You know they won't let me visit, else I would have been up there every day. Go and see her. Let her know you're thinking about her. Tell her that I'm thinking about her too. Please, if not for you then do it for me.'

Christopher watched as Joshua nodded. He wasn't convinced that his little speech had helped any. After all, he wasn't very good with all this emotional stuff himself, but he didn't like to think of Susan in there, he didn't like to think of her stuck with only Martin for company and he didn't like to think that she might never know how sorry he was.

16

———

JENNIFER

The hospital was quiet, quieter than Jennifer had expected. It made her feel uneasy, uncomfortable, even though she was used to muted places, often seeking them out. This stilted silence, however, was eerie. It made her want to hold her breath and walk on tiptoes.

The hairs on her arms rose.

Instinctively, Jennifer spun around on her heels and exited the main lobby, panic fuelling her decision. She strode out through the automatic double doors, all set on getting back in her car and driving home. But something had her stopping mid-step, some gravitational tug that she couldn't shake off.

With each breath she took the oppression she'd been imagining lifted and with it her mind cleared. She had come this far, she had to go in, had to see for herself.

She looked back over her shoulder at the building. Susan was in there, her little sister was in there. She owed her this much.

But I just need another minute first, she told herself as she moved to lean her back against the hospital wall.

For a moment, Jennifer watched as a few people drifted into

the building, a pregnant woman probably heading to a scan, an elderly man being pushed by a younger woman, perhaps his daughter, and a young boy with his dad, his arm in a plaster cast. None of them came running out in a flap, none of them looked as though they had given a second thought to what it meant to walk through those doors.

Stop being ridiculous. If they can do it then so can you.

With a small burst of assurance, Jennifer pushed away from the wall. Shoulders squared, she retraced her earlier steps into the lobby of the hospital.

Susan was in the ICU. On the eighth floor, the wall sign indicated.

For a split second Jennifer considered taking the stairs, an obvious delay tactic, only she didn't want to be out of breath when she got there, didn't want to look any less put together than she already felt.

She took the lift.

Approaching the double doors for Susan's ward, doubt washed over her once more.

Am I really ready to see her like this? What if Susan doesn't want me there? What if I make things worse?

She was being silly, she realised, and yet the thoughts continued to spiral through her mind even as she pressed the buzzer, as she explained who she was and as she stepped into the ward itself.

It was only when she was faced with the reality of an intensive care unit, the beeping and hissing of machines, the clinical smell of disinfectant and soap, the hushed voices of staff and visitors alike, that Jennifer's mind stilled.

'You're here to see Susan Grey?' the man behind the reception desk asked gently when Jennifer remained rooted to the spot.

She hoped that this was his usual tone with visitors, but in reality she knew that fear was radiating from every pore in her body.

She cleared her throat and took a step forward. 'Yes. I'm her sister.'

'Have you been before?'

Jennifer shook her head, guiltily.

'Okay, so Susan is in that room there.' He indicated a door to his left. Despite there being a large window looking in, the blinds were closed. 'Her nurse is with her at the moment, but when she comes out you can go in. You will just need to sign in to our visitors log,' he smiled, pushing a large book towards her on the desk, 'and ensure that you've washed your hands.' This time he indicated a basin against the wall.

'Thank you.' Jennifer smiled tentatively.

Her heart was racing and as she raised the pen to fill in her details, she realised that her hand was shaking.

Get a grip.

Having scrawled her name in the ledger, Jennifer followed the instruction to wash her hands, all the while she focused on her breathing. *In and out, in and out.* It was keeping her calm, it was keeping her from bolting.

'You can go in now.' Looking up, Jennifer realised that the receptionist was talking to her. From the corner of her eye she saw the nurse exiting Susan's room. Annoyance flared under her skin as Jennifer silently cursed that woman striding purposefully away with a paper tray in her hand. She wasn't ready, she just needed another minute or two to compose herself.

Why do I never get the things I want, not even the small ones?

Jennifer turned to face the room. A lump had formed in her throat, she swallowed hard against it.

In and out, she reminded herself, moving slowly.

Jennifer had watched enough dramas, enough soap operas to have a good idea of what to expect when she went in there.

She pictured an archway of machines adorning Susan's head, beeping intermittently with Susan lying statue still below, an oxygen tube in her nose perhaps. There would likely be a few wires here and there, not to mention the obligatory cards and flowers displayed on the windowsill from her many well-wishers.

Should she have brought flowers? The thought had her pausing with her hand braced on the door-handle. It was too late now, she realised, feeling somewhat of an idiot.

Jennifer slowly shouldered open the door, coming face to face with Martin.

'I didn't think that you would still be here,' she said honestly, the words shooting from her mouth before she had time to push them back down. He was standing at the end of the bed, blocking Susan from view, with his coat on.

He cleared his throat before answering. 'Jennifer,' he said, formally, hiding any surprise that he may have had over her arrival. 'I was just heading off actually.'

Martin didn't look at her, instead he looked past her, through the open door which Jennifer was still holding and out into the reception area. Without another word, Martin stepped to Jennifer's side as though to slide past her.

'Martin?' There was a note of disbelief in her voice.

'I really do need to go,' he responded, continuing out of the small room. Jennifer could only watch as he strode away.

The last time they had spoken, when they were together, Jennifer had said some very unkind things, words thrown at him in anger and spite, words to hide her vulnerability, her pain. Perhaps his reaction was warranted but still it stung.

Had Martin paused to look at her, had he given her his time she might have apologised, might have retracted her threats, but he didn't. Instead, he had chosen to ignore her, to pretend she didn't exist, the same way the customer had the other day in the shop.

Fury tingled under her skin, her fingers itching with it. Her body going rigid with it.

She desperately wanted to chase after him, to tell Martin Grey that she wasn't someone he could dismiss so easily.

But as usual she didn't move. Didn't act on the impulse.

Instead, she mentally balled up all those feelings, all those unspoken words, and shoved them into the depths of her mind, where they would fester, resurfacing later when she was alone and they meant nothing to anyone but her.

Only this time she would make sure that they meant something to Martin, she wouldn't allow him to walk away from this scot-free.

She deserved better than that.

A whooshing sound punctured its way into Jennifer's brooding.

Remembering where she was, she looked back into the room.

At Susan.

Any balance, any resemblance of togetherness left her then. This wasn't like any of the programmes she'd seen. Between the bandages encompassing Susan's head and the breathing tube obscuring her face, Susan was practically unrecognisable.

Jennifer was afraid.

Letting go of the door, she moved further into the room, but stopped short of the bed.

She didn't know what to do now, what to say. She had hoped that the words would come to her in the moment, that she would feel able to talk to her sister but instead she found herself shaking her head.

'It wasn't supposed to be like this.' A solitary tear ran down her cheek as she finally moved to the chair beside Susan.

Jennifer sat down heavily, as though the weight of the world had forced her into the seat. With her head bent, she didn't say anything else, she just sat there for a time before she stood up and silently left, not looking back as she went.

17

———

GRACE

'Nice part of the world,' Harry commented absently as Grace drove through Storrington.

Grace had asked Harry, now that his prior case had concluded, to accompany her to the Greys' house.

He had been updating her on his meeting with Beth Green, the young girl who had stumbled across Susan Grey's injured body.

DI Amberidge reported that he had only been able to ask a few questions. Beth's mother, clearly not understanding the importance nor the necessity of his visit, had been exceedingly protective of her daughter, fussing over Beth throughout the conversation and interrupting at every opportunity.

Harry had, however, been able to establish that this had been the first, and only time Beth had worked for the catering company.

'I didn't learn anything new to be honest. She stated that she ducked out to call her boyfriend, apparently he's able to corroborate this as they'd been texting and he was awaiting a call from her. However, as she moved into the house, which was dark, she literally stumbled over Mrs Grey's body. Beth said she'd been focused on her phone and hadn't seen her. She reports she then screamed and everyone arrived. She couldn't be any more specific as to who "everyone" was.' Harry was looking at his notebook as he recounted the conversation.

'Why was it dark?' Grace asked, trying to smother her annoyance that they hadn't gained anything from the interview.

'I asked that, Beth didn't know. Perhaps Mr Grey will be able to shed some light on it.'

Grace didn't need to look over to know that Harry was smiling at his own stupid pun.

She had asked him to join her, concerned that she may miss something, seeing as how the crime scene was never treated as one.

Although a uniformed unit had attended as first responders, they had quickly assessed the situation, deeming Susan's fall to be nothing more than a tragic accident, and handed over to the paramedics. No evidence had been recovered or recorded, no witness statements obtained, no documentation apart from a log of their attendance submitted.

And it would have remained that way had there not been a tip-off, Grace thought to herself.

Harry worked intuitively, Grace knew, and that was exactly what she needed in this situation, not to mention some moral support. She suspected they would be working blindly, trying to find the tiniest specks of information on an otherwise clean canvas.

She in turn had filled him in on the case details during their drive from Worthing. She'd outlined her main suspects and the rough timeline of events which she had pieced together from the statements taken so far, not to mention the recent and very significant payout made from Susan's account. Harry had asked some questions, clearly working over the scenarios in his head before they had fallen into a comfortable silence.

'It should be up here on the left.' Grace indicated, slowing the car down and leaning a fraction forward in her seat.

As expected, the house wasn't numbered, but rather named, Hillside Farmhouse. Harry spotted the slate sign up ahead, displayed proudly on one of two brick pillars.

Grace took the turning.

Despite there being an intercom unit below the sign, the gates had been left wide open.

Following the gravel driveway away from the main road, they soon found themselves pulling up in front of a sprawling Georgian mansion. The kind of property you would expect to see featured in a period drama on the TV.

Disembarking, Harry let out a low, impressed whistle, his head tilting back as he took in the estate. Grace would have reacted the same had she not already researched the property. Still, she couldn't deny that it was utterly breathtaking with its symmetrical brick façade, the decorative window headers and the highly embellished entrance. In truth, she suddenly felt a little underdressed in her work suit, to be approaching the building. A formal gown would have been more fitting.

'I am obviously in the wrong job,' Harry joked as they took the steps up to the front door. Without hesitation he pressed the bell then crossed his hands behind his back as they waited. Grace found herself mirroring his posture. It was relaxed, inoffensive.

After a minute, the unmistakable scrape of a lock alerted them to someone's presence, before the heavy door was pulled open just enough to reveal the pointy features of Martin Grey.

Grace watched as Martin's eyes drifted curiously over Harry first before shifting to her, a look of recognition flashing across his face before being quickly chased away with a wide-eyed look of horror.

'What are you doing here?' His indignation was unmissable.

'Hello again, Mr Grey. I have some further questions for you regarding your wife. This is my colleague, DI Amberidge. Do you mind if we come in?'

Martin screwed his eyes shut, the gesture making him look birdlike. When he opened them, he let out a sigh of resignation. 'Fine, but I do have to go to the hospital soon,' he conceded.

Grace suspected that had she attended alone, Martin would have possibly reacted differently, slamming the door shut in her face, refusing to cooperate with her further. It was very interesting, or was that infuriating, how the public responded to male officers compared to their female counterparts.

Mr Grey stepped back and Grace gestured for Harry to enter first. She followed on his heels.

The outside grandeur continued seamlessly inside the house. The foyer that Grace found herself standing in, the one that was nearly as big as her entire flat, boasted high ceilings with decorative cornices framing the walls, a large mahogany table positioned against one wall, and the staircase.

Had that staircase not been central to the critical condition of her victim, Grace would have been in awe. It dominated the space with its ostentatious balustrades and hourglass shape, not to mention the arched window at its landing.

'What do you want to ask me, Detective Roth?'

The atmosphere was unmistakably prickly.

'Shall we sit down?' Grace suggested in an attempt to diffuse the hostility.

'Fine. We can go in the kitchen.' Martin reluctantly led them through a doorway to the left, along a short panel-lined corridor and into a very spectacular kitchen.

The kitchen was large with enough space to house a long wooden dining table and a small sofa tucked beneath the window. The décor was surprisingly modern, with glossy units and chrome accessories, a far cry from the traditional features of the lobby. Beyond the kitchen, through another door, Grace could see what appeared to be a more formal dining room, and on the opposite side, a utility room perhaps.

There were double doors leading out to the garden. Automatically, Grace walked up to them. She imagined the party in her mind. The catering staff busying themselves here in the kitchen whilst the partygoers revelled outside. Grace knew there had been a marquee of some description and even Portaloos.

'Detective.' Mr Grey's voice filtered into Grace's thoughts. She turned back to see him indicating a seat at the table. Harry had already sat down.

'Thank you,' she said, joining her colleague and extracting her notebook from her pocket.

'Mr Grey, I wanted to talk to you some more about the business meeting that you had with Joshua Maddison.'

'Oh?' Martin responded, sheepishly.

'I have spoken with Mr Maddison.'

'I see.'

'Would you like to tell me again about your movements before Susan's fall?' Grace had been very careful not to give away any of the details from her conversation with Joshua. She wanted to know if their stories would marry up. She also secretly hoped that Martin would give her more information, walking himself into a confession even.

Mr Grey looked awkward, as though he didn't seem to know what to do with his hands. He finally settled on linking his fingers together and letting them rest limply on the table in front of him.

Such a peculiar man.

'Fine, it wasn't a business meeting in the traditional sense. I'm sure Joshua told you that much, but it was about his next business venture.' The way he said *next*, the tone of his voice which sounded like an eye-roll, had Grace glancing in Harry's direction. He met her stare with equal interest. 'I didn't want Susan investing in it, in him, again.'

'And why was that?' Grace had her notebook and pen poised in her hand.

'Because Joshua doesn't have the commitment nor the determination to stick at anything. He always bails at the first sign of difficulty. Susan has wasted thousands on his projects in the past already. But this one sounded bigger, more expensive. I didn't want her getting caught up in it, especially when it all falls apart, which it undoubtedly will. Knowing Joshua, he would just walk away, leaving his mother to pick up the pieces.' Anger seemed to fuel his words.

'But Susan never did think rationally when it came to that boy, he often got away with murder...' Realising his own faux pas, Martin stopped talking, his mouth still open. He snapped it shut and looked to Harry, perhaps hoping to find some camaraderie. When he didn't, he blew out his cheeks and added, 'Susan wouldn't have listened to me, even if we'd...' He waved away his last words before adding, 'It doesn't matter. I thought I might be able to get through to Joshua instead, but I should have known that it was a waste of time even trying. As far as that boy is concerned, Susan has a money tree hidden in her bedroom.'

'Do you know if Susan did invest?' Harry intervened. Like Grace, he was obviously thinking about the payment Susan had made prior to her fall.

'No.' Martin was shaking his head for good measure. 'She said that she would look over his business plan. He had actually brought it with him to the party. Can you believe the audacity of it?'

Grace thought back to Mr Maddison's flat, there had been a folder on the desk that he'd glanced at, was that his proposal, the one he'd brought to the party? Why hadn't he left it with her?

'So your discussion didn't go well?' Grace pressed, wanting more details.

'No, it didn't. I am ashamed to say that I lost my composure. I'd had a couple of drinks and I ended up shouting at him. He yelled some things in return, told me he hated me, hated his mum for marrying me, that sort of thing, and then Susan burst in. She was seething, told us we'd both let her down for causing a scene on her birthday.'

'Then what happened?'

'Joshua stormed off, having told his mother that she was unsupportive and uncaring of all things. I tried to reason with Susan again, but she just shot me down, told me she didn't want her night ruining further, and then she left. I stayed in the study. Alone.' His attention flashed back towards the corridor, presumably towards the staircase. 'Then there was all the commotion when Susan was found.'

'I would like to see the study before we leave,' Grace said. A thought was floating in the periphery of her mind, she just couldn't seem to reach it at the moment. Perhaps seeing the study would help bring it into focus. 'Have you noticed if anything is missing?' she asked, changing course.

'Missing?'

'Yes, devices, jewellery, precious items? Anything unaccounted for?'

Clearly confused, Martin shook his head slowly. 'Not that I've noticed, but then I haven't really looked. Why?'

'There were a lot of people at the house the night of Susan's fall and I don't want to overlook any possibility...'

Martin looked genuinely worried. 'Do you think someone was attempting to rob us?'

'It's a theory that I don't want to discount yet.'

'I don't know about Susan's things but I can check in her room. But no, nothing obvious is missing. Do you want me to look?'

'I would appreciate it if you would. Perhaps once we've gone,' Grace offered, not wanting Martin to wander off and derail the progress she felt she was making with him.

As Grace turned her attention back to her notebook, Harry cleared his throat pointedly. She glanced at him from the corner of her eye, he clearly wanted to ask a question. Grace gave a subtle nod, grateful he'd refrained from taking the lead, seeing as how he was the more experienced detective.

'Mr Grey, I spoke with the girl who found Susan at the party–'

'Oh yes, how is she?' Martin interrupted, genuine concern in his voice.

'Shaken, as you would expect. She indicated to me that the lights in the house, particularly in the lobby, were turned off, which is why she didn't notice Susan initially. Why was that?'

Martin unlaced his fingers and withdrew his hands from the table. 'Susan had suggested they stay off so as not to draw the guests inside. It's a grand house, people can be nosy.'

Grace suspected that, from the matter-of-fact tone in Martin's voice, he was telling the truth.

'Were you aware that Susan had planned on making an announcement at the party?' Grace asked.

'No, not at all. An announcement about what?'

This was obviously a red herring, one which she wouldn't waste any more time on. 'I was hoping you would be able to tell me. Another guest suggested that Susan may have had something she wanted to share but no one else seems to have any knowledge of this.'

'No, I haven't got a clue either.' Martin sounded almost annoyed at the admission. Something about Martin and Susan's relationship wasn't sitting comfortably with Grace. It wasn't anything Martin had said particularly but more his reactions.

'How is your relationship with your wife, Mr Grey?' Harry asked, clearly picking up on the same vibes as Grace.

Martin's cheeks reddened immediately and he rose to his feet. 'I don't think our relationship is any of your business, do you? Now if you've finished interrogating me, I will show you the study but then I really must be leaving.'

Both detectives stood up and followed Mr Grey, Grace raising her eyebrows at Harry. Something was definitely off in their marriage.

They retraced their steps back to the lobby before heading up the grand staircase. Surreptitiously, Grace eyed the stairs, looking for anything amiss, any clue as to why Susan fell. Obviously she didn't find what she was looking for, she wasn't that lucky.

On the landing, Martin turned right, indicating the first door with a slight wave of his hand.

'Thank you,' Harry offered, moving past Mr Grey and stepping into the room.

Grace followed, the distinct smell of alcohol greeting her as she stepped nearer to Martin. *Has he been drinking?*

She checked her watch; 12:15. Normally, Grace wouldn't have given it a second thought, but it was barely midday and Martin had indicated that he planned on visiting the hospital. She would say something before leaving, she couldn't knowingly allow him to drink and drive, no matter his situation.

The study wasn't as impressive as Grace had imagined. Yes, there were books, but only a few shelves full rather than the rows and rows that the name suggested. It was definitely more of an office than a study.

Grace eyed the solid wooden door.

'Mr Grey, you said that you remained in here after the

altercation with your wife, am I correct?' she questioned, closing the door.

'I wouldn't call it an altercation, but yes, Susan left and I remained in here.'

She reopened the door.

'And you only knew of Susan's fall because of all the commotion, when she was found?'

'Yes, I have just told you all of this.' Martin's frustration was becoming obvious.

Grace knew that Harry was intrigued, his eyes boring into her as though he was trying to read her thoughts.

'What I am struggling to understand is how you heard the disturbance downstairs, yet you failed to hear your wife fall?'

'I don't understand.' Martin looked confused, but Harry got it, his head bobbing in understanding.

Susan wouldn't have fallen silently, so why hadn't Martin heard that?

'When Susan fell, she probably would have shouted out for help, perhaps even screamed. Why do you think it is that you didn't hear that but you did hear the panic that soon followed at the bottom of the stairs?' Harry explained, picking up the thread of Grace's enquiry.

Martin instantly looked like a deer in headlights, his eyes wide, his features frozen. 'I don't...' He began to stutter. 'There was music. From the party. That must have drowned it out.'

'But that still doesn't explain why you heard voices, shouts from downstairs, which is further away?' Grace pointed out with authority.

Martin Grey looked between the detectives, before he spoke again. 'I don't think I should answer any more of your questions until I have spoken to my lawyer.'

'I think that's a very sensible idea,' Grace agreed, feeling a swell of excitement. *If he had nothing to hide, he wouldn't need a lawyer.*

Although they didn't have enough for an arrest, they did schedule for Martin to come into the police station, with his lawyer, for further questioning before they left. Grace also suggested that Martin should wait a while before driving, owing to the drink he had obviously had. Martin's cheeks coloured at the warning.

Getting back into her car, Grace allowed herself to smile, to feel the modicum of success that they had just had. With Harry's help, they had uncovered a hole, a flaw, in Martin's story, an error which may be all they needed to prove his guilt.

18

────

SUSAN

SEVEN DAYS BEFORE SHE FELL

Susan trailed her fingers over several dresses. They were all lovely in their own way, but none of them were for her.

'Why is it that when you're not looking for clothes, you always find something but when you are looking, you can never find anything?' she moaned to Rachel over the clothes rail.

Today had been just like when they were younger, they had jumped on the train at the local station and made their way to London, the whole day ahead of them, both with money to burn and a party to buy for.

Susan had pictured the sort of outfit she wanted to wear for her birthday: fitted, black and glittery. Only all the dresses that even moderately resembled what she had imagined made her look, well, old, with bingo wings and a soft middle. Both things she didn't recall from her youth.

'I know exactly what you mean,' Rachel agreed with a smile. She was currently holding a cream jumper against her body. 'What do you think?'

Susan glanced up, eyed the bland top and shook her head. 'Yes, but you've found your outfit. At this rate I'll be wearing my birthday suit.'

Rachel laughed. 'Well, that would be one way of making the night memorable, not to mention the few heart attacks you'd cause.' She put the jumper back on the rail. 'I still like the last one you tried on.'

The last dress had been approximately three shops ago and the best of what Susan felt to be a bad bunch, but Rachel was right, she needed something to wear or else she would cause a stir. 'Okay, let's do one more shop, grab some lunch and if I haven't found anything better then I'll get that one.'

Wordlessly they both exited the store.

Covent Garden was humming with the excitement you only got on a Friday. The working week was almost at an end and the anticipation of the weekend's plans were building. Susan smiled as she spotted a hen do, the bride wearing a cheap veil and sash, tottering on high heels into a restaurant. She couldn't help but think back to her own wedding.

It had been nothing like the bash she'd planned for next weekend. No, it had been a quiet, low-key affair with only a very select few friends and family members invited. They had married in a registry office before heading to a little Italian restaurant for a meal. Martin had gently pressed her to go bigger, to consider a church service, but she hadn't wanted to make a fuss.

Even then, having said yes to him, she had felt conflicted. Not that she had or would ever admit this to anyone, not even Rachel. The truth was, it wasn't something she even liked to admit to herself.

She loved Martin, she had from the first moment they'd met. He had been kind and caring and reliable. All things she'd been left craving for with Christopher. But Christopher, despite his shortcomings, had always been embraced by her family, accepted as one of their own. Martin, on the other hand, was and would always remain an outsider, his middle-class upbringing, the suits he wore, the job he had, marked him as different, and that hadn't sat well with her working-class family.

Not to mention Joshua had practically detested him from the moment they'd met. Martin, not having kids of his own, didn't seem to know how to relate to Joshua.

And what was more was the fact Martin's dependability, his attentiveness, soon began to leave her feeling smothered. A feeling which had only expanded over the years.

He would blatantly refuse to argue with her, instead sidestepping important issues in an attempt to prevent any confrontation. She didn't look for fights, didn't nit-pick in the hope of starting something, but the more he denied her the opportunity to disagree, to have an independent voice, the more she found herself looking for those opportunities. Until they had ended up where they were now.

'How about that one?' Rachel nudged her, derailing her thoughts. She was pointing to a shop across the road.

For a split second, Susan considered shaking her head, looking for another option, the shop outwardly posh. That was the sort of place Susan had always felt beneath, believing she would be ushered out in a flurry of disgust and perfume if she dared to step over the threshold.

Silly, she knew, but then she hadn't always been well-off. She had worked damned hard for her money and perhaps that was the reason she was ambitious, ruthlessly so if needed. Still, it didn't change who she was underneath, the values and beliefs that she held. Deep down, Susan believed she would always be that girl who grew up in a council house wearing her sister's hand-me-downs, which were already second hand before Jennifer even wore them.

'Okay,' she eventually responded with more force than was necessary. She wouldn't let her irrational fear stop her today, she could and she would walk in there as though she belonged. Because she did.

Stepping into the boutique, it was exactly as Susan had imagined. The clothes, hanging sparsely on rails and mannequins, were stunning, the detailing exquisite. Every garment looked as though it were handmade.

It didn't take long for Susan to find herself trying on several dresses, prices be damned. Surprisingly, it was a silver, floor-length, fishtailed gown that had won her over. It hugged her tightly in all the right places, her hourglass figure looking timeless. *This is the sort of dress you wear when you are planning on making a big announcement, when all eyes are going to be on you as you tell everyone your news,* Susan thought excitedly.

The bank had approved her loan, she'd received confirmation only yesterday, and she had already put out some feelers about properties. The excitement and anticipation was almost too much to bear, she had nearly spilled the beans to Rachel on the train journey this morning. But she hadn't, she'd managed to rein the words back in before they'd left her mouth. She wanted to surprise everyone, together.

'Well, what do you think?' She held her hands out in a tah-dah motion and stuck her hip out to the side.

Rachel tilted her head, her lack of immediate response had Susan turning back to the mirror once more. It looked wonderful, she knew, reassured.

'Are you sure you don't want to get the other one?' Rachel offered. 'I mean, that one is pretty and all but I bet it's expensive.'

Of course, Rachel was fretting about the cost. 'It's on sale,' Susan lied to ease her friend's worries. 'And it's my favourite by far. I'm going to get it.' Susan smiled. Her mind made up.

An unreadable look flashed across her friend's face before

she responded with cool indifference. 'It's your money.' Rachel promptly turned back towards the front of the store leaving Susan wondering what that was all about.

'I'll have the goat's cheese salad and a glass of house white please,' Susan said, returning the menu to the waiter.

'And I'll have the Caesar salad also with a glass of house white,' Rachel added.

The waiter dutifully noted down their orders before confirming, 'Would those be small or large glasses of wine?'

Without looking over to her friend, Susan responded, 'Definitely a large glass.'

Lunch was Susan's treat, a thank you to Rachel for coming all the way to London, dress shopping, with her. The least she could do was go large with the wine.

They had managed to nab one of the remaining vacant tables outside in the restaurant's courtyard. The space, which was bustling with diners, was canopied with luscious ivy-covered posts and trellises, giving the area a midsummer's night feel. Susan imagined that it was magical in the evenings sitting out here, especially with the twinkling lights she'd spied hidden within the foliage, glowing.

With their shopping bags squirrelled under the table, they spent a moment in companionable silence watching the world pass them by.

Eventually it was Rachel who spoke. 'So, you haven't updated me on the Martin situation?'

'Ah,' Susan responded as she surreptitiously looked for their waiter and more specifically for her glass of wine.

She hadn't mentioned it because she was doing her

damndest not to think about it, not today. But it was inevitable that her friend would ask, why wouldn't she?

'Nothing's changed,' she finally said with a sigh. 'We tiptoe around each other, offer the occasional pleasantries but we don't talk. He's still sleeping in another room, still spending his evenings locked away in the study. I don't even know if there is a way back from this,' Susan said, the final part spoken quietly, talking more to herself than to Rachel. They had definitely grown apart these past few months, their differences becoming like a chasm they could no longer bridge, because the truth was that neither of them really wanted to talk about it.

Rachel waited until the waiter had placed their drinks and food on the table. After he had retreated, she frowned. 'It's really that bad, huh?'

'Yep.'

'I'm sorry,' Rachel offered, clearly not sure what else to say.

'It's fine, it is what it is.'

'Is there someone else?' Rachel blurted out loudly, drawing a few stares from other diners.

Susan spluttered on her drink, then offered an apologetic smile to the couple at the table beside them. 'What? Of course not,' she whispered across the table. 'Well, not on my side anyway.'

'So this isn't about Christopher?'

'Christopher? What would make you think that?'

'Well, you have been stringing him along all these years, haven't you? I think you liked knowing he was still there, pining for you, waiting for you, just in case things didn't work out with Martin. And now that they're not, I just thought...?'

'Well you thought wrong,' Susan replied vehemently, not able to meet Rachel's glare. 'That is not what I've been doing and Christopher knows that. He's been with other women over the years. He knows we are just friends. For Joshua's sake.'

Christopher was Joshua's father after all. True, she had wanted them to remain amicable, to be friends even, but she hadn't been stringing him along, hadn't offered him any reason to believe there would ever be a reconciliation. Had she? Why would Rachel think that?

'I hope so,' she responded somewhat sullenly. Susan glanced up to see that Rachel was now digging into her food, the accusation already a thing of the past.

After a minute Rachel suggested they should look for shoes next, making it obvious she wanted to move the conversation on, recommending a couple of shops to try.

Susan nodded, trying not to dwell on Rachel's prior words which had stung more than they should have, the words which had been unmistakably tinged with bitterness.

19

______

JOSHUA

Joshua found himself out in the centre of Brighton, the hustle and bustle of the endless nightlife exactly the sort of distraction he had needed.

The club was busy but not yet heaving. He checked his watch, 23:00.

Still early.

Joshua had positioned himself purposely at a table near to the bar beside the dance floor. He was visible, without standing out. He could drink his beer, watch and wait. Not that he felt he needed to hide, the bouncer knew him, had bought some gear off of him in the past. Still, he didn't want to make it too obvious, didn't want to presume that what he was doing was okay.

But he needed to keep himself occupied.

His contact, Gav, hadn't called yet and Joshua was getting nervous. He'd said a couple of days and that was three days ago now. Maybe he shouldn't have trusted him? No, he couldn't think like that, Gav had always come good for him in the past and this would be no different.

As Joshua watched a large group of lads stride in, laughing and joking with each other, his thoughts digressed, back to his chat with his dad. Joshua hadn't been able to face his mum, not after, well, everything. Did that make him a coward? If it did, he didn't care, he just knew he didn't want to sit there talking crap to himself. Besides, she couldn't hear him, she wouldn't know if he'd visited or not.

He had, however, plucked up the courage to call the hospital as a means to quell any rumours, any gossip that may be rumbling, as his dad had indicated. He certainly didn't want that woman detective poking too closely into him and his private affairs. Especially not now.

The nurse had reassured Joshua that his mum was the same as before, critical but stable. Having made it this far was a positive sign and the doctor was hoping to start reducing the sedatives shortly which had kept her unconscious whilst her brain healed.

If she woke up, he would work out what to do then, how he would explain himself.

Joshua downed the remainder of his beer, washing away the trail of thoughts with it.

A familiar figure trotted up to him, unabashedly, and leant in close enough to whisper, 'Buy a girl a drink?'

Joshua smiled wryly. 'What do you want?'

'The usual.'

Jessica wasn't his type. Sure, she was pretty, stunning in fact, but she was too self-absorbed, too self-assured. In truth, she was too like him and that was why they would never work long-term. Regardless of this, they did occasionally find themselves in bed together, they were only human after all. But Joshua didn't feel that way inclined this evening, his brooding and waiting was consuming his thoughts, he was too distracted to fulfil someone else's needs, their desires, tonight.

Still, he strode to the bar and ordered a drink for both of

them. Returning, he handed Jessica a glass then clinked his bottle against it. 'Cheers.'

'Cheers.' Jessica took a sip, her eyes never leaving Joshua. 'You by yourself tonight?' Jessica tilted her head to the side, the movement made her look very feline, he thought, like a big cat assessing its prey.

'For now.'

'You should come and join us.' With a sideways glance, she indicated a group of women on the dance floor. They were all looking at Joshua, watching him.

'No thanks, not tonight.'

Jessica pouted but didn't look genuinely upset by his refusal. 'Well, you know where I am if you change your mind.' She leant into him again then, her lips practically brushing his ear as she whispered her next request.

Joshua knew it was coming, the small clear bag already out of his pocket and concealed in his closed fist.

'Twenty pounds.'

Knowingly, Jessica pulled a note from inside her purse and tucked it straight into his shirt pocket as she planted a kiss on his cheek, in return he slid the packet into her waiting hand.

'Enjoy your night,' Joshua offered dryly.

Jessica turned on her heels. 'I intend to,' she said, the words drifting to him as she danced back to her friends.

By 2am, Joshua was up a couple of hundred quid, having sold all of his wraps. It was always a precarious decision, deciding how much to take out. He needed to have enough to make sure it was worth his while but not too much that if he got caught he couldn't feign personal use as an excuse. Tonight he had got that balance right. He smiled to himself, profiting always did make him feel happier, the hint of success lightening his step.

He exited the club, patting the bouncer on the back as he left, and headed towards Brighton seafront.

The night was surprisingly warm but the air was refreshing, clean even after having spent hours inside the club with its smoke machine, the pungent mix of perfumes and aftershaves and the occasional hint of body odour and vomit.

Joshua breathed deeply as he began the short walk home.

He hadn't gotten far when his phone started ringing. Shoving his hand into the depths of his pocket, he retrieved it and glanced at the screen.

It was Gav.

About time.

Joshua's heartbeat quickened as he answered. 'Gav, mate. I thought you'd skipped out on me.' Despite his jovial tone, his words rang surprisingly true.

'Yeah, well, I had to be extra careful this time. Wanted to be sure this couldn't be traced back to me, didn't I? Seems like you've got a genuine item here. How did you say you came to have it again?'

'I didn't,' Joshua responded dryly as he continued to walk slowly. He had said very little other than he needed the best price. 'So...'

'So, I've got a buyer for you.'

Joshua punched the air triumphantly. 'Excellent.'

'Obviously it's not as much as if you'd shopped around openly, got a few offers on it, that sort of thing, but I think you'll be happy.'

Cut to the chase already.

Joshua stopped mid-step. 'How much?'

There was a pause on the other end of the line, just long enough for Joshua to start to worry that he wasn't going to like what he was about to hear.

'Fourteen.'

Joshua pressed his lips together and screwed his eyes shut, his free hand balled up into a tight fist which he swung out in front of him as though he was defending himself against a ghost, before mouthing, 'Fuck, fuck, fuck.' Thankfully there was no one around to see his silent outburst.

'It's worth way more than that,' he finally responded, a note of desperation seeping into his voice.

'You're welcome to sell it yourself, but that's the best I've got. If it helps any, I've already accounted for my cut.'

'Okay, fine. How quickly can you get the money to me?' Joshua suspected that he was being screwed over, but he also knew he had no other options. Without any paperwork it would have been near impossible to sell on himself. Gav at least had some contacts who would turn a blind eye to the missing authenticity documents.

'Tomorrow. I take it, you want it wired into your account?'

'Yeah, the one you used before.'

'Fine, I'll get the buyer to transfer your cut to you directly. Pleasure doing business with you,' Gav offered before ending the call.

Joshua shoved his phone away and let his head fall to his chest. He knew it was worth twice as much as what he'd just accepted for it. Fourteen thousand was barely going to secure him a building let alone cover the cost of renovating, decorating and stocking a bar.

For a moment, he let the guilt he'd suppressed wash over him, let it ravage his insides for a minute. He had practically given it away without even attempting to barter for more. He should have at least tried a little harder.

Voices from up ahead had Joshua looking up. It was a couple, talking animatedly as they headed towards him. Judging from the way they were weaving from side to side, they were drunk, but happily so. For some reason, unbeknownst to Joshua, this made him smile. And just like that, his guilt and any lingering moroseness that it had created was gone, boxed up and stowed away.

Joshua resumed a brisk pace, his mind already working out where to spend the money, how he would use it to start his business.

Detective Roth was working late. She had spent the day calling and subsequently crossing off the remaining names from the guest list. No one stood out as a possible suspect and no one reported having seen anything untoward, other than reports of both the argument in the house and the one between Christopher and Rachel. Grace had even double-checked them all against the police database just to be sure. There were a couple with historic minors, but nothing that would suggest they would be capable of an assault of this nature.

We still have the catering staff to contact, Grace attempted to reassure herself. The company's owner had finally gotten in touch, providing the details of everyone who had been working at Susan Grey's birthday party. DS Cartwright was diligently making her way through those names. They needed to yield something from this extensive search, an eyewitness ideally, having spent too many man hours on it already.

Discarding the guest list, Grace turned her attention back to the email she had received from Mr Grey. Martin had been in touch pretty swiftly after her visit with DI Harry Amberidge.

Having suggested that this could have been a robbery gone wrong, he had willingly carried out an inventory of the house.

Martin was subsequently reporting that a necklace, a very expensive necklace to be more precise, was missing.

Was Grace surprised? Not really. Call her cynical but up until now Martin had been her prime suspect, this new allegation would obviously divert some of the attention away from him.

Grace looked at the image of the item in question. An image, one for insurance purposes he had claimed, that he had dutifully attached. It wasn't Grace's cup of tea, too ostentatious, but the graduated emerald and diamond tennis necklace with a large oval emerald at its centre, had been valued at over thirty grand. Grace clearly had cheaper taste.

It was a plausible theory, DI Roth realised. Admittedly it was one that she had suggested, but that didn't mean she had to like this new twist or that it was what had happened. She couldn't help but find the sudden loss of such a valuable piece of jewellery as, well, convenient to say the least.

On the car journey back from Hillside Farmhouse and their interview with Martin Grey, Harry had returned to the idea that all may not have been well in the Greys' marriage prior to Susan's fall. Martin had inadvertently disclosed they had separate bedrooms, having clearly said that he would check in Susan's room. What if the truth was that she was planning on divorcing him? Could that have been the motive? Quite possibly, Grace thought, and yet it was also possible that they simply preferred their own space, that having separate rooms meant nothing more than enjoying some time apart as a way of keeping their marriage together.

She would revisit this possibility later.

Still, Grace had to thoroughly explore every avenue of the case, including this report of a missing piece of jewellery, it was the responsible thing to do. Only, she would be utterly pissed if this turned out to be some wild goose chase orchestrated to deflect the heat away from Martin for a time.

Grace's mobile vibrated noisily on the desk next to her, drawing her attention.

With a small smile, she answered it. 'Hi.'

'Hi, pumpkin. I'm not disturbing you, am I?'

Pumpkin had been her childhood nickname, one her dad continued to use despite her repeated pleas to stop, seeing as how she was now a grown woman and a detective to boot. Her dad had simply responded that she would always be his little pumpkin, no matter how big and how important she got. And that had been the end of that discussion, apparently.

'No. I needed to wrap up anyway.' She glanced at her watch. 'Oh, it's later than I thought.'

'Are you working on a case?'

Her dad, Marcus, knew that she wasn't allowed to talk about the specifics, but he still tried to take an interest, asking a few safe, generic questions.

'Yep. Bit of a needle in a haystack at the moment though.'

Perhaps sensing his daughter's discord, Marcus responded lightly. 'Anything worth doing often takes time and effort to get it right. You'll find it, your needle, I'm sure of it.'

Even though he had no clue what she was working on, how little real evidence Grace had or the implications if she didn't find her assailant, the sentiment still made her smile.

'Thanks. But that's not why you called, is it?'

'No, you got me there. Just checking you're still coming round on Sunday?'

'Dad.' Grace's tone conveyed the eye-roll he couldn't see. They had a standing date on Sundays, so long as she wasn't working, and so far she had only missed two that she could think of, one due to illness and the other due to unexpected work commitments. And yet he called, without fail, every week to remind her. But then she knew that it was an excuse really, a reason to call, to touch base. 'Of course I'll be there. Aren't I always?'

After her mum had died, it was fair to say that the job had saved Grace. It had given her a purpose, a reason to get up every morning and slap a smile on her face, even when all she wanted to do was ball herself up in the corner of a dark and quiet room and sob. Her dad, however, hadn't been so fortunate. He had been utterly lost without his wife, like a balloon without a ribbon tethering it to the ground. His home and his heart were suddenly, if not expectedly, empty.

Thankfully he had never been a drinker so he hadn't had that vice to drown himself in. Instead, he just seemed to stop living; he stopped washing, barely got out of bed some days, often he forgot to eat unless Grace reminded him. He had been fading away.

That was until something snapped, or more precisely someone. Grace. She had screamed at him, telling him that when her mum had passed away she'd lost not one but both of her parents. Her words had been harsh and they had obviously stung, but they'd had the desired effect, dragging him out of his depression, and with it he'd found a new life passion: cooking. A task which had previously befallen his wife.

So now every week, he would delight, and very occasionally petrify, his daughter with a new recipe. Sundays were not simply for roast dinners in the Roth house. Oh no, it could be anything from a stew to a curry to a homemade quiche.

'You know I just like to check. I best let you get back to finding that needle. See you Sunday, pumpkin.'

'Bye, Dad.'

Grace spent several more minutes staring at her case notes, before she huffed out a sigh and swept the pieces of paper into a pile. She'd had enough, she was tired and hungry and she had the first niggles of a bloody headache. Begrudgingly, she recognised that she wasn't going to solve the case tonight, and especially not if she was feeling like crap.

Some food, some paracetamol and some rest. Then back on it tomorrow with fresh eyes.

With the file stowed safely in her bag, Grace switched off her computer, shouldered the leather satchel and made her way to the door, car keys in hand.

The building was quiet but not deserted as Grace made her way towards the car park. She offered a cursory smile to the few faces she saw before she stepped outside into the warm night.

Striding purposefully towards her car, Grace was already thinking through the meagre offerings her fridge held when a voice had her turning on her heels.

'Detective Roth?'

A uniformed officer Grace recognised but couldn't name was standing in the doorway, one hand holding the door ajar.

'Yes?'

'I'm glad I caught you. Do you have a minute?'

'Is it important?' Grace asked flatly, the headache which had centred itself behind her left eyebrow seemed to have ramped up its assault in the past three minutes.

'I think you're going to be interested in this.'

Curiosity piqued, Grace found herself automatically moving back towards the building. 'What have you got?'

She followed the officer who guided them back into the building and down a long corridor towards the holding cells. 'We picked them up about an hour ago.'

'Them?'

'Rachel Burstow and Christopher Maddison.' Grace barely managed to hide her surprise. But before she could say anything the officer continued. 'Drunk and disorderly, were causing one almighty scene by all accounts. Rowing in the street. Several neighbours called it in. Oh, and she's made an accusation of physical assault against Maddison, says he struck her across the face.' The officer glanced sideways at Grace. 'The holding sergeant seemed to think that you'd want in on their interviews?'

'Yes. Yes I would. Thank you.'

What a turn-up for the books, one of her suspects and a person of interest both arrested. She wondered what they had been arguing about, perhaps it was about Susan? Grace's headache receded as her excitement swelled. This could just be the needle that she'd been hunting for, the break in the case that she had been waiting for.

21

CHRISTOPHER

Christopher had been left to 'cool off' *all* night in a fucking cell. But the time on his own, with the thoughts he had been doing his damndest to ignore, had had the opposite effect. He was seething. His skin was practically tingling with built-up negative energy.

He hadn't done anything wrong. He hadn't started this. She had. He had only been defending himself. But as always no one was prepared to listen to him.

Christopher paced backwards and forwards in the small space afforded him like a caged animal. The tracksuit, police issue, that he'd been forced to wear, rubbed annoyingly against his skin as he moved.

Occasionally he would slam his fist into the wall, the door. It smarted but it was something to focus on, something to distract him.

They can't keep me locked up indefinitely.

As though someone had heard his thoughts, the annoyingly familiar scrape of metal on metal drew his attention as the bolt slid open on the cell door, the sound echoing ominously in the near-empty room.

'Step forward,' a large, or more precisely a fat officer demanded, a set of cuffs hanging in his hand.

'Where am I going?' Christopher countered before taking a step.

'Interview. Couple of nice detectives want to have a chat with you.'

Grunting in acknowledgement, Christopher did as he was told, stepping closer to the officer with his wrists held out in surrender. He had been here before.

He was cuffed. *Like a fucking criminal.* Christopher barely managed to bite down the words, to hold in the fury which was building like a pan of boiling water about to spill over.

Christopher was led to a room, the laminated sign on the door identifying it as Interview Room One.

He wasn't the least bit surprised to find the room already occupied by a tired-looking middle-aged man, dressed in an ill-fitting suit, his tie sitting just off to the side. He looked like he was the one who'd been in a cell all night.

'Your legal representative,' the officer identified. 'Coffee?'

'Yes please, black with one sugar,' the lawyer requested.

'Same.' Christopher sat down in the chair which was obviously for him.

With the officer retreating, the lawyer put his hand out. 'Good morning, Mr Maddison, I am Alexander Franklin, I'm the duty solicitor.' Christopher shook the man's hand, his cuffs jingling like he was a court jester. 'We only have a few minutes, I'm afraid. But in your own words, can you tell me why you've been detained?'

'You tell me.' Christopher responded like a petulant child. Franklin had a file on his lap which in all likelihood had all of Christopher's charges and his history listed.

This was a waste of time.

Unfazed by Christopher's attitude, the solicitor gave him a

stern look. 'Mr Maddison, I am here to protect your legal rights, to advise you on how best to move forward considering there are charges being brought against you. It would be in your best interest if you started cooperating with me.'

Christopher sighed. 'I was drunk, had an argument with a friend, Rachel. It got a bit heated, I wanted her to leave, she wouldn't, so I pushed her outside. She went nuts, scratched my face. The neighbours called the police. That's it.' Christopher knew that he had a scratch on his face, he'd felt it earlier. He resisted the urge to run his fingers along it now.

'Rachel Burstow?' Franklin clarified, his eyes scanning the file.

'Yes.'

He nodded once. 'Anything else?'

'No.'

'Mr Maddison. Your friend, as you have called her, states that you struck her first, slapping her across the face. Is this true?'

Christopher blew out a short, sharp breath through his nose and shook his head. *Of course that's what she said. Bitch.* 'No, it's not true. Although I doubt you or anyone else is going to believe that, what with my history 'n' all.'

'So tell me what did happen.'

'She was screaming at me, swinging her fists, punching my chest, my arms. As I said, I did push her to get her out of my house, I may have caught her in the face, but not on purpose. Not to actually hurt her.'

'I see.' Franklin fell silent for a moment then asked, 'And what about Susan Grey?'

Christopher's eyes widened, like he was the one who had just been slapped round the face. 'What about Susan?'

'I believe the detectives are going to ask you some questions pertaining to the ongoing investigation into her accident. Were you responsible for her fall?'

'What? No. Of course not.' Christopher hadn't even realised that he had risen out of his seat, that he was now towering over the suddenly nervous-looking solicitor.

'Sit down now,' the officer demanded as he pushed through the door, a Styrofoam cup in each hand.

The tension in the room was palpable, for a heartbeat no one dared move. It was only then Christopher realised that what happened next hinged on him, on his actions. His gaze flew between the cop and the solicitor and for a second he wondered how the hell he had gotten himself into this situation.

Regaining his composure, Christopher slowly straightened up, putting more distance between himself and his representative. The atmosphere instantly dissolved. In turn, the copper carefully placed the drinks on the table, but not before throwing a meaningful, *'are you all right?'* look at Franklin. Luckily for Christopher, Franklin nodded.

'Two minutes. And I'll be right outside.' The officer's words were obviously a warning.

With a fleeting glance towards the door, Franklin sucked in a deep breath. 'I am not sure what they have regarding the Grey case, but either way I would stick with "no comment". If they have anything concrete we can discuss it later.'

The door swung open once more, this time revealing the familiar face of DI Roth and another detective that Christopher didn't recognise.

Christopher watched as the detectives wordlessly took their seats.

'Hello again, Mr Maddison,' Roth offered, placing a file and large notepad on the desk in front of her. 'I am Detective Inspector Roth, in case you've forgotten, and this is my colleague Detective Inspector Amberidge.'

Christopher didn't respond, he didn't feel that this was a *hi, how are you* sort of moment. Instead, he watched them with eagle eyes, desperately trying to read their expressions, their movements, to gauge how serious this was, how much trouble he was about to find himself in.

'I'm just gonna get everything ready and then we can begin the interview.' Christopher sat motionless as, with practised efficiency, Detective Amberidge set up and turned on the recorder.

'The time is,' Amberidge checked his watch, 'nine thirty-eight. Present are DI Roth, DI Amberidge, duty solicitor Alexander Franklin and Christopher Maddison.'

'So Christopher, do you want to tell me what happened, why you're here?' Roth asked, obviously feigning ignorance. Christopher knew as well as she did that everything she needed to know was right there in that file, the arresting officer would have made sure to document everything.

Christopher shrugged. 'Nope.'

'Nope?' Roth parroted. Christopher couldn't help but notice the flush of red in her cheeks. That had gotten under her skin. *Good.* He didn't want to make this easy for her, after all, she wouldn't think about going easy on him, not if she thought she could pin something on him. 'Is that nope you don't want to tell me or nope you can't remember?'

'No comment.'

Roth smiled tightly. She was clearly used to her suspects clamming up; still, it must be annoying. *Never mind.*

She opened the file on the desk. Slowly, pointedly, she ran her finger down the page, stopping near the bottom. 'The report sheet identified that you were drunk and disorderly in a public place.'

She looked up expectantly.

Christopher blinked. 'No comment.'

'It also states that an allegation of physical assault has been made against you?'

'Yeah, well, that's bullshit,' Christopher spat, forgetting himself.

Roth didn't flinch at the outburst. Instead she said, 'So tell me what happened?'

'No comment,' Christopher replied, regaining composure. He folded his arms.

'All right. I am sure that you've been advised to "no comment" your way through this interview. But clearly you don't think this report is correct, so at the very least set the record straight, set me straight if you believe that I've got it wrong.'

'I am not the villain here.' Christopher glanced towards his legal representative. With the slightest of movements, Franklin shook his head. A warning. *Don't talk, don't say anything that will and can get you into more trouble.* Christopher hated being told what to do.

'Yes, I'd had a drink, yes, we had an argument, but I didn't hit her. If anything she's the one who assaulted me,' he said, defiantly pointing to the scratch on his face.

'What did you argue about?'

He knew exactly what the argument was about. He had called off their arrangement and Rachel had totally flipped out. She'd started mouthing off, firstly calling him names and then she'd dragged Susan into it, blaming her for his decision.

In truth she hadn't been wrong.

He had never made it a secret that he still loved Susan, that he had never stopped loving her in fact, and being with Rachel had made him feel shit about himself, guilty even. He had been lonely, but Rachel had been a mistake, one he'd repeated too many times. She had told Susan, when their arrangement had been private, making Susan believe there was more in it than there was.

Not that Christopher planned on telling the coppers all of this of course.

Finally he said, 'I broke it off, she was angry. That's all.'

Christopher could feel Amberidge's eyes on him. He looked up, meeting his hard stare. It felt as though he was attempting to be intimidating, perhaps taking on the role of bad cop to Roth's good cop. It wasn't working. Christopher wasn't easily intimidated.

'Why'd you end things?'

Christopher merely shrugged.

'You say you didn't hit her, then how come she has a bruise on her cheek?' Roth asked as Amberidge slid a picture across the table towards him.

Christopher could feel Franklin leaning in closer to get a better look, could sense his growing discomfort.

Christopher glanced down. He audibly clenched his jaw at the image of Rachel sporting a nasty-looking bruise below her left eye.

'You don't need to answer that,' Franklin advised, his voice barely a whisper.

Perhaps I should be listening to the lawyer. Perhaps I should have stayed away from Rachel. Perhaps I shouldn't have done all the things that I had.

Christopher leaned back in his chair, his mouth pursed into a thin line.

'It's not the first argument the two of you have had, is it?'

Again Christopher maintained his stony silence.

'We have witnesses who saw you arguing on the night of Susan's party. Who saw Rachel leaving the party right after you two had a fight.'

The look Roth gave him sent a chill down his spine. *They*

know then, that my alibi, the one which Rachel had been so quick to lie about, is a farce.

He'd laid into her for telling Susan about them, for making it sound like it was something more than it was. Rachel had retaliated by slapping him before storming off and leaving him alone. That was before Susan's fall, before he'd tried to find her to tell her the truth.

'Okay, what about Susan?'

'What about her?' he replied without thinking, without hesitation.

'Did you hurt her?'

White-hot anger burned beneath his skin. She was pressing too close, asking questions that were too raw and too personal.

'Did you argue with Susan as well, perhaps about the fact you were seeing her best friend? Did it escalate? Did you lash out, causing Susan to fall?'

Christopher's blood was pumping so hard, so fast, it rang loudly in his ears. He couldn't hear the questions, the accusations the detective was making, but he knew they were awful, that they thought he was guilty of hurting Susan.

He couldn't bring himself to deny them though, so instead he simply said, 'I love Susan, always have, always will.'

Roth asked more questions, an endless stream of questions, none of which Christopher heard, his mind whirling furiously. He was in real trouble, he realised, as they pressed and pressed him.

After what felt like hours, Roth finally signalled to Amberidge who in turn checked his watch. 'Interview terminated at ten twenty-six.'

'I suggest you spend some more time talking to your lawyer,' Roth offered as she swanned out of the interview room, file in hand, with a confidence that had Christopher swallowing hard.

22

———

JENNIFER

To say she was surprised by the phone call and subsequent couple of hours would be something of an understatement. In fact, she didn't even know that Rachel had her number in the first place.

Still, what was she supposed to do when someone asked for her help, she couldn't very well say no. Even if she'd really, really wanted to.

So with reluctance and an undertone of anger at having her day disrupted, Jennifer grabbed her car keys and headed to the police station, an establishment she'd never visited previously and one she didn't plan to frequent again.

'I just can't believe he would do that.' It was the third time Rachel had repeated the exact same phrase since she'd picked her up.

Oddly though, Jennifer agreed with Rachel. Only, Jennifer genuinely couldn't believe it whereas Rachel obviously did, if anything she was basking in the fact.

Or so she says.

Jennifer had known Christopher for more years than she cared to remember. He was practically family. Yes, he had been

133

in a few scrapes and yes he had a fiery temper but he had never lashed out at Susan, or any other woman that Jennifer knew of. That just wasn't Christopher. He had always respected women. He was one of the few good guys.

Also, why had Rachel spent the night in the police station if she was the innocent victim she made herself out to be? Surely the police would have taken a statement and then taken her home. But that wasn't what had happened. She'd been taken to the station, put in a cell and treated like a criminal.

There was more to this story than she was letting on.

With scepticism swirling round in her mind, Jennifer glanced over to Rachel, who was sitting in the passenger seat of her car. They were parked outside Rachel's tired-looking block of flats, only she didn't seem in any hurry to get out.

Still dressed in what was obviously last night's outfit; a tight pair of jeans and a top which showed off more cleavage than Jennifer felt was necessary, Rachel looked misplaced. Her straw-like bleached hair hung limply around her face, the grey roots a reminder of her age whilst her mouth, more wrinkled than it should have been from years of smoking, was pursed into a pout.

'I have known Christopher for a long time and I honestly can't imagine it. What were you fighting about again?'

Rachel lifted her chin in what was unmistakably defiance. 'It doesn't matter.' A false smile crept onto her face then as she crossed her arms and with a nonchalant shrug, said, 'And he did do it, didn't he?' Purposely she turned her face towards Jennifer, so she could see the bruise which shadowed her cheek. 'He deserves whatever he gets as a result.'

Despite the evidence, Jennifer didn't believe Rachel. Perhaps it was a gut feeling, or more likely experience. She'd proven repeatedly that she had her own agenda, that she couldn't be trusted, to the point where Jennifer had actively avoided her for fear of being caught up in one of her dramas. Rachel would push and provoke, exaggerate and even downright lie to get what she wanted. She had done it time and time again and now felt no different.

Despite the vagueness of Rachel's story, as to why she was at Christopher's in the first place, '*to discuss Susan,*' she'd said with a dismissive wave of her hand, Jennifer knew that they'd been dating. Or at least seeing each other in some capacity. Really, Jennifer didn't want to think about it beyond that. But it had become obvious at Susan's party that something was going on between them, Rachel had practically spent the evening hanging off of Christopher's arm.

She had always done a poor job of hiding the crush she'd harboured for Christopher as they were all growing up. She would blush when she talked to him, fiddle annoyingly with her hair and she seemed hell-bent on twisting and expanding any little tiff between Susan and Christopher until it became a huge issue. Jennifer had tried to warn her sister once, just to be shot down, to be told that she didn't know what she was talking about. So she hadn't bothered again, even when it was clear that Rachel's devious, spiteful words were working.

So she finally got what she wanted, Jennifer thought somewhat unhappily.

'You two looked very close at the party,' Jennifer eventually commented, wanting Rachel to respect her enough to tell her the truth.

She hated the feeling of being lied to, it felt uncomfortable, like something was swelling beneath her skin, threatening to push its way out. No, she preferred to deal in the truth, or if that wasn't possible, oblivion worked just as well.

Rachel turned in her seat, then sighed dramatically. 'Fine. If you must know we were dating. Not anymore. Obviously. But we had been seeing each other for a while.'

'Did Susan know?' This seemed like the logical thing to ask.

'I told her at the party. I had no choice. She would have found out eventually and it would have been worse if I hadn't been the one to tell her,' Rachel said as justification for her actions, actions which Jennifer couldn't help but suspect that Rachel had just rewritten.

If Jennifer had been anyone else, she would have spoken up then, told Rachel what a shit friend she was. Not only had she been dating her supposedly best friend's ex, which was definitely something you didn't do, or at least that was what she'd read in her many books, but she'd also chosen Susan's party as the time to break it to Susan.

What an absolute bitch.

But Jennifer was Jennifer. She knowingly avoided conflict at all costs, keeping her thoughts, right as they were, to herself. She would hold on to them tightly, nurturing them, internalising them until they soured another part of her. The anger she felt with the world multiplying as a result.

'What did Susan say?'

'Hmm?' Rachel responded, her attention now turned to her reflection in the sun-visor mirror.

'When you told Susan about Christopher, what did she say?'

'Oh, well not a lot actually. I mean, she was obviously pissed but she was dealing with Joshua at the time. Did you know Joshua and Martin got into a big fight?' She licked her finger before trailing it under each eye, eradicating some of the smudged mascara.

Despite Rachel not presently paying Jennifer attention, she still found herself nodding. Of course she knew, she thought sourly. In truth, everyone at the party had been aware. Their argument had been loud enough to be heard over the music.

'How do you know she was pissed if she didn't stop to talk to you?'

Rachel flipped the sun visor shut, and with eyebrows raised said, 'Firstly, she gave me that look, you know the one: eyes wide, nostrils flared and lips pursed so tightly they practically disappear.' Jennifer did know that stare, she had been on the receiving end of it a few times herself, but strangely the fact Rachel knew that look irritated her. She didn't like to think that Rachel was perhaps closer to her sister than she was. 'And then she said, "We'll talk about this later", in that stern mummy voice she has when you know she's pissed.'

'*Did* you talk about it later?'

A look that Jennifer couldn't read passed across Rachel's face, before she quickly smothered it with a wry smile. 'No. She fell before we got the chance.'

Rachel babbled on a few more minutes about Susan, bemoaning the hospital's visitation rules, but Jennifer didn't hear her. She was lost in her own thoughts, wondering what Susan really thought about the whole situation, if she remembered Jennifer's warning to her all those years ago that Rachel was after Christopher for herself.

'Well, thanks for picking me up.' Rachel touched Jennifer's arm, dragging her back to the present. 'I should try and get some rest seeing as how I didn't sleep much last night. It's fucking noisy in those cells, especially with all the drunks shouting and screaming.'

Before Jennifer could respond, Rachel exited the car, slamming the door behind her. Jennifer didn't wait, she started the engine, stuck the car in drive and swung out into the road. She wanted desperately to get back to the shop, to her ordinary, routine existence. She didn't want to be part of any more dramas, didn't want to be sucked into anyone else's problems, not when she had her own to contend with.

23

———

GRACE

Sitting at the table in the dining room, Grace waited with trepidation for her dad to reappear from the kitchen with Sunday lunch.

As always she had supplied the dessert, a traditional trifle today. The rest was left to him.

She hoped that his latest concoction wasn't anything too spicy, her dad seemed to have an iron stomach when it came to spices, whereas Grace had taken after her mum in that department. She liked a little bit of heat but anything more just wasn't enjoyable.

Glancing around the room, Grace smiled sadly to herself. Her dad hadn't changed a single thing since her mum's death. Every picture was in its usual place, every ornament positioned just as it always had been. Not that she wanted him to rip it all out and start again, but he could adapt, could make gentle adjustments if he wanted to, Grace wouldn't mind. Perhaps she should suggest as much just in case he was keeping it this way for her.

'Here we go,' her dad announced proudly as he strode into the room, a large silver tray in his hands.

Grace eyed the tray as he placed it on the table in front of her. It was roast chicken. *Thank God for that.* A bubble of laughter found its way out of her mouth, releasing the anxiety she'd been holding on to.

'What's so funny?'

'Nothing, Dad. Sorry. But a roast chicken, that's very mainstream for you for Sunday lunch?'

'Well, I just thought I would cook something I know you like. You sounded a bit,' he paused for a moment as though searching for the right words, 'flat when I spoke to you the other day.' He held up his finger as though to say wait one minute, before dashing back out only to return a moment later with a bowl of potatoes and another one of mixed vegetables. 'Is everything all right?'

'Of course,' she replied automatically whilst serving herself a generous portion of lunch.

'You can talk to me, you know. I know that your mother was always better at this sort of thing than me, but,' he pointed to his ears, 'I have a good set if you do want to talk.'

Grace smiled. 'Thanks, Dad. It's this case I'm working on, it's turning out to be, well, tricky. I mean, I knew it was going to be difficult but I haven't got any solid leads yet, just a few suspects but nothing to pin them with.'

'You mentioned a needle in the haystack, is this the same case?'

'Yep.'

Her dad was silent for a moment whilst he spooned vegetables onto his plate. 'Don't be disheartened, pumpkin. Often what we're looking for finds a way of presenting itself when we stop looking for it.'

Her dad's philosophical statements were often obscure, but deep down she hoped there was some truth in what he was saying.

'I hope so,' Grace replied, forking a piece of chicken and popping it into her mouth. 'Dad, you could have told me it was lemon chicken before I smothered it in gravy.'

Her phone beeped ominously just as Grace was finishing her last mouthful. Giving her dad an apologetic smile, she pulled it from her pocket and glanced at the screen. Her eyes skimmed over a message from DS Cartwright.

'Sorry, Dad, it's work. I just need to make a quick call.'

'Don't apologise. I'll make a start on the washing up.'

With her dad back in the kitchen Grace dialled her colleague. 'Tell me you've got something good?' Grace said the moment DS Cartwright answered.

'I think so. I was finally able to check out all the staff working the night of the party. At first they all checked out, but then when I cross-checked their details with our database, it flagged up a Lisa Hatton. She was one of the waitresses. Turns out she's previously done some time for theft, breaking and entering and handling stolen goods.'

Shit. So it could have been a theft gone wrong all along.

When Grace didn't immediately respond, Amy continued talking. 'I'm betting that if that necklace was stolen, then this is a good place to start.'

'Agreed. Have we got a current address?'

'Yep. I'll send it to you now.'

'Thanks. Can you meet me there...' Grace glanced at her watch. It was just before four. That was a good time to catch people at home, she decided. 'In an hour?'

'Of course.'

Grace's phone beeped with Lisa Hatton's address almost instantly after she'd ended the call. A quick search told Grace that the address was a property on the outskirts of a village not too far from where Susan Grey lived. She could be there in thirty minutes.

Perhaps sensing that she was no longer on the telephone, or more likely because he had been listening from the kitchen, her dad popped his head round the door. 'Do you still have time for dessert?' he asked, eyebrows raised hopefully.

Grace smiled. 'Yes, I think I have time.'

Grace pulled into the lay-by behind DS Cartwright's vehicle. The house they were looking for was on the opposite side of the road.

It was the sort of property that would put you off buying the neighbouring house. The front garden of the semi-detached brick building, was littered with a rusting old motor which may or may not have been red at one time. It didn't look as though it would move under any circumstances unless it was towed. Beside it was an old chest freezer and several black bags, one of which was split open, its contents spilling out onto the overgrown path.

Lisa Hatton was clearly not a woman who was house-proud.

DS Cartwright tapped on the passenger window of Grace's car. Grace signalled for her to get in.

'Didn't interrupt anything important, did I?' Amy asked, sliding into the passenger seat.

She was wearing a black suit and a crisp white shirt, her hair was pulled up into a neat ponytail.

'No, not at all. What do you think?' she asked her colleague, indicating with a nod of her head towards their suspect's house.

'I think I wouldn't want to live next door to that. Here, I printed off Hatton's file for you.'

Grace took the file, flipping over the front page and scanning the first page.

'Wow, she's certainly got form.'

'Yep,' Amy agreed. 'Looks like this could have been a robbery all along.'

Grace knew she was frowning at that idea, something about it not quite fitting correctly and yet her head bobbed in a nod. 'Certainly starting to look that way. Right, come on then, let's find out what Lisa Hatton has to say.'

The two detectives exited the car simultaneously and crossed the road.

The small metal gate which should have acted as a boundary for the property was hanging limply on one hinge, the other having been snapped off. Grace, suspicious as ever, guessed that it had been kicked open, perhaps during some kind of argument.

She could feel herself tensing in anticipation as she neared the front door.

With a final glance over her shoulder, to ensure that DS Cartwright was still a step behind, Grace knocked loudly.

Dogs began barking. There could be two, perhaps even three, and one sounded big.

Her heart began pounding but she stood her ground, refusing to move back even an inch.

A woman's husky voice echoed from within the house, shouting at the dogs to get back, to get down before a door was slammed shut, the barks instantly stifled.

Thank God for that.

It wasn't that Grace didn't like dogs exactly, she just hadn't grown up around them so didn't know what to do or how to act which often meant that the dogs didn't warm to her. This would definitely go smoother without the animals there.

Through the frosted glass, Grace watched as a blurred figure approached.

A key was turned and then the door was pulled open to reveal a sliver of a woman's face. 'Can I help you?'

'Lisa Hatton?'

'Yes?'

Grace pulled her badge from her pocket and flashed it towards their newest suspect. 'I'm Detective Roth and this is Detective Cartwright. Can we come in for a minute?'

Grace watched as Lisa looked back into the property, fear shining in her eyes. Was she thinking about running? Or was there something in there that she didn't want them to see?

Finally she turned back to the detectives, perhaps realising that she didn't really have any other option and asked, 'What's this about?'

'We are investigating an incident which occurred at a party you were waitressing at. We are talking to everyone who was there,' Grace offered vaguely. She didn't want to spook Lisa now. *Although if she did try to run then it was likely she was guilty,* Grace reasoned.

The door opened a fraction more, revealing more of Lisa Hatton. She was attractive, Grace thought fleetingly, with large brown eyes, a small delicate nose and full lips. Her hair, a brown so dark it almost looked black, was swept up into a knot on the top of her head.

Just as she was about to say something, a male voice from within the property had Lisa's head whipping to the side. 'Coppers,' she called back.

It was hard not to hear the swearing and commotion which ensued from within the property for the next few seconds.

'You'd best come in then.' Lisa finally sighed, stepping back, the unrest from within having subsided.

Grace, with Amy a step behind, moved into the small hallway and followed Lisa into the lounge.

The inside of the property did not reflect the outside, much to Grace's surprise.

Although the furniture was dated and the carpet clearly worn, the room was clean and well-presented.

In striking contrast to the old-fashioned furnishings, however, was a bearded man sitting in a flowery armchair. He was perhaps in his late twenties. His light-brown hair was cropped short at the sides but was fashionably longer and slicked back on top. He was well-built and both his arms were decorated with whorls of elaborate tattoos. Grace made a mental note of a few of them, they were very identifiable, meaning that she could check the system, find out if he was known to the police.

Dressed casually in grey joggers and a plain white T-shirt, he seemed very at home. But it was his eyes which Grace couldn't help but notice, they were aquamarine-blue and they held Grace firmly in his stare.

'Sit down.' Lisa motioned with a wave of her hand whilst she perched on the armrest of the chair, the man's arm automatically looping around her waist.

'Good afternoon, I'm Detective Roth, this is Detective Cartwright, and you are?'

The dogs, stowed away in what Grace presumed was the kitchen, started barking and pawing at the door, aware that there were strangers in their home. Their cacophony of excited and disgruntled noises echoed through the room making it sound as though Lisa could be housing ten animals back there. Grace swallowed down her own unease.

'Shut up,' Lisa called out with little effect. 'They'll stop in a minute.'

Grace smiled wryly, then in a voice loud enough to compete with the incessant cries of the dogs, Grace asked once more, 'Sorry, what did you say your name was?'

'Lisa's boyfriend,' he replied, his voice rough.

Grace pulled her notepad and pen from her pocket. She

wasn't in the mood to play games, so with a stare to match his own and an edge of contempt to her words, she repeated 'Lisa's boyfriend,' jotting it down on a fresh page. Then she frowned, showing her displeasure. 'Got a first name to go with that?'

Perhaps feeling the rising tension, Lisa intervened. 'This is Jonny. You said you wanted to talk about a job I waitressed at?'

Noting down his name, confident that between the tattoos and his first name, she'd be able to identify him, Grace nodded. 'Yes, it was a fiftieth birthday for a woman called Susan Grey, she–'

'I know the night you mean,' Lisa interjected. 'Fucking horrible what happened to that lady.'

'Can you tell me about that night? What do you remember?'

Lisa gripped her lower lip between her teeth. She looked worried, Grace decided. She hadn't been truly convinced that this investigation, this case, was going to end up being a robbery gone wrong. In fact, Grace had turned up suspecting that this was going to be an utter waste of her time, but that look, the apprehension which had filled Lisa's face had her doubting herself.

'I was waitressing, as you know already. I mainly worked outside in the marquee, handing out canapés, topping up wine glasses, that sort of thing.'

Grace smiled. 'I see. Am I right in thinking that the catering company had full use of the house kitchen?'

'Yes. There were two guys, Steven and Matt, they do all the cooking and then there were about eight waiting staff to collect and serve.'

'When you were in the house, collecting food, did you notice anything unusual? Anyone who shouldn't have been there?'

Lisa looked to Jonny briefly. Had Grace not been paying attention, had she not been watching closely, she might have missed it, the warning imperceptible but there nonetheless that passed between Lisa and her boyfriend.

He was telling her not to say too much, not to tell Grace everything, but why? What did this waitress have to hide unless of course she was the thief. Perhaps Jonny was also involved, selling on the stolen jewellery for her?

Grace's mind began racing almost as fast as her heart as she started considering all the ways that this could tie together her investigation.

She wished the dogs would shut up, she couldn't concentrate to follow the threads of her thoughts.

'There were constantly guests wandering in, getting in the way.'

'Anyone in particular that you remember?'

Lisa stuck out her bottom lip and shook her head. 'No.'

'That's okay. You said that it is horrible what happened to Mrs Grey, can you tell me what you know about the incident?'

There it was again, that look between Lisa and Jonny.

'Just that she fell down the stairs and that she's in a bad way.'

'Yes she is. Her injuries are very serious.' Grace placed her notebook on her lap and leant forward, clasping her hands together and resting them on her knees. 'I am investigating Mrs Grey's fall as there has been an allegation of theft and it may be that both incidents are related.'

'Theft?' Lisa questioned, confused.

Grace nodded, then turned to DS Cartwright who knowingly handed her a picture. 'A very valuable necklace is missing, presumed stolen. Did you happen to see this at any point during the evening?' She passed the image across to Lisa.

Lisa looked at the image, studied it before shaking her head. 'No, I didn't see this.'

She looked as though she wanted to say more, to ask something, but she didn't, instead she handed back the picture.

Time to be more direct.

Leaning back, Grace asked, 'Did you go into the main house for any reason?'

'She didn't steal it, if that's what you're getting at.' Jonny's words were laced with anger and Grace couldn't help but notice that his free hand, which had been resting on the arm of the chair, was now gripping the fabric. Hard. His knuckles had turned white from the effort.

Grace chose to keep her attention focused on Miss Hatton. 'As a matter of routine we ran a background check on everyone working there that night. You have previously served time for similar offences, haven't you?'

Lisa tilted her head up in what was unmistakably arrogance. 'Yeah, that's right and I've served my time for what I did.' Then after a moment's hesitation, she added with more modesty, 'You've got the wrong woman. I didn't do it. I don't ever want to go back to prison, I can assure you of that. I didn't take anything. And besides, I didn't ever hurt anybody. I'm working two jobs to make a living and still I get picked out. Can you fucking believe it?'

Once again, Grace had nothing to base it on other than a gut feeling, but she genuinely believed Miss Hatton. She had looked almost haunted when she mentioned prison as though that experience had burned itself into her soul. Yes, many convicts reoffended, but for a few the shock of prison was enough to turn them around. And Lisa Hatton's words suggested that she'd fallen into the latter category.

'You can understand why we would want to talk to you though, can't you?'

She shrugged. 'I guess.'

'Cos she's an easy target for you lot,' Jonny commented unhelpfully.

Ignoring his remark, Grace glanced at her colleague. Amy nodded her head in understanding. 'Okay, well, we have some further enquiries to make. We may need to talk to you again. Thank you for your time.'

Lisa followed them to the door and as Grace left she said, 'For what it's worth, I hope you catch 'em.'

So do I, Grace thought.

Grace and DS Cartwright left the property and got back into Grace's car.

'She didn't do it,' Amy said instantly, confirming what Grace already suspected. 'The boyfriend though, I wouldn't put it past him. Shame he wasn't on one of our lists.'

24

SUSAN

FIVE DAYS BEFORE SHE FELL

Susan slid back into her car, placing her handbag and leather folder on the passenger seat. She couldn't suppress the Cheshire-cat-like smile which was fixed into place.

'It's really happening,' she whispered to herself, a note of disbelief in her words. *And yet no one knows.*

But they would do soon, very soon in fact.

Susan hadn't originally planned to keep it a secret but she hadn't wanted to get ahead of herself, or to feel like a failure if it hadn't happened, hadn't been achievable. She especially never wanted to hear the words, *'really, at your age?'* Words which someone would have used without malice but they would have stung, would have made her feel redundant, past-it even.

So she had kept her plans to herself. Not even Rachel knew. They'd never had secrets from one another before, in all their years of friendship, and that was the one which Susan had found the hardest. Not that she had lied of course, she had just omitted the truth when they'd been chatting. But she was confident Rachel would understand, once she'd explained everything.

Her heart was racing from the adrenaline, the excitement.

Her eyes drifted to the leather folder, the folder which contained the premises details.

It was going to be a new beginning.

Now she needed to get home and put all the wheels into motion. She had a lot to do.

Susan didn't know where Martin was. Surprisingly, he wasn't at home when she returned.

Perhaps it's for the best, he would only spoil my good mood, she thought.

Still, it felt peculiar coming home to an empty house. He was always here, always milling about. In all honesty, Susan had started to believe that he had become something of a recluse, hauled up in his study doing God knows what for hours on end.

It's not as if he's working. There might have been a touch of malice to that thought.

The kettle boiled, snapping her out of her own head.

Susan made herself a strong but sweet coffee then headed to her usual seat at the kitchen table.

She hadn't wanted to seem too keen during the viewing, but she had known that it was the one the minute she'd walked through the door. It had ticked every box. She just wanted to double-check all her figures, to make sure she hadn't missed anything before putting in an offer.

With her laptop on and several pieces of paper positioned around her, Susan set to reviewing her workings out.

Before her coffee had even had a chance to cool, her productive silence was shattered, first by the opening and then subsequent slamming of the front door, quickly followed by the rustling of a bag and the familiar clinking of glass on glass.

Susan suppressed her disapproval as she realised that

Martin had been out to buy alcohol. Whisky or brandy, or both, she guessed.

As the sound grew closer, Susan shifted uncomfortably in her seat and began shuffling the papers around her to hide anything incriminating. She knew she would have to tell Martin at some point, knew that really he had a right to know what she was up to, but she couldn't seem to bring herself to find the right time, to find the right words. The chasm between them just felt too vast.

So vast in fact, that she hadn't even told him about the birthday party that she was hosting in their home in a few days' time. Perhaps she would start with that.

Martin strode into the kitchen and Susan kept her gaze trained on her laptop. She kept her features neutral, relaxed, hoping to hide any residual guilt.

Martin had seen her, she knew, and yet neither spoke as he busied himself with unpacking his purchases on the counter. Without raising her head, Susan glanced up to see a bottle of whisky, another of brandy and a third of vodka lined up on the side.

Her heart sank.

The tension was palpable, neither wanting to break the stalemate, but Susan had had a really positive day, she didn't want to let it be ruined so easily, plus she should tell him about Saturday, so she said, 'The kettle's not long boiled if you want a cuppa?'

He turned round and looked at her with an expression she couldn't quite read, before responding, 'I'm okay, but thank you.'

Susan didn't know what else to say and Martin didn't seem to want to grab hold of the olive branch she'd offered him as he turned back to his bottles, his back facing her.

Come on, she internally chided, *just get it over with and tell him.*

She knew she was procrastinating, knew that it was his silent yet obvious disapproval that she was avoiding. Despite sidestepping an argument at all costs, Martin had still become adept at making Susan feel small, silly even. It would be a throwaway comment, or a statement which undermined what she'd just said or sometimes he would redo something that Susan had already done, like loading the dishwasher, or cleaning out a pot she'd already cleaned, just to demonstrate how it was done properly.

It should have been water off a duck's back, easy to dismiss in a happy marriage, but in a struggling one, these things had and were chipping away at her.

Still, she should be the bigger person.

'Martin,' she broached tentatively.

Perhaps hearing the uncertainty in her voice, he turned around slower this time, a wariness in his eyes.

'I don't know if you've remembered but it's my birthday on Saturday, my fiftieth.' Martin opened his mouth but Susan forged on, determined to get this over and done with. 'I'm having a party, a garden party to celebrate. I've invited some family and friends, a few work colleagues, the neighbours. You're welcome to attend. If you want to, that is?'

She watched as Martin's mouth fell open and his brow creased. 'This Saturday?'

Susan nodded.

'Forgive me for asking, but that sounds like a lot of people. Why am I only just hearing about this now?'

Damn him and his passive-aggressiveness.

'Because I didn't think you'd be interested, and it's not like we have been on speaking terms lately, is it?' She was being honest but she also knew that deep down she wanted to rile him, to get a response. *Anything would be better than this.*

He blustered at her honesty, before collecting himself. 'That may be, but this is my home too and out of respect you should have consulted me.'

'You're right,' Susan conceded, because he was. At the last head count, she estimated that there would be over a hundred guests. She should have told him sooner. Still, it's hard to do that when you're not talking.

Martin looked at Susan over the rim of his glasses, a look which reminded her of a teacher she'd had as a teenager. It was an authoritative stare, condescending even. She'd loathed that teacher and she loathed that look.

'Susan, I know it's your birthday and a big one at that, but I am not sure I am really comfortable with having so many people in the house, especially at such short notice.' Martin turned away as though that was the end of the conversation.

Susan could feel her anger rising. Perhaps she should have said something sooner, given him more warning, but she'd be damned if he thought she was going to cancel it now.

'I appreciate that it is short notice, however as I said, it is going to be in the garden, so no need to feel uncomfortable about people in the house. In fact, I'll make sure the guests know to stay outside.'

When Martin faced Susan at last, she saw a flash of his fury before he quickly buried it. Ever the pacifist, Susan knew that Martin wouldn't pursue this further. He had voiced his disapproval and Susan had chosen to ignore it.

'Fine then.' His tone was clipped. Susan watched as Martin grabbed hold of one of the bottles, the whisky, clutched it tightly to his chest and shuffled back out of the door, muttering under his breath as he left.

Susan clenched her teeth together to prevent the tirade of angry words which were burning their way along her tongue from spilling out. She resented him for his passiveness, she desperately wanted him to finish what he'd started, to have enough gumption, enough fire to say what he wanted, damn the consequences. After all, things clearly couldn't get any worse between them.

But that just wasn't Martin, and it infuriated her.

Susan realised then that she had risen out of her seat, the adrenaline and irritation having pushed her to her feet. She was leaning forward, over her laptop, hands braced against the table.

Slumping back into her seat, deflated, Susan listened to the familiar sound of Martin's footsteps as he ascended the stairs. Heading to his study, she knew, to the solitary existence which he had created for himself.

She didn't know how he didn't go mad, spending all that time alone; she would have. But then he had always been her polar opposite, comfortable in his own company, or rather in the company of a good bottle of something.

God knows why he'd wanted to marry me. Or me him.

The thought took Susan by surprise. It was sad really, their differences had been what had drawn them together in the beginning but now it seemed as though they were becoming more insurmountable with each day that passed.

25

MARTIN

Martin was pacing, his footsteps trying desperately to keep up with his racing heart.

He had been interrogated for the best part of two hours and he was feeling aggravated, and justifiably so.

Thank God for the solicitor. His sturdy, calm presence was the only thing that had got Martin through those long hours.

His mouth was dry, his tongue heavy. He took another swig of his drink, the tumbler remaining cradled in his right hand.

Despite having been let out, it was clear the police thought it was him, that he'd pushed or thrown Susan down the stairs. It felt as though they were closing in on him and there wasn't a damn thing he could do about it no matter how brilliant his solicitor may be.

He had been the last person to see her before it happened and they knew that they had been arguing, screaming in fact, which was something that Martin rarely ever did. Plus, they believed that he stood the most to gain were Susan to die.

He couldn't help flinching as the word *die* flew through his mind.

Martin took another gulp of whisky. It was medicinal, he

reassured himself, to prevent him from having some kind of emotional breakdown.

He had of course mentioned the missing necklace again. Only, Detective Roth seemed to brush the information aside. Admittedly, she had said that they were looking into it, but she hadn't sounded convinced.

Who knows how thoroughly though? Probably not very, considering they believe me to be their suspect.

Perhaps he should tell them about what happened after the argument?

He shook his head. No, that would only stir up more trouble and raise more questions. If anything he would in all likeliness come off looking worse. Better not to say anything, he decided.

But what was he going to do, how was he going to deflect their attention?

He honestly didn't know.

Martin found himself wandering into the kitchen. He wasn't sure why, he wasn't hungry, not that he could remember when he last ate.

He switched the light on.

Necking the dregs of his drink, Martin stood motionless in the middle of the room.

The house, large as it was, had never felt empty before, but now it felt abandoned, creepy even.

An uneasiness slithered up his back, the hairs on his arms standing up. The darkness outside seemed to be pressing against the doors and windows as if it wanted to be let in.

In a burst of movement, Martin strode to the counter and turned the radio on. He didn't know if he'd done it to drown out the silence of the night or whether it was to mute his own turbulent mind.

'How is your marriage, Mr Grey?' 'Were you and Susan on

good terms before the party?' 'Do you know you are the sole *beneficiary of the house were Susan to succumb to her injuries?'*

The detectives had been trying to bait him, trying to use the current discord in his marriage as motive.

Ludicrous.

But what if it was enough to charge him?

Don't be stupid, they would have done it already if they had the evidence.

Martin recalled how her eyes, the detective's, had been fixed on him the whole time, gauging his every reaction, his every move to each of the probing, invasive questions.

He wasn't accustomed to his every word, his every move being scrutinised. Why would he be?

Not that he had contributed very much to the interview. Under his solicitor's instructions, Martin had largely executed his right not to comment.

Still, he knew that Detective Roth had decided he was guilty, she just couldn't prove it. At least that's what his solicitor believed, or else Martin would have been locked in a cell now.

He shivered involuntarily at the prospect. He had been in one of their holding rooms momentarily and that was horrendous enough, the stark, sparse room had left him feeling cold and strangely dirty.

He didn't know why but he suddenly found himself wondering if his solicitor believed that he'd done it. Would it have mattered to him if Martin was guilty or not? He had asked him several times for the truth.

If he didn't believe Martin, was he the best person to represent him? Perhaps he should look for someone else, another professional?

He shook his head, aware that he was being irrational. The solicitor had done his job efficiently, he had supported him, told him when to speak and when not to. That was all he needed him to do for now.

He hadn't wanted to be affected by it, by the whole situation or more precisely by Detective Roth, but he clearly was.

She believed him to be capable of hurting Susan, of attempted murder. He'd never hurt anyone, not intentionally.

Only... what had happened before her fall had been a mistake. It had been a horrendous error in his judgement, one fuelled by anger and alcohol.

Martin's phone began to ring in his pocket, dragging him back to the moment, back to the kitchen, which felt too exposed, too open against the black night.

He fished it out. He had taken to keeping it on him at all times in case the hospital rang, in case there was a change in Susan's condition.

But seeing the mobile number flashing on the screen, his heart sank.

It wasn't the hospital.

He didn't know why but he moved to the double doors which opened out onto the garden, phone still in his hand, and pressed his face up against the glass. He had the overwhelming feeling that he was being watched, but he couldn't see beyond his own reflection in the glass.

His nostrils flared in anger as he turned away.

'Stop calling,' he growled at the phone.

He hadn't answered any of the calls, so why keep trying?

He desperately wanted to forget, to pretend it hadn't happened, but they wouldn't let him.

Martin stared at the screen until it finally stopped ringing, stopped taunting him. He shoved the device back into the depths of his pocket in an effort to forget. But he couldn't.

Why was everyone out to get him, to paint him in a bad light, as a villain?

It was just a mistake, a moment's lapse.

Every which way he turned someone seemed to have it in for him, wanted to destroy his life, his reputation.

Martin looked over his shoulder, to the doors again.

Was someone out there, in the garden? Was it the police, were they watching him, or was it the caller?

He turned quickly and checked the door. Locked.

'You're being absurd,' he said to himself, and yet he wasn't convinced that he was.

Dropping his gaze, Martin noticed the empty glass then, stared at it as if he couldn't recall how it was that it came to be fixed in the palm of his hand. He walked to the counter and practically threw the glass down as though it had burnt him.

His drinking had got somewhat out of control, he knew and yet it made all the emotions, the built-up anger and resentment and guilt, all the things he didn't want to deal with, seem a little less important, a little less overwhelming. Everything felt hazier around the edges, even the secret he'd been keeping didn't feel as awful.

But it is awful, he reminded himself as he moved away from the glass.

Despite his best efforts to forget, snippets would jump into his mind when he least expected it; Susan's face contorted in anger, the wave of humiliation he'd felt at her words, the sudden desire that had grabbed hold of him, the shame that still stung now.

He shook his head to dispel the memory, causing a bead of sweat to run down the back of Martin's neck, slipping beneath the collar of his shirt, quickly followed by another. The fabric, he realised, was damp. He hooked a finger into the collar and pulled it in an attempt to remove the wetness from his skin.

It didn't help.

His phone began to ring once more, baiting him with its chiming. He didn't want to look, but he knew he had to.

The same number as before.

'Please leave me alone,' he shouted into the emptiness, into the night.

26

———

GRACE

'Tell me what you've got so far?' DCI Potter asked. She had called Grace into her office first thing that morning.

Grace had known she was going to have to report in sooner or later, she had just been hoping for later, when she had more to offer.

Sticking to the facts, Grace outlined the progress that she and her team had made with their investigation. All the while DCI Potter nodded along, her eyes remaining unreadable until Grace eventually fell silent.

'Tell me more about this possible theft?'

'Martin Grey claims there is a missing piece of jewellery, a necklace. It's worth a small fortune, and as you'd expect, it is a listed item on their insurance.' Grace kept her expression neutral. She didn't want Potter registering her scepticism, or she may demand that further time be assigned to what was undoubtedly an unnecessary treasure hunt. 'We've made several inquiries into it, followed up a couple of leads but they were all dead ends. If I'm being honest there is nothing to substantiate his claim. I strongly believe that it's a diversion tactic, he's using smoke and mirrors to take the heat off of himself.' Grace spoke confidently as she summarised Martin's present position as her prime suspect, even though she knew she didn't have any evidence to back up her suspicions.

Potter gave Detective Roth a look, it was sympathetic mixed with something else, disappointment perhaps. 'It sounds like you have made some really positive progress with your investigation, however at present there is still no evidence to suggest that this was an attempted murder, nor that Mr Grey is our assailant. Is that correct?'

'Yes, although–'

DCI Potter held up a hand to cut her off. 'You know as well as I do that the CPS will throw it out if we don't give them something concrete. Do you have anything concrete?'

'Not yet, but I'm working on it. I would like to request a search warrant for the Greys' property. I believe that we have reasonable grounds to suspect Mr Grey and if we happen to find the missing necklace then that would prove his guilt.'

Potter sat back in her chair and sighed through her nose.

She was obviously turning over Grace's request in her mind, perhaps considering Grace's previous operation and the black mark which continued to linger over Grace's career. Eventually, she sat forward and said, 'Fine, put the request in. But, when I gave you this case, I told you it wasn't going to be straightforward. If there isn't a case to build then there isn't a case.'

Grace nodded, the subtext to her words unmissable.

Grace rose from her seat and headed back to her desk, her mood sour.

Before she'd even thrown herself into her chair, Harry was by her side. 'Come on, let's go grab a coffee.'

Grace was about to argue, to tell him that she had too much to do but she relented, realising that if nothing else she needed some fresh air.

'Fine, but you're paying.'

'Potter wasn't very supportive, I take it?' Harry guessed before taking a sip of his cappuccino.

'Can you blame her?' There was more bite to Grace's voice than she'd intended. She offered a brief, apologetic smile. 'We haven't been able to substantiate either the attempted murder or the theft.'

Harry had been doing some digging on the latter, putting feelers out to a few jewellers in the local area, not to mention a couple of auction houses. Nothing matching the description of their necklace had surfaced. Unsurprisingly, it was a dead end.

'So what's our next move?'

Grace swished her coffee around in her mug. 'Potter has reluctantly agreed to support my request for a search warrant for the Greys' house.' She looked up to meet Harry's waiting stare.

His left eyebrow was cocked in a silent question.

She hadn't told him what had happened during her previous job, she didn't like to discuss it, but Grace knew that rumours had circulated.

She sighed. 'My last case,' she began tentatively. 'It was a sexual assault.' She shook her head as though to dispel the details of the crime. 'We had a guy in custody. He matched the vague description our victim was able to provide, he could be tied to the area at the right time and he had a previous allegation made against him for something very similar, although that one fell apart because of lack of evidence.'

Pausing, she took a sip of coffee.

Harry continued to sit silently, so Grace continued. 'We had everything except DNA to tie him to the crime. He'd done it, there was no two ways about it, we all knew it, we just couldn't prove it.

'The case was therefore flawed and as you know any half-decent lawyer would have got him off. He had been careful, he'd used protection, covered his face, disposed of anything incriminating like his clothing. He knew he was going to get away with it, he was so damned cocky.'

Grace paused as guilt and embarrassment flooded through her. 'I should have suspected, should have questioned the new evidence more thoroughly.' She was talking more to herself than Harry at this point. 'The victim reported that she had been bound with a rope of some description but we couldn't find anything at our initial search. That was until my superior, DI Gould, found a length of rope in the suspect's shed during a subsequent search. The shed had already been checked and Gould was alone when he found it.' Grace watched as understanding flashed across Harry's face. She knew she didn't need to say anything further, Harry got it, but now that she had started, she just wanted to get it all out in the open.

'It was sent for forensic testing and surprise, surprise, there were traces of the victim's DNA on the rope. I was just so relieved to have the evidence we needed that I discounted the report filed by a uniformed officer identifying that he had already searched that same area and found nothing. He was obviously suspicious.

'The case recently went to trial and as anyone with any sense would have known, the defence attorney was all over that officer's report. Turns out similar reports of misconduct had been made against the DI in a previous case. It fell apart and the guy got away with it.'

Grace's phone rang in her pocket. She chose to ignore it. 'I might not have been the one who planted the evidence but I should have known better, this guy was clever, he wasn't about to leave a crucial piece of evidence lying around in his shed. And because of my ego, my desire to catch the bad guy, I slipped up. He's now out there, free to offend again.'

Grace was furious with herself as she realised that a tear had slipped down her cheek. She wiped it away with a firm hand. It was an angry, regretful tear but it made her look weak.

Harry put his cup down on the table and leant forward. In a low yet serious voice he said, 'You didn't plant the evidence. The investigation cleared you of any wrongdoing, don't let it eat away at you. You're a good copper. We all make mistakes. Learn from it and move on.'

'It's not that easy though, is it?'

'Why not?'

'Potter doesn't fully trust me. I can tell. She said something about not trying to make a case when there isn't one to make.'

Harry's mouth opened as though to say something, but clearly he didn't have the right words. So Grace continued. 'And secondly, that prick is walking around probably eyeing up his next victim. If he offends again, which he will, that will be on my conscience.' Her tone was matter of fact, but those thoughts ate away at Grace in the middle of the night. Perhaps that was why she was so determined to solve this, to put all the pieces together. She didn't want to let another guilty person walk free.

'You're hoping to find the necklace, stashed somewhere in the Greys' house?'

Grace nodded. 'I'm not going to make the same mistake twice, but I just know that this is a red herring. Until I've proved it, however, it feels like the case keeps being pulled in the wrong direction. If we find it, it would be a clear indication of Martin's guilt and we can confidently focus all of our efforts on proving as much.'

Harry's phone, which was lying face down on the table, began vibrating. He turned it over then looked at Grace. 'It's Amy,' he offered before answering.

Grace drank the dregs of her drink, all the while keeping her gaze fixed on Harry.

'Yes, she's here with me,' he said to Amy.

He paused, listening intently whilst Amy relayed some news.

'When?' he said, his voice dark.

He didn't look happy at all. *This isn't going to be good news.*

Grace had a sinking feeling. Her heart began to beat a little quicker in anticipation.

'Yep, I'll tell her. We're heading back now.'

Grace watched as Harry carefully replaced his phone on the table before he met Grace's stare. 'It's not good news I'm afraid. Martin Grey was pronounced dead at the scene of an RTA last night.'

It took a second for the information to filter through Grace's mind, for the words to sink in. As they did her eyes widened in disbelief. If she had been able to find her voice in that moment, a tirade of curses would have streamed from her mouth. But she couldn't.

There were no words.

27

SUSAN

THE DAY BEFORE SHE FELL

Susan bustled into her appointment ten minutes late. She had been held up on a call with the caterers. There had been some issue with some of the ingredients, so they'd had to make a couple of last-minute changes.

Thankfully everything else seemed to be on track; the marquee was being erected in the garden as she sat down, the cocktail bar and dance floor were being assembled later this afternoon and the Portaloos – to ensure the house was off limits to keep Martin happy – were supposed to arrive first thing in the morning.

Oh, and she'd already worked a couple of hours in the shop alongside Jennifer. She may have inadvertently suggested to Jennifer that she hoped to share some exciting news tomorrow, before brushing away her comment, annoyed with herself for saying anything. Thankfully Jennifer hadn't seemed to be listening, too preoccupied with a table display she was arranging.

Susan was unsurprisingly flustered.

Dropping her bag by her feet, she laid her hands out on the table in front of her.

'Hectic morning?' her beauty therapist, Bethan, questioned.

'You could say that,' Susan responded. She had been visiting Bethan's small, independent treatment rooms since moving to the area and felt very comfortable chatting to her. 'I'm having a party tomorrow evening and there have been a few last-minute hiccups. It's to be expected, I suppose.'

'Yes,' Bethan agreed. 'But I've got you all booked in for a manicure, pedicure, eyebrow and eyelash tint, so you've got some time to unwind.'

Susan smiled, her shoulders, which had only moments ago been tense, relaxed. 'Fantastic, thank you.'

The garden had been utterly transformed in the few short hours that Susan had been gone.

In place of the large, flat lawn was now a glittering marquee decorated in yards of fabrics.

Susan wandered around inside the large space, her excitement almost tangible.

The dance floor was being assembled whilst tables were brought in and positioned around the edges.

It was going to be a fabulous night, she knew, surveying the area as it continued to evolve.

Susan found herself turning sharply, a sudden feeling of unease creeping down her spine, as though someone was watching her. And yet everyone was busy working, going about their tasks, oblivious to her presence.

She turned and looked out of the marquee's entrance, back towards the rear of the house. There, standing at the vast window was Martin, his arms folded. Susan couldn't quite make out his expression, but she could imagine what it looked like.

Lips pursed tightly, eyes narrowed, nostrils flared as he breathed out his anger.

The atmosphere had been even more frosty than usual between them, her refusal to cancel the party had seemingly tipped the very delicate balance which they had been living by.

Now there were no polite conversations, no curt smiles as they walked past one another in the mornings, in its place was total disregard. As far as Martin was concerned Susan may as well have been a ghost. In fact, he probably would have been more interested, paid more attention to her were that the case, she thought sourly.

With a sadness that she hadn't been anticipating, Susan turned away from the house, putting her back to Martin and forced herself to concentrate on the blossoming venue before her, difficult as it was.

After a brief chat with the party organiser, Susan headed back to the house.

Her phone rang before she stepped through the door into the kitchen.

She recognised the number. 'Hello, Susan Grey.' Her breathing quickened in nervousness. She was desperately hoping that this call was about to bring some very exciting and potentially life-changing news.

'Good afternoon, Mrs Grey. It's Matthew Gregory. Is now a good time?'

'Yes, just give me one second please.'

'Of course,' Matthew responded.

Susan, clutching the phone to her chest, strode into the kitchen, walking past the caterers who were unpacking crates of glasses and plates. She moved down the hallway and across the entrance hall – with a sideways glance she noted that Martin was no longer lingering at the top of the stairs – before she pushed open the door to the living room.

Once inside she shut it firmly behind her.

This wasn't supposed to be all cloak and daggers, but she didn't want anyone to overhear, or more precisely she didn't want Martin to overhear.

She would need to talk to him separately, to gently explain everything she had planned and she hoped he would understand, that he wouldn't fight her on it.

'Sorry about that, Matthew. Go ahead.'

'Well, I have some very positive news for you. The vendor has accepted your offer.'

'That is absolutely fantastic. Thank you. Oh my goodness.' Susan was ecstatic. She wanted to rush outside and tell everyone but she couldn't of course.

'I'm pleased that we could get a deal done.' Susan could hear the smile in his voice.

'Yes, me too. So what happens now?'

'Well, as we discussed, there is the initial down payment to make. I think it was that which really sold your offer. I will email across our bank details, if you could get that sent across to us I can let the seller know that we have it in holding for him. I already have confirmation of your agreement in principle with the bank so I can inform them that it's a go. After that it's just some formalities, paperwork and surveys, that sort of thing.'

Susan was attempting to remain professional, composed, but inside she wanted to skip around the room and cheer. She cleared her throat. 'Wonderful. Yes, send me the details and I'll get the money across to you today.'

'Great. Let's talk again on Monday, but go and celebrate.'

'Thank you, Matthew. I intend to. Have a good weekend.'

'You too.'

Disconnecting, Susan stood motionless for a moment, the phone still poised in her hand before she punched the air with both fists. 'Yes, yes, yes.'

Then a noise from outside the door had her standing still, arms still raised in celebration. She turned her head a fraction, ear trained towards the space beyond.

She listened for a few seconds.

Nothing.

Why are you being so paranoid?

She lowered her arms slowly and shook her head, feeling a little silly. As Susan turned away from the door, she thought she may have heard the faint echo of footsteps receding.

28

———

GRACE

Grace was standing in front of the whiteboard once more. DI Harry Amberidge and DS Cartwright were also present, along with DS Richard Shore. An older officer, with salt and pepper hair, thick-rimmed glasses and kind eyes. He had recently returned from leave, having had a knee operation and had been assigned to Grace's team to aid their investigation. Grace wasn't sure whether she should be insulted or grateful for the extra pair of hands; Richard was still recovering after all and his input might well be limited. Still, Grace couldn't deny that his extensive experience might be helpful.

The past twenty-four hours, since the news of Martin Grey's death, had been somewhat of a blur. Were it not for the absurdity of it all, Grace might have actually laughed. Her prime suspect, the man she had released without charge – admittedly due to lack of evidence – was dead.

She shook her head. This case was supposed to be a fresh start, a way to shake off the remnants of her past, of a previous fuck-up, to prove she had deserved her promotion all along.

But it was slipping away, like water between her fingers, she had nothing to grasp hold of and the clock was now ticking.

Grace had found herself once again in DCI Potter's office.

The DCI's words still echoed in Grace's mind. '*I know how much this case meant to you. But we now need to focus our efforts on Mr Grey's death,*' Potter had said in earnest, her face so full of sympathy. Sympathy that Grace hadn't wanted.

No, what she wanted was answers, to know what had happened to Susan and why. And to know what the hell had happened to Martin.

An endless stream of theories plagued Grace's mind. Had he done it on purpose, his guilt weighing too heavily on him? Had it been an accident, a drunken one perhaps? Was anyone else involved? Where had he been going? Did he even have a destination in mind?

She wouldn't be able to rest until she'd gotten her answers, some sort of closure, which was why she had practically begged Potter for more time when she'd suggested archiving Susan's case, stating that as yet there was still nothing to indicate that it was anything more than an unfortunate accident. But Grace had a gut feeling and now with Martin, that had only strengthened Grace's resolve.

She had argued that the two investigations were likely to overlap. 'Please just give me forty-eight hours to focus on Susan. There are some loose ends that need tying up and I suspect that in addressing those, I will also learn more about Martin's death.'

She hadn't wanted to sound desperate, but she had, she could tell from the expression on her superior's face. Thankfully Potter had conceded.

Grace sighed heavily before she spoke to her team, her voice solemn. 'As you are aware, Martin Grey was pronounced dead at the scene of a road traffic accident. He was our prime suspect in the attempted murder of his wife Susan Grey, who continues to remain in a critical condition in hospital. So it appears that our investigation is now two-pronged.

'We need to understand the circumstances leading up to the moment Mr Grey's car ran off the road. Where was he going? Had he spoken to anyone prior to the crash that we can talk to? Ultimately we need to know if this was intentional or not. A post-mortem is scheduled to be carried out and hopefully that will tell us more. I do believe Mr Grey may have had an issue with alcohol but that doesn't mean this was an accident.'

Grace had been careful with her choice of words, she didn't want to prematurely besmirch his name but she had previously smelt alcohol on Martin's breath in the middle of the day. It was a possibility not to be ruled out, although she would suspend her opinions until she knew what the post-mortem gleaned.

'Potter wants our main focus to be on Martin's death, she has however granted us forty-eight hours to work on our investigation into Susan's fall. I have submitted a request for a search warrant for the Greys' house, which I am hoping will arrive shortly–'

DS Shore cut in then. 'What are we looking for when we carry out the search of the house?'

Grace quickly outlined her theory regarding Martin's claim that there was a missing piece of jewellery. 'It just feels too convenient to me. Harry has made some inquiries and as yet, nothing matching the description has turned up in any of the local jewellers or auction houses.'

Richard nodded and made a few notes. Satisfied that he wasn't about to offer an alternative theory, Grace continued. 'There are still a few unknowns that I think we should focus on until the warrant comes through. Firstly, what was that large sum of money for, who was its recipient? The fact that we are having trouble answering these questions makes me suspicious. Was Susan being blackmailed, and if so, what did they have over her? Did that person or persons have something to do with her attempted murder? Secondly, can we find anything else out about our anonymous caller? I think it's worth revisiting the call. Is there anything we can utilise from the recording to help us narrow down our search? The caller obviously saw something or else they wouldn't have phoned it in. And thirdly, let's reinterview some of our other witnesses, Susan's son Joshua, her sister Jennifer. I want to know more about the state of Susan and Martin's marriage. There have been some hints that it may not have been in a good place, let's see if that leads us anywhere.'

'And what about Martin's death?' Harry asked.

Grace thought for a moment. 'Let's start with his phone records, that might tell us if he was planning to meet someone. If he was then perhaps we can rule out suicide. When we have our warrant we can also review his digital devices. Talking to Jennifer Russell and Joshua Maddison may also shine a light on Martin's state of mind before the crash.'

For a few minutes Grace assigned tasks to each of her team before they began to file out of the room. Harry, however, lingered.

His hand came up to rest on the small of her back, his eyes boring into hers. 'We will solve this, we are onto something, I know it.' He then removed his hand and left Grace alone with her thoughts.

She wanted to feel the same conviction Harry did, wanted to believe his words but she couldn't shake off her doubts, couldn't brush them away as insignificant. Instead, they had sprouted, shooting off in all directions within her mind. She believed Martin had done it for the financial gain, their marriage was on the rocks, perhaps Susan had indicated that she was leaving him and he had panicked. But she wasn't sure she would ever be able to prove that now.

The case, which should have felt as though it was winding up, seemed to be unravelling before her eyes. Despite having a plan and more avenues to explore, Grace was losing heart and with it the hope she'd had of securing a conviction.

29

———————

JENNIFER

Jennifer felt heavy, sluggish, with a tiredness that she couldn't seem to shake. As she ambled to work, every muscle in her body ached as though she'd run a race the day before.

It wasn't only the extra hours she had needed to work weighing her down. No, it was also the incessant worrying which was keeping her up at night.

Jennifer had continued to ruminate on Susan's undisclosed announcement. It was evident that no one else had known about it, thank the heavens, but Jennifer had figured it out, even before the accident. Susan had been planning on selling the bookshop.

I mean, what else could it be?

Jennifer had been aware that Susan had met with the bank, on more than one occasion in the weeks leading up to the party, and then there was the estate agent. She wasn't supposed to know about that but she hadn't been able to help herself, curiosity had gotten the better of her. She'd snooped through some of Susan's things when she'd popped out for lunch. It was there on her personal calendar, a meeting with an agent, probably to establish a value for the building itself.

Jennifer's heart hammered furiously in her chest at the thought of losing that place, the shop which had become like a home to her.

What Jennifer didn't know, however, was why. Why did Susan want to sell it? As far as she could make out the business was sound, turning a respectable profit each month. Admittedly it was never going to make Susan rich, but surely that was a title she already possessed from selling her previous venture? Perhaps that was what she did though, grew solid businesses and then sold them on, staff and family members be damned?

Or perhaps she was bored of the mundane chores associated with it, the inventory, the shift rotas, the stock ordering, all jobs which Jennifer silently enjoyed.

Disgust rolled through her at the idea of her sister hating something that she loved so dearly.

Jennifer had fleetingly considered if she could put herself in a position to make Susan an offer for the shop, before her fall, when she began to suspect that Susan might be considering selling. But she'd had to disregard the idea, aware that she would never be able to afford it, would never be able to raise the funds necessary. She dreaded to think what the stock alone would be worth.

A mixture of nausea and anger washed through her as she continued to navigate her way along the high street.

Although that prospect had been temporarily halted, Jennifer was now consumed by the real possibility that Susan might not survive her injuries, and then what?

She would be in no better position than if Susan had sold it.

What would she do? She had always dreamed of running a bookshop and now it looked as though that dream, that reality, was going to be ripped out from under her.

It had never occurred to Jennifer how intrinsically linked her life had become to her sister's, not until she'd ended up in hospital, not until Jennifer had had time to consider what would be lost.

And either way, it looked as though Jennifer was going to lose.

The morning had passed at a snail's pace with only four customers entering. Jennifer had been silently relieved. She'd plastered on her happy face, the one which said, '*I'm fine, you definitely don't need to ask me how I am, because as I said, I'm fine.*' It was the kind of smile which ensured that no one bothered to look any closer. And that was just the way she wanted it.

Anna, one of their part-time sales assistants, had glanced across to Jennifer a couple of times, a wariness to her gaze. Perhaps she sensed a change in Jennifer's mood, but she didn't comment. Maybe she thought that Jennifer was worrying about Susan, and Jennifer was worried but not necessarily for the reasons she should be. Not that she would ever admit it to anyone.

Wrapping up and labelling the last of several online orders, the bell above the door had Jennifer looking up. It was Kathy, a regular and also an avid member of their monthly book group.

Kathy was a sturdy-looking woman who always wore a bright shade of red lipstick no matter the occasion. She was straight-talking and Jennifer believed her to be fearless.

Working as a paramedic, she had seen some sights which would surely have affected a lesser person, not that she talked freely about her job, instead she would brush away the topic saying that books and the book club were her escapism, her place to forget her daily life.

That was something that Jennifer could relate to. Normally.

'Good morning,' Jennifer offered with a more genuine smile.

'Morning, lovely lady, how are you holding up? How is Susan?' Kathy's mother was Irish and Kathy had notes of an accent to her voice.

'I'm all right, thank you.' A lie Jennifer told without hesitation, she had said it so often throughout her life. 'Susan is still holding in there.'

'Your sister strikes me as a fighter, I am sure she will pull through.' There was sincerity in Kathy's words.

Jennifer nodded in response. 'Me too.'

After a moment's silence, Jennifer cleared her throat, dislodging the guilt that had found its way there. Guilt for her own lack of compassion, for her selfishness. She should be more worried about Susan, and not because of how it impacted on her own life, but because she was her sister. Only that didn't come naturally, had never come naturally for Jennifer. 'Are you looking for something in particular or just here to browse?'

Kathy's eyes were already scanning the various sections of the shop, as though hoping that a book would jump out at her. 'Just browsing today. Attended a nasty RTA the other evening. A man died at the scene and he just reminded me of my Jim. Something about his face.' She shook her head, clearly not wanting to remember. 'Matthew something, it'll come back to me. Anyway, you don't want to hear about that, you have enough on your plate without listening to me.'

Without further conversation, Kathy drifted away from the counter, her feet taking her to the fiction section. Jennifer was confident that she would find something distracting there.

After fifteen minutes Kathy returned, two books in her

hand. 'I couldn't decide between these two so I'd best buy them both.' She smiled as she justified her purchases.

'Sensible logic,' Jennifer agreed as she ran up the books and slid them into a bag.

As Kathy stowed away her purse, having paid, she offered a small smile and said, 'Look after yourself.' Then she turned to leave.

Kathy had reached the door when Jennifer found herself calling out, 'I hope that they do the trick. That they give you the escape you need.' She wasn't sure why she'd felt the need to offer those words, but she meant them. Kathy seemed like a genuinely nice person and Jennifer didn't like to think she might be struggling, that her resilience was under attack.

Kathy paused, an unreadable look flashing across her face before she finally said, 'Thank you, Jennifer. I appreciate it and I am sure that they will.'

Jennifer nodded, expecting her customer to leave but Kathy lingered in the door.

Finally she said, 'Strange, I've just remembered his name, the RTA victim. His name was Martin Grey.' She paused, before adding, 'Grey, just like your shop, Grey's books. I don't think I'll forget it again.' Kathy ducked out of the door without another word, the bell ringing after her as that name hit Jennifer with such force that she stumbled backwards a step.

Martin?

No, it couldn't be the same Martin, surely?

Jennifer let out a shaky breath. It had to be some sort of twisted coincidence. *It was another Martin Grey. Yes, that was it. After all, there must be more than one man with that name.*

And yet even as she attempted to convince herself, doubt forced its way through her mind.

She struggled to hold on to her conviction and with it her hope. It was as if they were made of nothing more than air, their weightlessness causing them to disappear before she could truly grasp hold of them.

Jennifer pressed her hand firmly against her chest, against her heart, in an attempt to hold it together, to keep it from breaking.

This isn't real. This isn't happening.

A sob escaped her lips. It was an unattractive, wet sound she tried to muffle, covering her lips with her other hand. But Anna had heard. She was walking towards Jennifer, a worried expression etched on her face.

Jennifer dipped her head to hide the tears which were filling her eyes. 'I'll be back in a few minutes.' Her voice broke as she spoke, but she didn't stop, didn't pause when Anna tried to intervene, to offer support for a situation she didn't yet understand.

Slamming the office door shut behind her, Jennifer rested her back against it, the solidness of the wood keeping her grounded as her mind whirled and the tears flowed freely.

Surely this can't be happening. Not Martin.

Without realising, she'd slid to the ground, her knees bent in front of her, feet braced against the floor.

Each breath she took was more erratic than the last. None of this was making any sense. Was she being punished? Was that it? Because she hadn't been a good sister, a good person? Was it because of what she had said, what she had done?

With her head in her hands, Jennifer sucked in a deep breath and tried to steady herself.

No. It isn't him. I would have known. I would have been told.

And then a thought drifted into her already tumultuous mind. *Was this my fault, was this because of me? Did I have something to do with it?* She shook her head, shaking away the preposterous idea, of course this was nothing to do with her. It was a car accident.

She refused to believe it. Any of it.

It is very sad for someone else, someone else who knew another Martin Grey, but it isn't the same man that I know.

Wiping away a remaining tear with the back of her hand, she slowly dragged herself back to her feet and moved to the desk where she'd left her bag. Digging through it she found her phone.

She would have to make sure of course, perhaps even send her condolences to the family of this other Martin.

But who should she call? She couldn't very well call the hospital. Should she ring the morgue? She considered these things with a strange sense of detachment.

Other than knowing it was a road accident and his name, Jennifer had no other details to offer even if she did know who you called in these situations. She wasn't even sure of the day it happened.

Then it hit her, she'd call Martin.

He would, of course, answer the phone and with that simple action, that single 'Hello', this nightmare would end.

Jennifer scrolled to her previously dialled numbers. Martin's was the last number she'd called. She chose not to think about that, about the reason behind the calls she'd made. This time was different, this time he would answer.

She hit the call button and put the phone to her ear.

It rang.

And it rang.

Finally it switched to voicemail. The sound of Martin's calm voice asking her to leave her name and number filtered across to Jennifer, and with it came a new wave of panic. She didn't leave a message. She ended the call.

He could be busy, she attempted to reason, or perhaps his

phone was in a different room. Maybe he was at the hospital with Susan and didn't want to answer.

Just because he didn't answer, does not mean that it was him.

But she still needed to be reassured. She scrolled through her numbers until she found another one. Joshua's. Surely he would have heard if something had happened.

She called her nephew in the desperate hope that he would be able to alleviate all of her fears.

30

GRACE

Joshua Maddison hadn't been the easiest of men to track down seeing as how he chose not to answer his phone.

So, she'd had no choice but to turn up at his flat, with DI Harry Amberidge in tow, expecting him to be there, that arrogant, cocky air of his greeting them. Only, there was no answer. Instead, a neighbour, having heard them repeatedly hammering at the door and shouting through the letter box, suggested they try here, a premises in central Brighton.

Grace found herself standing outside a narrow yet long shop tucked just off of the main street in the centre of the city. Glass double doors were positioned to the left side of the building's façade and a large floor-to-ceiling window on the right completed the entire front. A metal shutter had been raised just high enough to allow people to walk in and out.

It was clear from the remnants of graffiti and debris that up until very recently it had been empty.

The doors were open. DI Roth and DI Amberidge entered.

Despite the quietness from the outside, inside was a hive of activity. Several people were busy working; decorating and fitting new ceiling lights.

Grace couldn't help but be suspicious. Harry, clearly reading her mind or perhaps her facial expression, said, 'For someone who supposedly needed a loan from the bank of Mum only a few short weeks ago, Mr Maddison certainly seems to have pockets lined with cash.'

Grace nodded as her eyes drifted across the expensive and somewhat gaudy fittings of what was clearly going to be a bar.

Joshua had gone for a navy-blue and gold colour scheme. In the bright light of day, it was oppressive but Grace suspected that at night and after a few drinks it would make for a relaxed atmosphere.

Against the right-hand wall and running almost the entire length of the room was a bar. Its dark wood softened by gold leaf detailing and behind it rows of optics and empty shelves just waiting to be filled with bottles. The left side was occupied by several booths and tables.

'He isn't here.' Harry was peering over the bar as he spoke.

Grace was just about to ask a decorator, a young woman in overalls who was presently up a ladder with a roller in her hand when Joshua emerged from a door secreted at the far end of the space, a stockroom perhaps or a bathroom.

Evidently unfazed by the appearance of two officers, Grace watched as Joshua sauntered over to the bar, pulled out a stool and sat down. There was no shock in his expression when he'd registered Grace, she realised, or perhaps he was very adept at hiding his emotions.

As Grace thought about this, Joshua simply reached out his hand and slid out the stool beside him expectantly.

His arrogance knows no bounds.

Grace glanced at Harry, who unsmilingly met her stare. *Clearly not a fan of Mr Maddison either.*

She knew what Harry was thinking, that Joshua was an arse, and he wasn't wrong. Still, he was important to their investigation so Grace squared her shoulders, walked over and sat next to him. Without having to look, Grace knew that Harry had followed suit and taken the seat next to her.

'How are you, Mr Maddison?' she asked politely.

Joshua rolled his eyes. 'Mr Maddison is my dad. Joshua is fine. I am as well as can be expected considering the situation.'

His words lacked all sincerity, it sounded more like a line that he'd trained himself to say. In fact, despite his calm demeanour, Joshua looked as though he was absolutely buzzing. Excitement danced in his eyes and his mouth was curved up as though he was fighting against a smile.

'This is my colleague DI Amberidge.' Joshua nodded without comment. 'Nice place,' Grace offered, her eyes indicating their surroundings.

'Thanks. It's starting to come together.'

Grace cut straight to it, aware that she was against the clock. 'I'm afraid that we are here with some difficult news.'

'Is it my mum?' Joshua's eyes had widened enough for Grace to know that somewhere in that conceited exterior of his, he cared.

'No.' She put her hands up to placate him. 'As far as I am aware your mum remains critical but stable.'

His concern quickly changed to confusion. 'Then what's this about?'

'I'm afraid I have to tell you that your stepfather, Martin, was pronounced dead at the scene of a road traffic accident.'

Joshua's gaze drifted away from the detectives and across to the empty wall of optics. A slight frown was the only indication that he had heard Grace's words, that he understood what had happened.

Grace waited for a few seconds, sitting silently. She was just about to ask if Joshua was all right when he began shaking his head.

'Well, that is some insane bullshit that I wasn't expecting to hear.' He ran his hand through his hair, strands sticking out in all directions. 'Fuck.' Then he looked back at Grace. 'Seriously, he's dead?'

'Yes. I'm very sorry for your loss.'

Joshua blew out his cheeks and with it a sound that was unmistakably a laugh.

He isn't even attempting to feign grief.

What a dick.

Grace surreptitiously glanced towards Harry. He was struggling to mask his disgust for this man's lack of sympathy.

'I mean, that is awful and all, but it's not like we ever got on,' Joshua said as though feeling the need to justify his reaction. With some difficulty he did wipe the grin from his face before falling silent momentarily.

Had he been someone else, Grace would have suspected that he was wallowing in a little bit of guilt. But Joshua Maddison didn't strike Grace as someone who was capable of that emotion.

'Mum will be devastated,' he finally said.

'Yes, I am sure she will be.'

'Okay, well, is there something that you need me to do, some paperwork that I need to sign? I am really busy at the moment as you can see.' Joshua stood up and with a wave of his hand indicated the space behind them.

Grace heard Harry fidget in his seat, she knew that he was royally pissed off now. A man had just died and this prick didn't give a shit even though they had known each other for years.

'I am afraid that it is not as simple as that, Mr Maddison. Please sit down.' Grace's tone was now firm, bordering on harsh.

Joshua did as he was instructed but in an attempt to appear in control, he only perched on the stool's edge.

'As I am sure you will appreciate,' Grace continued,

unfazed, 'with there already being an ongoing investigation into your mother's fall, and now with Martin's unforeseen death, we have some questions.'

Joshua sat up straighter but his expression remained unchanged. The only thing to move were his eyes as they narrowed before he said, 'First you question me about my own mother's accident, as if you believed that I was the one responsible for her fall and now you're suggesting that I had something to do with Martin's death...'

Grace cut Joshua off mid-rant. 'I haven't made any sort of suggestion. You have not been accused of any wrongdoing at this time, unless of course there is something you wish to tell us?' Grace paused long enough for Joshua to shake his head once. 'Fine then. We are simply trying to get a better understanding of Martin, the relationship that both you and your mother had with him. We want to understand what happened leading up to his death.'

'What do you want to know exactly?'

'When did you last talk to Martin?'

Joshua didn't even pause to think before answering, 'The night of the party. I haven't spoken to him since.'

'Not even about your mother?'

He shook his head.

'How would you say things were between Martin and your mother, before her fall?'

Joshua shrugged. 'I don't know, the same as ever, I guess.'

'What does that mean?' Harry interjected, his tone clipped. His patience wearing thin.

'I don't know. I wouldn't say that they were unhappy but they spent more time not talking than they did talking.'

Grace had theorised as much, suspecting that the relationship may have been strained but it was good to have it confirmed. 'And before the party, were they talking or not?'

'I don't think they'd been talking for a few months.'

'Do you know what they had fallen out about?'

Joshua shook his head. 'Mum didn't exactly talk to me about the ins and outs of her marriage.'

'But they were arguing?'

'Not exactly, no,' Joshua said vaguely, then seeing Grace's frown, he sighed. 'They didn't argue. I think Mum would have but Martin would never rise to it. Except on the night of her party. I've never seen him so irate. It was rather surprising to be honest. That is the only time I have ever heard him raise his voice. He was obviously pissed off but then he was drunk. No, what typically happens is that they fall out about something trivial, don't speak for a while and then one of them eventually apologises, which is usually Mum, and all is forgotten.'

Grace thought about this for a moment, considering how to ask her next question. Straight to the point, she decided.

'Do you think Martin was capable of pushing your mother down the stairs?'

'Martin?' Joshua laughed loudly. 'Despite what I may think of the man, no, I don't believe that he was responsible for my mum's accident. He just wasn't that sort of man. If you know what I mean?'

That wasn't what Grace had wanted to hear and yet she strangely wasn't surprised. It was her experience that even the most laid-back individuals still had their limit and it sounded as though Martin had been pushed to that limit on the night of the party. He may not have meant to do it, it may have been out of character, but he could have lashed out, causing his wife to fall.

Joshua's mobile sounded from within his pocket, he slipped it out and peered down at the screen. Grace watched as he silenced the call and tucked it back in his pocket.

'Please do get that if you need to,' Grace insisted.

'It's my aunt, I'll ring her back in a minute.' From the emptiness of his words, Grace wasn't sure that he would.

Harry leant closer then and asked, 'Did Martin drink often?'

'All the time. He was, what do you call it? A functioning alcoholic. Although he didn't have any real functioning to do. He hated that Mum wanted to help me achieve my goals, to do something positive with my life when he obviously wasn't doing anything with his. He was such a jackass. No, a hypocrite, he was a hypocrite.'

'Am I correct in thinking that Martin hadn't worked for some time?'

'He was made redundant during Covid, I think. Mum had said that he was considering opening his own accounting firm, but he didn't. I don't know why though. To be honest, I have no idea what he's been doing these past few years except growing more miserable.'

'You said that Martin was irate on the night of the party, do you know why?' Grace wondered if Martin had known about the withdrawal from Susan's account, or perhaps the announcement that never was.

'Besides from me, do you mean? I think he was annoyed about the party.'

'Why do you say that?' Harry questioned.

Joshua glanced at the workers, perhaps to make sure that they were still busy working. 'Because Martin hated anything fun. He was a sad old man and I can't say that I am going to miss him. Now if you really don't mind.' He stood up once again.

Grace still had a couple more questions she needed to ask though. 'Yes of course, we can see that you're really busy. You seem to be full steam ahead. When is the grand opening?' She rose to her feet in an attempt to keep the conversation casual.

That spark of excitement was back in Joshua's face. 'Next Saturday. But there's still tons to do. I haven't even ordered all the whiskies. It's going to be a whisky bar, if you hadn't realised.' Then he blew a sharp breath out through his nose. 'That was probably the only thing that Martin ever did teach me, how to pick a good whisky. Ironic really.'

Grace couldn't see the irony, only tragedy. She forged on, desperate for a few more answers. 'This must be costing you a small fortune?'

Joshua offered a wry smile but deigned not to answer, instead he shrugged. 'It will be worth it.' He took a step towards the door, his arm held aloft in an attempt to usher the detectives from his premises.

Grace ignored it. 'Did you find an investor?'

Stopping mid-step, Joshua let out a single laugh. 'I'm not sure that that is any of your business.'

'If I am not mistaken, the last time we spoke, you informed me that your mother hadn't invested in your business. So forgive my curiosity but I am wondering how you are able to afford all this, how you've got so much done in such a short time?'

Grace knew that the decorators were now listening, the conversation which had moments ago been contained to three participants had now spilled over and everyone could hear. And Joshua knew it too, his gaze darting hastily around the room.

'If you must know, I cashed in some shares.'

Liar.

Gone was the self-assuredness which he wore so comfortably, in its place was a nervousness, an awkwardness which had Grace questioning herself.

Perhaps she hadn't truly entertained the possibility that there was a theft. After all, it had seemed too convenient, too well-timed. But if Susan hadn't lent Joshua the money then how was he affording all of this? What if *he* stole the necklace to fund his new enterprise?

Harry, one step ahead of Grace, pulled a picture from the file in his hand and held it up so that Joshua could see.

'Before we go, do you recognise this necklace?'

Grace watched as Joshua's gaze dropped to the picture before he looked back up to DI Amberidge. There was a moment's hesitation before he replied. 'That looks like one of my mum's necklaces.'

'Do you recall when you last saw it?'

Grace watched Joshua's facial expression as he considered Harry's question. He looked as though he was clenching his teeth, his jaw tensing against the effort.

'No, I can't say that I do. Why are you asking?'

Harry looked to Grace this time, who happily responded. 'It was reported as stolen. It would appear to be rather valuable.'

Before Joshua could say anything, Harry tucked the image away. 'Thank you for your time, Mr Maddison. I am confident that we will be seeing you again.'

Grace struggled to hide her smile. She did enjoy working with Harry.

'Mr Maddison,' she offered as she walked confidently out of the building, aware that Joshua Maddison was in all likeliness shitting himself right about now.

SUSAN

THE MORNING BEFORE SHE FELL

With some difficulty, Susan sat still, facing her vanity mirror whilst the hairdresser, Debbie, teased her hair into an up-do. She had a list of jobs still to tick off but Susan was making a concerted effort to try and savour the moment, the day, to not let it pass her by in a blur.

The house was buzzing with activity, with excitement as people rushed around purposefully.

The last time there had been this many people in the house, when there had been so much life in these walls, had been the day that they'd moved in, Susan realised somewhat sorrowfully.

That had never been the plan, in fact it was supposed to have been the exact opposite. They had talked about the dinner parties they would host, the barbeques, the parties. Only, by the time Susan had finished establishing the bookshop and felt able to focus her attention elsewhere, Martin had been made redundant and had started to grow distant, insular. He had isolated himself from all his London friends and acquaintances and from Susan.

She blinked hard to dispel the trail her thoughts were

taking, aware that it would only sour her mood and she was not going to let Martin muddy this day for her.

'You were lost in thought then,' Debbie said, eyeing Susan in the mirror. 'You all right?'

Susan forced a smile to her lips. 'Yes, I was just thinking how this party is long overdue, but I still have so much to do.'

'Anything I can help you with?'

Susan and Debbie had become firm friends over the past few years, bonding over the trials and tribulations of owning their own business, both of which were situated in the village. Not to mention the stories they'd shared which had them both bent over with laughter.

Debbie had recounted the time a gentleman had wandered into her hairdressers requesting a trim. Debbie had squeezed him in between appointments, only to find that he was wearing a toupée. When Susan had asked what she'd done, Debbie had replied, 'I did what any good hairdresser would do, I cut it.'

Susan's stories hadn't been quite as amusing but she had recalled one customer who had attempted to return a book which had obviously been well read, not to mention sporting a coffee cup stain. She had politely declined the customer's request, so they had stormed out, leaving the book behind.

Debbie's business was two shops down from the bookshop and a staple at the heart of the village, which was helped by Debbie's warm and friendly nature.

She had even gone out of her way today, offering to do Susan's hair at home for her.

'Thank you for the lovely offer but it is all in hand. And besides, you need to make sure that you're ready for the festivities.'

Debbie grinned. 'I can't wait.' She picked up a large can of hairspray, shielded Susan's eyes and sprayed vigorously all over her hair. 'Right, I just need to position your hair comb and then you're all done.'

The hair comb had been a last-minute purchase. Rachel had suggested that it was more suitable for a wedding than a birthday party, but it was stunning with its pearls and gems. Susan couldn't resist.

Debbie slid the comb in at the side of Susan's head as requested, then smiled. 'What do you think?' She held up a small mirror allowing Susan to see the back of her head.

'It looks fantastic.' Susan moved her head from side to side to get a better look. It really did look wonderful and it made her look a little younger, she thought.

'I'm pleased you like it. Right, I'll pack up then head off so that you can get on. Just be careful, I can always tidy up any loose strands later if needs be.'

'Thank you so much, Debbie.' Susan was already on her feet. 'Party starts at 6:30.'

'Can't wait.'

Susan left Debbie to tidy up and made her way downstairs. She wanted to run through all the final details with Jo, the events planner. Susan shouldn't be worrying, that was why she had hired someone else to organise everything, but she couldn't help it, it was in her nature.

Halfway down the staircase, Susan spied Martin exiting the lounge. She wasn't sure why but she found herself pausing.

He didn't notice her straight away.

Susan eyed him as he moved to the centre of the hallway, his gaze trained on the corridor opposite, in the direction of the kitchen, where the majority of the hustle and bustle was emanating from.

His face slowly distorted with a scowl and he shook his head in what was obviously annoyance. But it wasn't that which had

Susan inhaling sharply. No, it was his clenched fists, the knuckles bone white which sent a shiver shooting down her spine. Never, not once, had she seen Martin, a man she thought she knew inside and out, show any sign of aggression, any hint of anger. But then there was only so far that even the calmest of men could be pushed before they eventually reacted.

Had Susan pushed Martin too far this time? Were her actions, the desire to have a party to celebrate her birthday when she knew without a doubt that Martin would have done nothing, been too heinous for him to forgive?

As if Susan had spoken her thoughts aloud, Martin turned sharply towards the stairs, seeing Susan. They locked eyes for the briefest of seconds.

A look that she couldn't quite read flashed across his face before he quickly hid it, before he unclenched his fists and relaxed his brow. Before he donned his usual air of indifference and began to ascend the stairs.

Despite Susan forcing herself to resume her descent, to maintain a pretence of ignorance, she had to admit she didn't want to walk past Martin right now. For the first time in their marriage she felt uneasy. She wanted to turn around and dash back to her room. But she couldn't.

She forged on.

As they met at the stairs' narrowest point, Susan looked away, towards the corridor which led to the safety of the excited chaos in the kitchen. She didn't look at Martin, didn't want to know if he was looking at her or if he had also turned away.

Reaching the bottom step, Susan exhaled loudly and darted across the entrance and through the doorway of the corridor.

It was only once she knew she was out of Martin's sight that she stopped, back pressed against the wall.

Why had that affected her so much?

And then she realised, the look that Martin had attempted to hide from her was hatred.

He hated her.

32

GRACE

The warrant wasn't in yet. So Grace had sent Harry back to the office to get some more information on Joshua's current financial situation.

Joshua was flashing the cash and Grace wanted to know where he'd gotten it from. Had he stolen the necklace and sold it on? It was a reasonable assumption to make and both herself and Harry were certain that his accounts would show some red flags at the very least.

What Grace hadn't considered previously but was becoming more probable, was that there were two crimes which had occurred during Susan's party, a robbery and an attempted murder. She didn't like coincidences but she had to accept that perhaps one crime had obscured her from seeing the possibility of a second one.

Martin may have been telling the truth all along. *About the theft that is.*

With Harry looking into Joshua Maddison, DS Cartwright was busy digging into the payout that Susan had made. That was one question which Grace wanted resolved today, everyone they had spoken to so far had been dragging their heels on providing them with any useful information but Grace had instructed Amy to put some pressure on, threaten them with warrants and even obstructing an investigation if need be.

DS Richard Shore was making a start on Martin's phone records, for both his mobile and the home phone, trying to piece together the beginning of a timeline.

And Grace was back outside the bookshop, ready to reinterview Jennifer, Susan's sister.

Stepping through the door, the little bell announced her arrival.

Strangely there was no one manning the till but at a glance Grace noted several customers milling around.

Peculiar.

Grace walked up to the counter and waited a moment.

Eventually a woman, perhaps in her early thirties with brown curly hair and fashionably thick-rimmed glasses appeared from a section towards the back, looking flustered.

'Sorry,' she breathed heavily, 'how can I help you?'

'Hi, that's okay–' Grace glanced at the assistant's name badge, 'Anna. I was hoping to speak with Miss Russell. Is she working today?'

DI Roth watched as Anna's eyes flicked towards the closed door of the office then back to Grace.

After a moment's hesitation, Anna nodded. 'Yes she is, but I think she might be in the middle of something. Could you come back a little later?'

'I would really like to speak with her now if I may.' Grace pulled out her badge and held it out for Anna to see. 'Could you please tell Miss Russell that it's DI Roth?'

Anna bit the edge of her lower lip but nodded. With obvious reluctance she made her way to the door.

Grace watched as she knocked lightly.

There was obviously no reply because after waiting for a

few seconds, she tried again, only this time she rapped a little harder.

Grace didn't know if she had been granted entry or whether Anna simply decided the situation justified opening the door, either way she tentatively turned the handle. When the door was open just far enough, Anna peered inside.

Despite facing the door, Grace couldn't make out what was being said.

The not knowing only amplified Grace's impatience, her fingers drumming on the glass top of the counter.

A customer, a woman perhaps in her mid- to late-sixties with shoulder-length blonde hair, a straight, proud nose and tired eyes came and stood beside her, three books clutched to her chest. Grace couldn't help but look at them.

Following Grace's stare, the woman gave a guilty smile. 'I just love a good book, don't you?'

DI Roth nodded in agreement, but in truth she hadn't read a book since her mother had passed away. She had tried several times but each time the act of reading, the smell of the paper, the weight of it in her hands, transported Grace back to the hospital. Back to when she would sit beside her mother and read to her, unsure if she could hear the words or not. Regardless, she would read for hours, not knowing what else to do, not having any other words to say. She had said them all already, time and time again, telling her mother how loved and adored she was.

That had been towards the end, when her mother was barely clinging on, when she couldn't speak anymore and would only open her eyes fleetingly. It had been heartbreaking knowing that the end was imminent, that in a few days or even a few hours her mother would succumb to the bastard of a disease which had ravaged her body. Grace knew that her mother had been in tremendous pain, but she had forged on, fighting as hard as she could for as long as she could. At least the pain would be gone. At least she could finally be at peace, she had thought, like a mantra, trying to find the smallest of silver linings.

The cancer had won in the end. And Grace could no longer find any pleasure in reading.

She swallowed hard at the lump which had settled in her throat. Now was not the time to travel down that road.

Fed up of waiting for Jennifer to grant her entry, Grace strode away from the counter and to the door, which was ajar, Anna's body filling the small opening.

'I don't feel comfortable telling her that,' Grace heard Anna whisper.

So that was how this was going to be.

With a firm yet careful hand, Grace didn't want to accidentally hurt Anna, she grasped the door-handle and pushed the door open far enough to see in.

Anna gasped whilst Jennifer jumped out of her seat, a look of shock being replaced with a look of anger.

'There is a customer waiting to purchase some books,' Grace calmly informed Anna, who took the opportunity to retreat.

Stepping into the small yet well-presented office, Grace purposefully shut the door behind her.

Turning back, Jennifer didn't say anything but her irritation was obvious. Beyond that, however, Grace couldn't help but notice that Jennifer looked as though she was upset, as though she had been crying. Her eyes were puffy, the skin on her cheeks a little blotchy and her nose was red.

'Good afternoon, Miss Russell. I am sorry to drop by again but I need to talk to you about–'

'I already know.' Jennifer's voice wobbled.

With a tilt of her head, Grace asked, 'What do you know?'

'About Martin. Joshua told me.'

That explains why she is upset.

'I see. May I sit down?' Grace indicated the empty chair, seeing as how she suspected that Jennifer wasn't about to offer.

Jennifer nodded.

Taking a seat, Grace pursed her lips in what she hoped was a sympathetic look. 'I am very sorry for your loss,' she offered.

Miss Russell's tears began to flow freely. Grace, spotting a box of tissues on a shelf near the wall, stood up, grabbed the box and gently slid it in front of Jennifer before sitting down once more.

Jennifer took one, wiping at her cheeks first and then her nose. 'Thank you.'

'I hope you don't mind me saying, but I didn't realise that you and Mr Grey were so close.'

The comment seemed to pierce through Jennifer's grief, her tears stopping almost instantly, her attention suddenly fixed on the detective. 'I wouldn't say that we were close exactly, but he's family, and he's been a support to me, since Susan's fall. I think it's the shock that's got me all unsettled. First, my sister and now Martin. Anyone would think we're cursed.'

'May I ask what Joshua told you?'

Jennifer paused for a moment, then said, 'That it was a car accident.' Then she shrugged. 'He didn't say much else actually, just that Martin hadn't survived.'

'Did Joshua tell you that as a matter of course we are looking into the events leading up to Martin's death?'

Jennifer shook her head. 'Not specifically. He told me you had been to see him and were asking more questions, but not that there was a proper investigation.'

'Whenever something like this happens we need to establish a timeline of events to better understand what occurred and why.' What Grace didn't say, however, was that she was convinced that both Martin's death and Susan's attempted murder were linked because it was too much of a coincidence for them not to be.

There are just too many coincidences in this case for my liking.

What Grace believed in were facts and evidence, but with little of that to go on, coincidence was seemingly all she had.

'Can you tell me when you last spoke to Martin?'

A look of worry flitted across Jennifer's features. 'Do we really need to do this now, Detective? I am all over the place as I am sure you can understand.'

'I'm afraid that we do. Best to get it over with while it's all fresh in your mind. Wouldn't you agree?'

'I couldn't say for sure, but a couple of days ago.'

Grace took out her notepad and pen, she held the pen poised just above the clean sheet of paper. 'And by a couple of days would that be two, three or four?'

What is it with this family and their vagueness?

Jennifer looked flummoxed. 'Um, perhaps four.'

'I see. And what did you talk about?'

'I don't see why that would matter?'

Grace rested the notepad on her lap before levelling Jennifer with a stare. 'It matters because we are trying to get a sense of what state Martin was in leading up to the crash. Obviously his wife, your sister, is in hospital in a critical condition. How was he coping with that? I would expect he may have been struggling emotionally. Was the situation having an impact on his mental well-being? Was there anything else affecting him at the time of the accident? So whatever you can tell me about your last conversation with Martin could prove to be vital.'

Jennifer sighed under her breath but Grace heard it nevertheless.

Grace trusted herself enough to spot if there was an angle, a lead to chase, and if she wasn't mistaken there was definitely something in Jennifer's body language, in her attitude, which suggested she was trying to hide something.

'Come to think of it, I don't think that I actually spoke to Martin then. What I mean is, I did call him, for an update on Susan and to see how he was, but if my memory serves me correctly, he didn't answer. I think I had presumed he was at the hospital.'

Grace only nodded, because if she was being honest, words were failing her. Why was Jennifer Russell purposely trying to deceive her? Without a shadow of a doubt, that was what was happening here.

'All right, so the last time you actually spoke with Mr Grey was when?'

Jennifer missed the slightest of beats before she answered. 'A day or two after Susan's accident.'

Grace didn't even attempt to hide her confusion. 'Forgive me, Miss Russell, but a moment ago you said that you had spoken to Martin only four days ago for me to now find out that it was well over a week ago. And I am certain that earlier, when I arrived, you indicated that Martin had been a great support to you following Susan's accident, and yet you haven't actually spoken to him. What is going on here?'

Miss Russell looked spooked. 'I told you that now was not the best time for this. I am all sixes and sevens. Martin has been a support, but you are correct I haven't spoken to him for a while because he is so often with his wife.'

Detective Roth could see that she was losing Jennifer, so she abruptly changed course. 'Yes, I am sorry and I appreciate how difficult this must be. Last time we spoke, you indicated that Susan may have been planning to make an announcement at the party. I don't suppose you've had time to consider what that may have been about, have you?'

Jennifer appeared to be the sort of person who was easily overlooked, perhaps even underestimated, but Grace suspected there was more to her, that she was observant, clever even; it just went undetected or ignored.

Let's see what happens if I use that to my advantage.

'Oh, I'm really not sure, I would only be speculating.'

'So you have thought about it? I'm not surprised really, even if Susan was trying to keep it a secret, it's always hard to hide things from your sister, isn't it?'

'Susan never was as careful as she thought. As a kid I would always know when she'd snuck out to meet her boyfriend even though she'd deny it.'

'So what do you suppose she was planning?'

Jennifer curled her mouth to the side in contemplation. Grace knew Jennifer was debating what to tell her. Eventually, she nodded once to herself as though she'd made her decision. 'I think she was planning on selling the bookshop.' Grace couldn't help but notice an edge of anger to her words.

'Why would you think that?'

Jennifer shrugged. 'Because that is what Susan does, she builds up businesses and then she sells them on for a profit. She had been talking to the bank and to an estate agent.'

That was news to Grace. 'Do you know which estate agent she'd spoken to?'

Jennifer shook her head. 'Sorry. I guessed that she was having the shop valued though.'

That was certainly a new avenue to look into, Grace thought, pleased that she'd managed to get Jennifer back on side.

'Could I also ask you about Susan and Martin's relationship, how was it before Susan's fall?'

'Oh, I really don't think I could comment on that.' Her

defences were up again. Grace was getting dizzy from the momentous swings in this woman's attitude.

'But as you already said, you noticed things about your sister, things that she might have been trying to hide...'

For a minute, Grace didn't think Jennifer was going to buy it again, but then she rolled her eyes, an act so quintessential of a teenager that it appeared alien on this woman's features, before she leant forward, arms resting on the desk. 'I don't think things were very good between them. Susan would make the occasional comment about Martin, belittling him for not working and for not helping out with the shop. And I think he was drinking enough to make her worried.'

'What makes you say that?'

'Susan had borrowed one of the self-help books. It was about supporting people with addictions. It was in her desk drawer,' Jennifer attested.

'I see, but Susan never confided in you that she believed Martin had an issue with alcohol?'

'No.'

'Did you happen to see Martin on the night of the party, did you notice if he had been drinking?'

Jennifer pursed her lips as though she was trying to remember. 'I think I saw him in passing and yes, I think he'd had a drink, but then it was a party. Everybody was drinking.'

Grace nodded. 'Of course.'

Feeling as though her questioning had run its course, Grace was just about to excuse herself when her phone began ringing.

With an apologetic smile, Grace extracted the phone from her pocket. Amy.

Grace answered. 'What have you got for me?'

'I have finally tracked down the deposit made from Susan Grey's account. It was a down payment on another shop premises. I spoke with one Matthew Gregory. He deals in private acquisitions, and apparently Mrs Grey approached him to aid her in finding a new premises. She was planning on expanding her business portfolio by opening a second branch of her bookshop. There had also been talk of a third.

'Mr Gregory was very shocked to learn about Susan's situation. I have logged all his details and informed him that you will likely be in touch in the next day or so.'

'Good work. I'll be back in the office shortly.'

That wasn't exactly what Grace had wanted to hear, but at least blackmail could now be ruled out. Although it also disproved Jennifer's theory, Susan wasn't going to announce that she was selling up, quite the opposite in fact.

'Sorry about that,' Grace offered as she stowed her phone, notebook and pen in her bag then rose to her feet. She took a few steps towards the door. 'I need to head back now, although just for the record, my colleague has just unearthed Susan's plans.' Jennifer's eyes widened. 'She wasn't planning on selling the bookshop, she was looking to grow the business. She had just put a rather large deposit down on a second premises.'

Shock, or perhaps guilt twisted Jennifer's features. Grace didn't look back as she left, aware that Jennifer Russell clearly didn't know her sister as well as she had believed herself to.

33

CHRISTOPHER

The day had been totally turned on its head.

First, Joshua had stunned him with the news of Martin's death, a tragedy which for Christopher brought about mixed emotions. He felt sad knowing Susan was none the wiser about her husband's death and fearful of how she might deal with it but there was also some hope. Selfish as it was, he hoped that he could now make things right between them, that Susan may even, in the not-too-distant future, consider giving him another chance.

And it was that thought that had spurred Christopher on, giving him the courage to call the hospital once more.

He had spoken to the ward sister, Sally.

Despite having already been aware of the situation, Sally initially denied his request, falling back on ward policy as her reasoning. But Christopher had argued, with a fire in his belly that he hadn't felt for years, that without Martin, Susan would be alone. A patient who, owing to the stringent rules, rules which could easily be bent or changed, would be seemingly abandoned, even though there were visitors practically jumping up and down to be let in.

Sally had fallen quiet momentarily as though weighing up her options before finally relenting, stating that he could visit today if he wished.

Christopher hadn't needed to be told twice. With haste he had cleaned himself up, changed his clothes and headed to the hospital.

He hadn't known what to bring, but knew he couldn't turn up with nothing, so he'd grabbed flowers, he didn't know what they were but Christopher thought they looked pretty, a box of assorted chocolates and lastly, a couple of magazines from the hospital shop. Susan had always enjoyed reading those gossip mags, Christopher remembered.

With his arms laden, he had taken the lift up to the intensive care ward, where he'd stepped out, to be greeted by large security doors.

That was where he found himself standing now.

Nervousness, or was it fear, had rooted him to the spot. He desperately wanted to see Susan, to stride through those doors, into her room and into her heart. But deep down he knew it wouldn't be like that.

How could it?

She was fighting for her life. In all reality, she probably wouldn't even know that he was there, not that that mattered.

He looked down at the items in his hands, realising how superficial they were, how stupid he was for bringing them. Susan wasn't going to see the flowers or eat the chocolates. Yet he couldn't bring himself to throw them in the bin, to have empty hands which he wouldn't know what to do with.

Nausea swelled in the pit of his stomach but he chose to ignore it.

He wanted to be there for her.

Without further hesitation, Christopher pressed the entry button.

The ward was quiet, he noted as he signed in and waited to be directed to Susan's room. He liked the quiet, although he knew Susan preferred there to be a buzz, whether it was the TV, the radio or chatting, she had never seemed comfortable with silence.

Perhaps if they let him visit again he could bring a radio for her, he considered as he moved to the room the nurse had kindly indicated.

The door was already open and from the periphery of his vision Christopher could see the bed, could see Susan in the bed even before he'd entered.

Shock hit him like a bolt of electricity. A lump rose to the back of his throat. He swallowed against it.

Regardless of the shock, the anticipation which threatened to overwhelm him, he didn't miss a step, didn't falter.

Susan needed him now more than ever and he was damned if he was going to let fear keep him at bay.

Carefully he placed the useless things he'd brought on the tray at the foot of her bed.

With a sweeping glance, he noted that there were no other flowers, no cards decorating the window ledge or the top of the small unit in the corner. The room was utterly bare, void of any tokens from family or friends.

This isn't right. Susan has lots of friends, lots of people who care about her, but then why is her room so lifeless? Surely Martin had brought her flowers?

Perhaps it's another ridiculous hospital policy? No gifts allowed from well-wishers, although, no one challenged me about the things I brought in.

Choosing not to think about that further, Christopher sat in the chair beside her bed. He also tried not to think about how many other people had sat in this very seat before him, how many of them had slept in it even, waiting, praying for their loved ones to recover.

Now he was looking at the machines which were obviously helping Susan in some way. And there were a lot of them. Numbers were digitally displayed on most of them, beats per minute, units per hour, systolic pressure. None of it meant anything to him, and yet he took it all in until he was satisfied he had looked at each one in turn.

He was procrastinating he knew, putting off what was yet to come, and for good reason.

But with nowhere left to look, Christopher steeled himself and allowed his eyes to finally settle on Susan.

He hadn't thought about this part. No, he had thought about the things he needed to say, the conversations he should have had with her over the years, he'd even thought about helping her when she was better, when she was recovering, but he hadn't actually stopped to think about her now, like this, lifeless but still alive.

It caught him off guard.

He clenched his teeth, hard.

His throat bobbed as he swallowed, the lump which had risen refused to move. The nausea in his stomach spiralled and swelled. She was so pale and so thin. Her cheeks were too prominent, her eyes too sunken.

Christopher breathed slowly, in and out, he focused all of his attention on each breath until the rising sickness abated.

'Hello, beautiful,' he finally said. His voice sounded odd, as though it wasn't his own.

Gently he reached out and laid his hand on top of Susan's.

'I hope they're looking after you properly.'

Christopher couldn't help but think how unfair this all was, to have to see Susan lying there, crisp white sheet shrouding her broken body. She was a good person, one of the best. She didn't deserve this.

If he could, he would trade places with her in a heartbeat, he wouldn't even need to think about it.

'I'm sorry it's taken me so long to visit, they're a bit strict here about who they let in. Guess they'd marked my card already.' He smiled, but it didn't reach his eyes.

He stared intently at Susan's face, looking for even the most infinitesimal of changes, the slightest of movements to indicate that she could hear him.

She didn't move.

His chest ached.

'Susan, I need to apologise,' Christopher began because he was no good at idle chit-chat. In fact he wasn't very good at talking at all, still, there were things that he needed to say and he might never get another chance.

He glanced towards the open door, feeling suddenly vulnerable. Thankfully, there was no one there to listen, no one to overhear his heartfelt words.

'I have always been hot-headed, Susan. I think that at the beginning you loved that about me, only after we had Joshua you grew up, you had to. But me, I carried on just the same, an immature, combative dickhead, starting fights if someone even looked at me the wrong way.' He snorted through his nose. 'I think leaving me was probably the right thing to do, for you and Joshua. Not that I realised that then.

'But now I see it, if you had stayed, you would have grown to hate me, to resent me and that would have been worse than losing you. And for Joshua, well, I wasn't exactly a good role model, was I?'

Christopher fell silent. What he would give to be able to redo the past fifteen years, twenty years even. He wouldn't make the same mistakes twice, he wouldn't lose his family a second time.

'I wish I had listened to you then, when you'd threatened to leave, and looking back, I think you probably stayed longer than you should have, gave me more chances than I deserved. I've always been a bit slow though, haven't I? Always took a bit longer to see what was right in front of me.' He paused to collect himself, to push down his sadness.

'I had everything with you, with you both, but I threw it away. Only, by the time I'd realised what I'd done, you'd met Martin and you had moved on.'

Christopher chose not to tell Susan about Martin's death. If by some miracle she could hear him, he didn't want to tell her something which would undoubtedly cause her more pain, which might even affect her recovery.

And besides, it probably wasn't for *him* to be the one to break that news.

'Rachel shouldn't have said what she did to you at the party.' Christopher shook his head. 'What I mean is, that wasn't the right time or place to tell you, that was your night and she shouldn't have hijacked it the way she did. But then if I'd told you before, she wouldn't have felt the need.' Once again, he'd been an idiot and just like before he'd realised it too late. It suddenly felt as though all he seemed to do was fuck up when it came to Susan.

He looked at her again, she remained unmoved.

He would have given anything for her to shout at him, to yell, to swear. He would have welcomed it with open arms, but she was still, silent.

He sat back in the chair and continued to talk. 'The thing with Rachel was just a bit of fun, it didn't mean anything. Well, not to me anyway. That's what I wanted to tell you that night.'

Christopher raked both of his hands through his hair. It had all got so messed up. Rachel telling Susan about them, him racing to find Susan to smooth things over, to lie if that's what it took because the reality was he was afraid of what she would think of him, how she might hate him. But then she had fallen, or been pushed. He desperately wanted to know who had hurt her, because then he could hurt them in return, make them suffer the way Susan had been forced to suffer.

He sighed loudly, before reaching out for Susan's hand once more. He couldn't remember when he had last held her hand. His fingers slid around hers, rough against smooth, large against small.

'What I wanted to say, Susan, what I should have said a long time ago is that I'm sorry.

'I'm sorry for it all, for treating you the way I did when we were younger, for not appreciating you then when you were mine and for being stubborn enough to let you leave. And I'm sorry about Rachel, I'm sorry for what I said that night and I am sorry for what I did. I never meant to make things difficult for you, but everything I said was the truth. I love you, Susan, I always have and I always will, even if you never love me back.'

Christopher fell silent then, his chin dropping to his chest as he wept.

34

JOSHUA

The bar was finally empty. Everyone had downed tools for the evening and gone home, everyone except for Joshua that was.

Joshua would openly admit he wasn't typically a hands-on sort of person, he wasn't very good at anything manual, wasn't a grafter in the physical sense of the word.

He was more casual, more laissez-faire, in his approach to a task, taking his time, only doing what really needed to be done and if it could be delegated, then he would certainly try that first.

But he knew there were a lot of doubters out there, people who were hoping he would fail, that Joshua Maddison wouldn't succeed, and he desperately wanted to prove them all wrong. Plus, he had a lot on his mind and felt the need to be busy.

So with strict instructions from the decorator, Joshua was painting a single wall. She hadn't seemed exactly thrilled at the idea of leaving him with a paintbrush and a freshly primed wall but he had assured her that even he couldn't muck this up.

With as much care as he could muster for the job at hand, Joshua was cutting in the edges first. Thankfully the decorator had already masked up the adjoining walls, skirting boards and ceiling because admittedly some paint had accidentally found its way onto the tape.

Joshua was running through a mental list of jobs still to complete in the next few days before his big unveiling. And top of that list was to confirm a supplier. Despite having spoken to a couple, there still wasn't a drop of whisky in his whisky bar. He had been attempting to haggle on price, to score a better deal but they had all said the same thing, his initial order wasn't big enough to warrant the discount he was hoping for.

He knew he would have to make a decision tomorrow, it would never do to have supermarket-level brands lining his shelves.

No, he planned to offer more sought-after, exclusive whiskies. Not only would his profit margins be healthier that way but it would also ensure he was attracting the right sort of clientele. He didn't want just anybody frequenting his premises after all. It was important to get his business off on the right foot and reputation was everything in this game.

But that required spending more of his ever-dwindling reserves.

And they were diminishing quicker than he had expected.

But then what was a whisky bar without whisky?

A flop, that's what.

So he needed a plan to increase his funds, and one that would pay quickly. Fleetingly, he considered broaching the subject with his dad, to see if he would be interested in investing, but then just as quickly as the idea popped into his mind, he discounted it.

Over the years Joshua had proposed numerous ideas to his dad, suggesting that they could work together, could build up a family business.

Admittedly, Joshua had been hoping his dad would stump

up the capital for the venture in question, but each and every time, he'd declined. *'Thanks for thinking of me, son, but I don't think running a business is for me.' 'I don't know the first thing about importing and exporting, you're better off finding someone who understands all that stuff.' 'I like to keep life simple, go to work, come home, enjoy a beer, I don't think that's for me.'*

The funny thing was that, with each rejection, Joshua found himself wanting to work with his dad more. But he suspected his dad didn't trust him enough to invest in him.

Perhaps he would consider a loan?

He didn't want to ask anyone for help, didn't want his critics to be able to say that he could only pull this off because he had financial backing from his parents.

So if he couldn't borrow the money, he would have to find another way of raising the extra cash. Only, from the way that woman detective had asked him how he'd afforded all this, how she'd then questioned him about his mum's missing necklace, he knew the police were suspicious. That they were likely to be keeping an eye on him and on his financial affairs.

He didn't want to do anything that might raise their suspicions further, which ruled out most of his options.

Before Joshua could contemplate his remaining choices, his phone, which was on the nearest table, beeped, making him jump, navy-blue paint flicking across the adjoining wall.

'Shit.' He sighed, but without making an effort to clear up the splatter, he dropped the brush in the tray, stood up and moved to the table.

Coincidentally, it was his dad.

> I am at the hospital with your mum. They finally let me in. You should visit her.

Joshua pressed his lips together tightly. That was all he needed, his dad making him feel guilty about not going to the hospital. He had considered it, in fact he nearly went after seeing his dad at the pub the other day, but he'd bottled it.

He had said some real shitty things to her at her party, unforgivable nasty things that he didn't particularly want to recall. What he couldn't forget, however, was the hurt expression she'd tried to hide, the way she turned away from him a fraction too late to mask her pain, her disappointment. There was also the pawned item. He knew when he'd done it that it was a mistake, one he might regret, but Joshua was always able to swiftly move on, his mum, however, probably wouldn't see it like that, she wouldn't be so quick to forgive him when she realised.

It was for the best if he didn't go.

He put the phone down without responding. He was about to walk away when an idea hit him. He picked up his phone once more.

Dialling the number, he waited.

'I hadn't expected to hear from you,' the voice on the other end said, although there was no surprise to his tone. 'You still owe me a grand. I thought I was gonna have to chase you down.'

'Yes, about that. I need some cash–' The man on the other end laughed. It was a hollow, chilling sound but Joshua didn't stop to pay attention to it. 'I've got some gear, it's worth about three times what I owe you. How about you buy it off me, minus what I owe you of course?'

There was a pause, which Joshua knew to be a good sign. So he waited. 'Interest has been added to your debt.'

'Of course,' Joshua responded smoothly.

'Another three hundred pounds.'

Damn.

But then what did he expect when he dealt with these lowlifes? He needed the money and at least this would ensure he had enough to stock the bar for opening night.

'Fine, but I need it tonight. In cash.' Best not to have any money transferred into his account now. Just in case.

'I'll meet you at the pub.'

'I'll be there in an hour.'

Problem solved, Joshua thought to himself smugly. He pocketed the phone, grabbed his bag and headed to the door with a triumphant swagger. Flicking off the lights, the bar fell into darkness.

He exited, locking the door behind him, leaving the paint and paintbrush abandoned on the floor.

35

———

GRACE

Grace was poring over the case files, her head in her hands. She had revisited Martin Grey's interview to see if there was anything new to glean from it, anything she had previously missed.

There wasn't.

She was acutely aware that the time she'd been afforded was running out and they were no further forward with Susan's case.

But, understanding there wasn't much more she could achieve this evening, she was debating packing up.

Decision made, she began shuffling the papers back into order. She was already thinking about stopping for a takeaway on her way home, a Chinese perhaps, aware that her fridge was lacking enough of anything to make a decent meal.

'I think I've got something,' Harry said loudly from his desk, drawing her attention.

Grace was on her feet and moving towards him, file discarded. 'What is it?' She wasn't going to get her hopes up, but Harry wouldn't have said anything unless he thought he was truly onto something.

'I've been looking into Joshua's finances.' He shook his head as though he couldn't quite believe his luck. 'He obviously isn't the sharpest tool in the box or at least he hasn't been as thorough as he should have. He recently set up a business account for the bar, transferring in approximately fourteen grand from another account. That in itself isn't unusual, but it's the other account which got me suspicious. It isn't registered to Joshua Maddison but rather Josh Maidstone.' He looked up at Grace with eyebrows raised.

'So he's got an account registered under a false identity?'

'Exactly. He obviously made a mistake in transferring straight from that one to the business one. All I had to do was work backwards.' Harry glanced up at Grace to make sure she was still with him, she was. 'So I checked the account and there have been multiple payments made to Joshua or rather Josh over the past couple of years, including one for fourteen thousand a few days ago. Most of them unfortunately are untraceable. But this account,' he pointed to an account or rather a set of digits on his computer screen, 'this last one, the one for the fourteen grand is a registered business account. So with a little digging I have an address. And guess what? It's a pawn shop in Brighton.'

A huge grin spread across Grace's face. 'Gotcha,' she said.

'We can wait until tomorrow morning to confirm it's the necklace but I'm pretty sure it will be.'

'Let's go and arrest our man now, we've got enough evidence.'

'I'll drive,' Harry offered as he grabbed his keys.

They eventually arrived at Joshua's flat having tried the bar first which was shut up tight for the night.

The detectives were about to exit the vehicle when Grace spotted Joshua leaving his apartment building, a duffel bag slung over his shoulder.

Typically, Grace wouldn't have paused, wouldn't have given

her suspect an inch of distance in which she might lose him, but there was something in the way that Joshua glanced around before he set off. He was nervous and that made Grace suspicious.

'Where do you suppose he's going at *this* hour with *that* bag?' Grace thought aloud.

'Gym?' Harry guessed, clearly playing along.

'He doesn't seem like the sweaty gym type, if you ask me.' Joshua had had several run-ins with the law so Grace didn't feel she was making an impossible leap in suspecting Joshua was up to no good.

'Well, in that case, I would suggest that he looks as though he is up to something unsavoury and possibly even illegal.'

'That is exactly what I was thinking. Shall we follow him?'

'Good idea,' Harry replied, starting the engine. 'Let's radio for backup just in case.'

DI Roth and DI Amberidge tailed Joshua Maddison as he darted through the streets of Brighton. A couple of times they lost sight of him; firstly when he'd headed down a one-way road and then again when he crossed a pedestrianised area.

Harry, despite appearing calm, cursed under his breath as he sought out an alternative route, hurtling this way and that until he thankfully led them back to their man.

Harry had grown up in and around Brighton, he'd informed Grace when she commented on his luck with routes. He knew most of the roads, he'd said, although he did acknowledge that things had changed in the last couple of years.

Eventually Joshua paused outside of a pub, The King's Arms. He seemed to be readying himself, Grace decided as Joshua straightened the strap of the bag on his shoulder and ran his fingers through his hair.

Harry tucked the car at the end of a row of parked vehicles and cut the engine, the lights turning off.

Joshua, perhaps sensing their stares, or simply uneasy, glanced over his shoulder.

Grace held her breath momentarily.

But he didn't turn far enough to see the two detectives secreted in the darkened car, who were watching his every move, he also didn't notice the patrol car which had pulled in at the top of the road and had purposefully obscured itself behind a van. He didn't see anything other than an empty street.

Without any cause for concern, Joshua ducked into the pub.

Grace didn't want to waste a minute.

Climbing out of the car, Harry in tow, Grace strode up the slight incline of the street to the patrol car.

She flashed her badge at the uniformed officer in the driver's seat, a tall, thin man with a sharp nose and large eyes, then looked across to his colleague, a younger woman with round yet serious features. 'I'm DI Roth. Our suspect has entered the pub, he's wanted for theft and possibly attempted murder, but we suspect he may be selling illegal items in there. He entered with a large duffel bag.'

Whilst the officers joined her beside the car and Grace provided them with a description of Joshua, Harry jogged off to check for rear access to the pub.

Grace watched from the corner of her eye as he disappeared down a small side alley. After a minute he reappeared, giving a thumbs up and indicated that he would cover that exit.

Grace nodded.

'Right, let's get our man.'

Her heart was racing with excitement and her stomach was twisted with anticipation. There was a thrill that came with making an arrest, one that couldn't be replicated. There was nothing like knowing you had got your man, or woman, that you had taken a dangerous individual off the streets and served them with the justice they deserved.

This was the break she had so desperately needed, that she deserved. And it couldn't have come sooner. Grace would make the arrest and in the morning she would trace the necklace back to Joshua. She couldn't say for definite if this meant he was the one who'd injured Susan, but it would give her grounds to hold him for longer, to question him more intensely.

Striding towards the entrance of The King's Arms, the two uniformed officers flanking her, Grace only halted to radio through to Harry, to let him know they were moving in.

Harry's reply was brief: 'In position.'

Opening the door, Grace was hit by the overwhelming and unpleasant smell of stale beer, an odour which seemed to be coming from everywhere and nowhere at the same time. Perhaps it was seeping out from the very foundation of the building, she considered fleetingly.

Thankfully there was a glass divide behind the door screening them off from view.

DI Roth peered around the wall.

The pub was dark in an oppressive way, not simply because of the low lighting but because the walls were a shade of burgundy. The carpet which was well-trodden and likely to be very sticky, was a matching deep red and all the mismatched furniture was a collection of dark wood.

It was depressing but also the perfect place for some underhand dealings, Grace decided instantly.

Sweeping her gaze across the few drinkers bent over their pint glasses, she easily spotted Joshua. With his crisp white T-shirt, clean-shaven face and good posture, he stood out like an oasis in the desert. His companion, however, fitted in with the décor, dark and shady.

And there on the table between them was the duffel bag.

She watched as Joshua casually slid it across towards his acquaintance, the gesture disguised as a move to make room for his pint on the small round table. The man, accepting the bag, took it off the table, tucking it beside him on the bench as though it were a beloved pet, before reaching for his drink.

That was a handover, if ever she saw one. But of what? Grace wasn't sure. She wasn't going to wait any longer to find out.

Indicating to the officers where her suspect was, Grace strode confidently out into the pub's main area and straight towards the table.

It was Joshua's associate who looked up first, aware that someone was approaching their table. Spying Grace, his expression was one of curiosity but it was as he registered the uniformed coppers behind her that his face distorted into a mixture of anger and fear.

He was on his feet instantly, bag clutched in his hands as he pushed the table over and dashed for the small corridor indicating the toilets. Grace didn't need to look to know that her colleagues were chasing him.

At the same time Joshua also rose to his feet, not because of the police but because he was now covered in beer. He was holding out his hands in disbelief as he looked up to see Grace closing in on him.

Surprisingly, he didn't look afraid, although his gaze did flick beyond Grace towards the door as though he was considering the possibility of making a run for it. With Grace now in front of him, he returned his stare to her, obviously deciding against it.

'Detective Roth, I didn't know you frequented this pub.' He subtly wiped his hands down the sides of his legs before plastering that cocky smile on his face.

What a cock.

'I'm afraid that this is not a social call, Mr Maddison.'

'Oh, that is a shame. Then what can I help you with?'

'Mr Maddison, you are under arrest on suspicion of theft and attempted murder.' Grace couldn't pretend that it wasn't utterly satisfying to say those words. Reaching out, she clasped her left hand onto Joshua's wrist before hooking the cuffs on.

'What the fuck?' Joshua began fighting against her then, but she was too swift, too well versed in this situation. She had the other cuff on him before he could pull away. 'I didn't do anything,' he protested, shouting now as Grace held him fast.

Unperturbed, she proceeded to read Joshua Maddison his rights.

'You have got to be fucking kidding me,' and then when Grace chose not to reply, 'Are you serious?'

'Very,' was Grace's only response.

A tap on Grace's shoulder had her turning round. She came face to face with a withered old man who looked as though he could do with not only a good bath but also a healthy dose of vitamin D.

She wasn't sure what she expected him to say but she readied herself for his interference. For some reason the public always seemed to feel the need to get involved, to intervene when they saw someone being arrested. It was as if they couldn't believe you had the just cause to be carrying out an arrest or that they somehow had the right to stop you from doing your job.

Admittedly there were the rare few who assisted, helping to secure a suspect but somehow Grace didn't feel that this was one of those times.

'Can you take this outside? You're disturbing my other customers.'

Whatever Grace had been expecting it wasn't that. The man looked a decade past retirement age for starters. But with a smile she replied, 'My pleasure.'

With her forearm pressed firmly against Maddison's back

and her other hand securely gripping the cuffs, she pushed him towards the door, all the while he continued to protest his innocence.

Outside, DI Amberidge, with the help of the male officer, struggled to detain Joshua's buddy. They had him on the floor with Harry wrestling his wrists into cuffs whilst the officer encircled the guy's legs with his arms, fighting to keep him from kicking out. All the while the man on the floor spat a tirade of expletives at them.

Evidently he wasn't going to go quietly.

'Nice company you keep,' Grace commented.

'I don't know him,' Joshua lied, poorly.

Grace gave a half laugh. 'Pull the other one. I just watched you having a drink with him, and that's not even mentioning the bag that you slid across to him.'

'I don't know what you are talking about. What bag? This is a set-up.' Joshua began squirming against his restraints once more. 'Take these things off.'

'Gov?' It was the female officer. As Grace looked up the officer tilted the now open duffel bag in Grace's direction so that she could see its contents. Weed and pills. Enough to get half of Brighton high.

The smile that lit up Grace's face was large and genuine. She was finally getting some results.

'I've never seen that before. I'm being framed.'

'Save it for your interview,' Grace scoffed and began pushing him towards the police van which had just pulled up.

36

SUSAN

AN HOUR BEFORE THE PARTY

Susan carefully zipped herself into the silver, floor-length gown. It was even more stunning than she'd remembered.

Keeping her eyes fixed on her reflection in the full-length mirror on the door of her solid wood wardrobe, Susan turned a half circle, to see herself from every angle, one hand pressed against her stomach and the other on her hip.

It was perfect.

She ran her hands down the dress as though smoothing out an invisible wrinkle, her eyes never leaving her reflection.

Pleased with her appearance, she moved to sit on the vanity table stool. She slid her feet into the audacious shoes she'd also bought, and once again rose to assess herself.

With her hair up and her make-up carefully applied, Susan thought she looked almost ten years younger. Well, maybe five, she corrected modestly. But still. She did look lovely.

Checking her watch, there was still an hour to go before the first of her guests would arrive.

Knowing that her feet would likely be killing her within twenty minutes, she slipped the shoes off and placed them by the bedroom door. Perhaps she should have attempted to wear them in, she considered fleetingly before dismissing the idea.

She would have felt ridiculous waddling around the house in those unnecessarily.

Susan's gaze drifted around her bedroom aimlessly. She didn't know what to do to occupy herself, to kill the remaining time. The caterers had everything in hand and the events coordinator had gently yet firmly shooed Susan away earlier, saying, 'I have everything under control, go and relax.'

Susan's attention fell upon the nightstand, one of a pair, furthest from the door, hers was on the right, his had been on the left.

There was a book, abandoned there. She had dusted around it more times than she cared to count, thinking he would come back sooner or later and pick up where he had left off. But he hadn't and Susan honestly didn't believe he would. She wasn't even convinced that she wanted him to.

And today, the sight of that book, what it symbolised, was proving too much for Susan to stand.

She made her way around the king-size bed, dress swishing satisfyingly around her ankles as she moved. She picked up the novel in question.

Fleetingly she perused the blurb, a crime novel, not her cup of tea at all. Without another thought she moved back to the vanity table and dropped it in the bin.

It landed with a thud. A sound that seemed so final, Susan's heart ached unexpectedly.

She debated retrieving it, went as far as to bend down and then chastised herself, withdrawing her outstretched hand.

It is only a damned book.

She left it in the bin.

Susan sat down on the stool once more, only to almost instantly bounce back up onto her bare feet.

There was a nervous energy tapping away beneath the surface of her skin, the kind that kept you on your toes, stopped you from sitting still, made relaxing an impossible task.

What if nobody showed up? What if only a handful of people bothered to come? What if the entire night was one big flop?

She hadn't realised she was pacing the length of the room, hadn't noticed that she was wringing her hands together.

Susan knew that it was normal for the host to feel jittery before a big event, but she felt ridiculously like a teenager throwing their first party, worrying about her popularity, her standing within her small world.

But still, what if?

She caught sight of herself in the mirror and had to stifle a laugh. If no one turned up, then no one turned up. There was plenty to eat, plenty to drink and she for one certainly planned to enjoy herself.

Right now though, she needed to be busy. Susan found herself leaving the confines of her bedroom. She drifted along the corridor towards the top of the staircase.

For a moment she paused, ear trained towards the opposite corridor, the one that housed both Martin's study and the bedroom which he had now commandeered on a permanent basis.

What was she listening for? She didn't know, signs of life perhaps. Maybe even some indication as to his mood.

She knew he was fuming about the party, that he had taken it as some kind of personal insult, especially once she'd decided to ignore his request to cancel.

The atmosphere in the house had turned from chilly to downright freezing.

Susan really hoped he wouldn't cause a scene tonight,

wasn't going to find some way to embarrass her in front of her guests.

Of course he wouldn't, she chided herself. This was Martin after all. Giving Susan the silent treatment was one thing, but Martin, ever the pacifist, wouldn't seek out drama and he definitely wouldn't instigate it.

Martin probably wouldn't even venture out of his study, despite knowing almost everyone invited, and if he did, Susan was confident he'd quickly find the bar, sedating any complaint he was going to make.

She couldn't hear a thing. Absolutely nothing, no sign of life whatsoever coming from that part of the house.

Turning her attention to the garden, she watched from the large window as all the waiting staff scurried around like ants. Crates of wine and glasses were being carried into the marquee.

A loud burst of noise came out of the giant tent, disturbing the low hum of activity. Susan jumped. The DJ testing his sound equipment, she realised with a soft laugh.

But it was the second thud, a quieter sound but one that was full of emotion, that wiped the smile from her lips. It was a sound that only Susan had heard and it unsettled her.

It was Martin, banging his fist against the door or a book against the desk. She wasn't sure of the specifics but it was certainly a bad sign, he was obviously reacting to the burst of noise.

Susan wondered if she should go and talk to him, attempt to appease him somehow, just enough to get through this evening. However, before she'd made a firm decision she was accosted by the chef.

'Ah, Susan, I was just looking for you. The first dishes are ready and I wondered if you wanted to sample them?'

Susan's gaze flittered once more towards Martin's study

door before returning to the chef, a lovely woman called Claire who ran her own catering company. 'Of course, I'm starving.'

And with that she descended the stairs, barefooted, and followed Claire towards the kitchen; Martin, a problem to be considered later.

37

———

GRACE

Grace hadn't wanted to waste any further time, she had her man in custody so why wait for morning to interview him?

As soon as his appointed representation had arrived, Grace with DI Harry Amberidge beside her, sat down opposite Joshua Maddison in Interview Room One.

It was nearly two in the morning at this point and Grace had been awake for nearly twenty hours. She was running on adrenaline and caffeine.

Of course, Maddison's solicitor had protested, objecting to DI Roth's haste, arguing that she appeared to be pushing this through exceptionally quickly.

Perhaps she was, but Grace disregarded these concerns. Joshua wasn't drunk, he didn't need time to sober up, nor was he high, so why wait?

But that had been Grace's first mistake. One of several she had come to realise.

After only a couple of hours at home to rest, Grace was back in the office, the knot in her stomach twisted so tightly she felt nauseous. She hadn't been able to sleep of course. The events of last night had been replaying, on a loop, in her mind.

When they'd arrested Joshua Maddison, Grace had felt positive that she had her man. The money into Joshua's account from the pawn shop would most certainly prove to be payment for the necklace, his mother's stolen necklace. Grace theorised that this in turn would be grounds for proving Joshua had been responsible for his mother's fall and the motive, sad as it was, was money. Plus, Grace also had the bonus charge of drug possession with intent to supply.

Joshua had denied the accusations levelled at him of course. What Grace had failed to anticipate, however, was the detailed description of the item Joshua had sold to the pawn shop, written down on a piece of paper and slid across the interview desk to her by Maddison's solicitor. Grace might have ignored it, might have forged on, but the solicitor had given her a sympathetic look, the sort of look which said, '*Oh dear, don't you look silly.*'

She had needed to read the piece of paper through three times, the words refusing to register.

Despite Grace having initially approached the interview without reservations, she had known in that moment, in that one look, that she'd fucked up, that she hadn't got her man after all.

Yes, Joshua was guilty of drug offences, that she could prove, but the rest of it, she was no longer sure. Grace had quickly terminated the interview.

Now, she was waiting tentatively for Harry to call, to confirm what it was that Joshua had sold to the pawn shop.

Harry had been quick to volunteer to go and Grace had been happy to let him.

This was a formality, one which she should have undertaken before arresting Maddison, although she had to take some consolation in the fact that had they not followed him last night, they wouldn't have got him on anything. At least that was what she was silently repeating to herself like a mantra.

At quarter past nine, her phone, which she had placed on her desk, rang.

She jumped at the sound despite knowing it was coming.

'Roth.' Her voice croaked as she spoke.

She listened intently as Harry verified what Grace already knew.

It wasn't the necklace.

It wasn't anything even resembling the piece of jewellery in question.

This investigation was like a pendulum, swinging dramatically one way before tracking back on itself to swing the other way and Grace had had enough of it. She wanted to reach out, grab that fucking pendulum and yank it down.

She wanted to solve the case, to have answers and once again she had next to nothing.

With some restraint, she ended the call and placed the phone back on the desk, when what she really wanted to do was hurl it at the wall and scream like a banshee.

But she couldn't. Her reputation was dangling by a thread and it wouldn't take much for that last sliver to snap, she recognised.

'Thank you all for making the time to attend at such short notice.' In the wake of the morning's revelations, Grace had felt it only fair to update her team on the current state of play, especially with the leeway that Potter had afforded the investigation about to expire. 'I am sure that you are all aware we arrested Joshua Maddison last night.' Grace's heart sank as she noticed both Amy and Richard nodding enthusiastically.

Just get straight to the point.

'Despite having had a really good lead to follow, it doesn't look like Maddison is our man. Not for the theft that is.' Grace could feel her cheeks flush with shame, or rather embarrassment.

'We have got him on significant drug charges though,' Harry added pointedly, trying to put a positive spin on things.

'Yes,' Grace conceded. 'However, as a result we are currently without a suspect for the attempted murder of Susan Grey. Furthermore, there has been a hold-up with the warrant, some bureaucratic nonsense. DCI Potter has assured me that it will be back today, so we still have that avenue to pursue. Has anyone else got anything new? Richard, any progress with Martin's phone records?'

Richard nodded once but didn't smile. He pulled out a sheet of paper from the file in front of him. 'I have managed to track the number that was used to call Martin a couple of times on the day of his death and several times prior to that.' Grace watched as his eyes scanned the paper. 'It is registered to a Miss Jennifer Russell, his sister-in-law. There were no other unusual calls, numbers.'

Another dead end then. Jennifer had already admitted to calling Martin for moral support so that wasn't new information.

Of course, Grace didn't say this, she instead said, 'Good work, at least we can rule that out of the investigation. Amy, anything on the anonymous caller?'

Grace's hope was dwindling. Susan's attempted murder would soon become a cold case if they couldn't come up with anything, the team being dispatched to work on other, current cases.

'I have listened to it multiple times and there isn't anything that I can pick out. I have sent it for further analysis as I am positive that I am missing something, that there is something I'm not hearing.' She was shaking her head in frustration, before she added, 'I'll send it to you too, perhaps another set of ears will help.'

'Yes, do that.' Despite her own feelings, Grace rallied herself enough to offer her team some encouragement. 'Whilst we wait for the warrant, I think it would be prudent to reinterview Mr Maddison. Although he may not have stolen the necklace, as one of the beneficiaries of Susan's will, he still had motive to harm her. Richard and Amy, can you please revisit witness statements to see if there is anything we've missed, discrepancies in stories or times, anything at all.'

Grace turned to Harry. 'Fancy interviewing Maddison? I'm not sure I can stomach too much more of his smarmy remarks.'

'It would be my pleasure.' Harry smiled, rising to his feet.

38

———————

JOSHUA

Joshua, hands clasped behind his head, was laid on the bed, if it could be called that. In reality it was just a thin, hard plastic mat resting on a larger solid metal frame, uncomfortable as hell but he wasn't about to let that show, wasn't about to complain.

He didn't want them to see that this was getting to him, didn't want them to know how much he fucking hated these places.

Police cells always had the same smell, and Joshua had been in several to know. It was the stench of cheap disinfectant mixed with piss. Unpleasant and unforgettable.

He didn't know how or why but he had found himself locked up on several occasions. It was his opinion that he was often in the wrong place at the wrong time and in all but one case, he had been let go with nothing more than a slap on the wrists, proving him correct. The last time, however, they had charged him with handling stolen goods, those charges had stuck despite his best efforts of denial.

He'd found himself wearing his favourite suit and standing up in court in front of a judge. He was found guilty, but owing to the fact that it was technically his first offence, he was given a suspended sentence and community service.

The community service had been horrendous. He'd had to work alongside some downright awful people, the kind of men and women that even Joshua would cross the road to avoid, to clean up a community centre in one of the rougher parts of the city. The memory made him shiver.

Despite his hatred for these windowless rooms, Joshua hadn't been squandering his solitary time. He had been thinking. He was confident that several of the charges would be dropped, because they were utter bullshit. But the marijuana, the pills, that one was going to be trickier.

Joshua had been desperately trying to come up with some excuse, some reasonable explanation for having the drugs, for being caught handing them over, but the quantity he'd had was significant, he knew, and that was going to be a bit of a sticking point.

They had mentioned intent to supply. Admittedly they hadn't been wrong but hopefully his solicitor would be able to find some grounds, some means to get him out of here, personal use perhaps.

He sighed heavily.

Joshua was tapping his foot, the only outward sign of his building frustration. Time was not on Joshua's side at the moment, he had a deadline, a grand opening to be ready for and he couldn't afford to sit around here indefinitely.

He wasn't sure what the time was exactly, he'd had lunch, a microwavable pasta meal which he'd had to eat with a plastic fork of course. That was maybe an hour or two ago so he guessed it must be nearly three o'clock.

The thought had Joshua sitting up.

The decorator had a key, thankfully, so at least she could carry on but the plumber, the one who had squeezed Joshua in as a favour to his dad, who was due to connect up the two dishwashers, was supposed to be there today.

'Shit.' Now Joshua was pissed off. If the plumber wasn't able to come back in the next couple of days, Joshua might well have to delay the opening. He couldn't serve drinks in dirty glasses. Could he? No, of course not, he told himself.

Unless... what if he could hire someone to wash up all the glasses, at least for the opening night? Yes, that could actually work, Joshua realised. There was bound to be someone in need of some cash-in-hand work or who would like to be repaid in drinks or trainers, his cash flow was a little stagnant at the moment after all.

Feeling happier that he had sourced a workable solution, he laid back down once more, the mat creaking loudly beneath his weight.

Joshua tried not to think about how many other bodies had laid here before him, didn't want to know how many unwashed, sweaty people had slept where he was, no matter how temporary.

The small metal viewing window in the impenetrable door flipped open, the hinges squeaking. Joshua looked up to see a pair of serious eyes, framed with black glasses, staring in at him.

Just as quickly, the face retreated and the window was shut.

The door unlocked.

The custody sergeant, Joshua couldn't remember his name but he had booked him in last night, filled the doorway. He was well-built but old, probably counting down the months to his retirement, Joshua suspected. 'You're wanted for an interview.'

Joshua frowned. He'd already been interviewed. Still, it wasn't as though he could refuse. If he did, he would likely just be dragged there kicking and complaining.

Wordlessly, Joshua rose to his feet.

'Do I need to cuff you?' the officer asked earnestly. What he was actually asking was, 'Are you going to be difficult?'

'No.'

'Good. Come on then. Can I get you a tea or coffee?' he enquired as he guided Joshua down the corridor, past all the other cells, their doors shut, and to an adjacent corridor, also lined with several closed doors, only these ones were wooden and less intimidating. At least from the outside.

Fleetingly Joshua wondered what the residents of those brick boxes had done to end up being incarcerated, for however short a time, but just as quickly, he dismissed the thought. He didn't have enough headspace to think about anybody else, he needed to be concentrating on himself and the shit that he was in.

'Coffee, please, with two sugars.'

'No worries. You're in here, room two,' the man said, moving forward to open the door.

Joshua liked this man, there was something friendly yet firm in his voice, it kind of reminded Joshua of his dad.

Joshua moved into the already occupied room, his eyes quickly scanning the faces which had all turned to look at him. His solicitor and both detectives from earlier, Roth and Amberidge.

'Good afternoon, Mr Maddison, please take a seat.' Amberidge had half-risen out of his seat as he indicated the only vacant chair remaining in the room.

Joshua wasn't always the most observant of individuals, didn't always pay attention to others, to the smaller details, but as he took his seat, he couldn't help but notice that Amberidge, who had sat down once more, and Roth, had switched places.

Perhaps it meant nothing, but Joshua suspected otherwise.

Joshua watched as Roth set up the recorder and identified

who was present before stating the time: quarter past three. Joshua had guessed correctly.

'Mr Maddison,' Amberidge said, opening his notepad, 'I wanted to talk to you some more about the item that you sold.'

So he was in charge this time.

Joshua didn't respond, he simply lifted his eyebrows, silently waiting for the deluge of questions, questions he wouldn't answer.

'I have now been able to confirm with the owner of the shop that the item you described was in fact what you sold, so thank you for your honesty. But can I ask you, why did you sell such a unique watch and for half what it was worth?'

'No comment.' Joshua sat back in his chair, hands resting in his lap.

'I took a look at it, saw the engraving. I am gathering that it wasn't an easy decision to make?' When Joshua remained silent, Amberidge continued. 'It was from your mother, wasn't it?'

Joshua became aware that his teeth were pressing together, that his jaw was taut. He didn't see what relevance any of this had to selling drugs. It was his to sell and how much he got for it was no one's business but his.

Joshua shrugged his shoulders.

'Why didn't you sell it with the authenticating documentation, you would have made much more if you had?'

Because he didn't have the paperwork, because his mum had kept hold of it. At the time she'd said she'd keep it 'for safekeeping' but Joshua wasn't a complete moron, he knew that really, she had wanted to ensure Joshua wouldn't be able to sell it on, not without suffering a significant financial loss.

Her actions had spoken volumes.

She hadn't trusted him to cherish the gift she'd given him for his twenty-first birthday, hadn't believed him capable of holding on to something of such worth.

The fact that he'd sold it now was besides the point, she'd left him no choice.

All of this, however, he wasn't about to share with anyone, let alone DI Amberidge.

Instead, he inspected the nails on his right hand.

'All right,' Amberidge said with a sigh after a moment's pause, 'so it looks like the fourteen thousand pounds you received for the watch was then transferred into a business account set up for your bar.'

Again Joshua didn't react, didn't confirm Amberidge's assumptions, right or not.

'It must be very expensive, starting a business from scratch all by yourself?'

'You have no idea.' Joshua visibly winced. He hadn't meant to say anything, what he had planned was to keep his mouth shut for the entirety of this interview.

Sometimes he could kick himself.

The comment had just flown free from his mouth like a bird escaping its cage. He clamped his lips together, determined not to let that happen again.

'Is that why you were selling drugs, to fund your business?'

Shit. I walked into that one.

Joshua folded his arms across his chest, defiant.

'What were you getting again? Nearly two thousand? That would certainly help, wouldn't it?'

Joshua's jaw was starting to protest from the pressure.

'We know that you approached your mother about investing. Why do you think she declined?'

Joshua's hands were now balled up into tight fists, his nails digging into his palms. This copper knew nothing, he thought. She didn't decline, hadn't given him a firm no, she had just wanted more information. Joshua was confident she would have invested, would have wanted to help him eventually were it not for what had happened.

'Are you aware that now that Martin Grey is deceased, you are the only listed beneficiary of your mother's estate?'

Joshua swallowed hard. That fact had not been lost on him, but his mum was still alive, was still fighting, according to his dad. And besides, how would that help him now, with his immediate cash flow issues? It wouldn't. Again, Joshua didn't voice any of his thoughts.

'Mr Maddison.' Amberidge leant forward, his clasped hands coming to rest in front of him on the desk as he levelled Joshua with a stare that made him want to fidget, made him want to look away, but he didn't. He wouldn't. 'Did you push your mother down the stairs for your own financial gain? Are you responsible for her injuries?'

For a heartbeat, Joshua stared unseeing at this man, as the unpalatable question sunk in. Then he jerked forward, his hands gripping the edge of the table tightly. Amberidge, in response sat back, putting more distance between them.

Joshua was aware of his solicitor opening his mouth, preparing to either stop Joshua from doing something he may regret, or to protest about the question, but Joshua shot him a look, one which had him shrinking back in his chair.

'You can't seriously think that I did it?' Joshua said, his disbelief audible.

'At the moment, we are exploring several lines of inquiry related to your mother's fall. Unfortunately, as you have failed to provide us with an alibi for your whereabouts at the time of the incident, added to the fact that you stand to inherit a significant sum of money in the event your mother dies, then yes we are seriously considering the possibility that you are responsible.'

'I didn't do it.' Joshua's voice was calm, his tone deadly

serious. 'Whatever you may think of me, whatever assumptions you have made, you've got it all wrong. Yes, we argued on the night of her party, yes, I may have said some things that I regret but when I left she was absolutely fine. I had just got home when my dad called to tell me, check my phone records.'

Joshua watched as an unreadable expression settled on Amberidge's face. At a guess Joshua would have said he looked vaguely displeased, as though he had hoped for some admission of guilt from Joshua, but ultimately he knew that it was unlikely.

Did he believe him though? Did he think he was lying? Joshua realised he didn't really care. He knew the truth and that was all that mattered.

His mum was the only person in this world who had always been there for him, who had stood up for him when he'd gotten into trouble at school and after he'd left school even when others had been quick to judge him, quick to turn their backs on him. She had believed in him, in his potential and had wanted to see him succeed in life. That was why he kept trying, kept thinking up new ideas, new businesses to help him carve out a name for himself. He wanted to prove that he was worth believing in. He wanted nothing more than to prove her right.

He didn't do it.

Slowly, Joshua unpeeled his fingers from the table's edge and huffed out a laugh, it was a sound that lacked any amusement, any humour. He slumped back in his chair.

Amberidge didn't respond but instead turned his attention to his colleague momentarily, something silently passing between them before he looked back at Joshua.

'Yes, I have read through your previous statement. A phone call does not, however, prove your whereabouts. We are working to establish your movements, but I am sure that you will appreciate it is proving rather difficult without any witnesses or

CCTV evidence. Are you sure there isn't anyone who can verify your whereabouts?'

Joshua shook his head, then in a somewhat dismissive tone said, 'Apart from stopping at the corner shop to buy some beers, I went straight home.'

Roth, who had remained silent throughout the interview, spoke now. 'Mr Maddison, you never reported stopping anywhere on your journey.' She was obviously exasperated. 'That information would have been very useful to have much earlier. Which corner shop exactly?'

Joshua had honestly forgotten about dipping into the shop right up until a second ago when he'd said it, but he had. He'd bought a four-pack of beers and some crisps.

If he was being honest, he hadn't realised they were seriously considering him as their culprit, also he'd had so much else to think about lately that it had slipped his mind, but he didn't say that, Roth's admonishing tone still stinging. Instead, he simply gave them the rough address of the corner shop near his flat, with a bit of a shrug.

Both detectives and his solicitor jotted this down.

Joshua thought that the interview would terminate, that they'd get busy running off to confirm his whereabouts, but Amberidge shuffled through a few sheets of paper.

Finally he spoke, his voice serious. 'I am sure you've already been advised by your counsel but owing to the quantity of drugs involved, you won't be able to claim personal use. You are facing jail time.'

Joshua glanced across to his solicitor, his eyes questioning.

The suited man with deep frown lines scored into his forehead, met Joshua's stare before nodding just once, a small dip which felt as though he had just condemned Joshua.

Fuck.

What the hell am I going to do now?

'If you cooperate with us, Joshua, tell us about the deal you made, any previous deals that you had been involved in, we could put in a good word for you.' It was Roth who had offered him a lifeline, who had seen that flicker of fear in his eyes.

'What do you want to know?'

39

GRACE

The locksmith gave the lock one final tug before pulling it clean away from the door, a hole straight into the house remaining in its place. From his kneeling position in front of the door, he reached up with one hand and twisted the handle.

The door swung open.

As promised, the warrant had been approved.

In fact, it had been waiting for Grace on her desk when she'd left the interview room, when she'd left Joshua Maddison, who had given them more than they could have hoped for.

The information he'd provided didn't help with her investigation, but he had offered up a few names, a few locations which would most certainly aid her colleagues in their efforts to dampen down the drug culture in the south.

He had grassed to save his own skin.

Grace found that she was often left with an unusual mix of emotions for men such as Joshua, it was a hearty cocktail of both disdain and respect. Such an odd feeling.

He had helped to potentially take some dealers off the streets but he had only done so to help his own situation.

She shook away the trail of thoughts and focused on the building, the home in front of her.

'All yours,' the locksmith said, getting to his feet and dusting off his knees. I'll pop a new lock in there whilst you're doing your thing.'

'Thank you,' Grace replied then turned to her awaiting team consisting of DI Amberidge, DS Cartwright and DS Shore plus three uniformed officers. 'You all know what we're looking for. It is imperative we are thorough, anything that you're unsure of, bag it and we'll review it later.'

With her team splintering off into different rooms, Grace found herself pausing in the sprawling entrance.

The house felt bigger than the last time she'd been here. Was that even possible?

She struggled to imagine how this place could ever feel like a home. Her flat, compact as it was, sometimes felt too big, too empty when it was just her. She couldn't comprehend what it would feel like to be here alone. The word *scary* popped into her mind, quickly followed by *lonely*.

Perhaps that was why it felt so vast, because it was empty of all life, of happiness.

Grace sighed away her thoughts, she had a job to do and couldn't be distracted by her feelings, her emotions.

Heading to the nearest door, Grace found herself in a large but cosy lounge. The room was filled with all manner of furniture, two large velvet sofas, both positioned around a stone fireplace. There was a desk pressed against one wall while on the opposite wall a large wooden chest. On closer inspection the chest was decorated with ornate carvings. Like everything in this house, it looked expensive. There were also several small tables dotted strategically around the room.

The cream walls were punctuated with an occasional picture, large framed pieces of artwork, landscape paintings of places Grace had never seen. Grace had no clue as to their worth, if they had any, or whether they were simply framed posters. Although if she were to make an educated guess, she would say they were the real deal and probably worth more than she took home in a month.

Grace turned her attention back to the desk and with gloved hands pulled open the first drawer.

'Grace,' Harry called from the adjacent corridor approximately thirty minutes later. Grace, having almost finished scouring the lounge with little success, apart from finding what looked like an old mobile and bagging it up just in case, moved to the doorway. 'I think you might want to come and take a look at this.'

There was a note of excitement in DI Amberidge's voice which had her instantly abandoning the lounge altogether to join him.

He was standing in front of an open cupboard door. It was one of several floor-to-ceiling cupboards, all of which had been designed to look like an ordinarily panelled wall. There were no visible handles or locks to identify them as storage.

'How did you know this was here?' Grace questioned, eyeing the remaining wall.

'I leant on it and it clicked,' Harry responded earnestly.

Clever really, Grace acknowledged as she moved closer. Fleetingly she wondered if there were any other hidden cupboards or rooms in this labyrinth of a house before she focused her attention on the cupboard before her.

Inside were half a dozen drawers starting at the ground and moving upwards to approximately midway, the remaining space was shelved and housed cleaning items, bathroom cleaners, kitchen cleaners, sponges and other domestic items.

But it was the open top drawer which Harry was focused on, which had his full attention.

'What have you got?' Grace questioned as she followed his stare.

He didn't need to answer, however, because there, in the middle of the drawer filled with all manner of clutter, paperclips, pens, an assortment of wires for charging phones and other such devices, was the necklace.

It looked entirely out of place in its surroundings, as though it had been discarded.

With her gloved fingers, Grace carefully picked it up and laid it flat across the palm of her left hand.

'Well now,' she breathed, 'this does change the complexity of things, wouldn't you say?' With an air of reverence she slowly turned the piece of jewellery over, it perfectly matched the pictures provided by Martin Grey.

There was no theft, it had been here all along.

Triumphant at having been right washed over Grace, she felt vindicated, she knew Martin had been lying about the theft, the timing of it was too convenient for her liking.

Yet her assuredness was tempered by a gust of doubt blowing through her mind. She couldn't afford to make any more assumptions, didn't want to be caught chasing another dead end.

This was still circumstantial, she knew, aware that any barrister would explain away its presence as an oversight or a mistake. What she needed to quell her rising uncertainties about Martin was irrefutable, forensic evidence such as fingerprints. If Martin's fingerprints were on the necklace then he put it there, meaning: he lied.

If not, then God knows how it ended up in the drawer.

Pulling an evidence bag from her pocket, Grace carefully slid the necklace into it and sealed it up. 'We need to get this tested for fingerprints,' she said, 'as a matter of urgency,' handing the bag to Harry. 'Great job though.'

The search had yielded more than Grace could have hoped for, not only had they found the necklace but there were also numerous devices which might hold some useful information.

Grace gazed out of the passenger window at the tree-lined roads, as Harry drove them back to the station, back to the chaotic and noisy building which was in stark contrast to the stillness of the Greys' house, which was once more locked up.

A companionable silence had fallen between them.

It was Harry who broke through the quiet. 'Do you believe he was purposely misleading us or do you think that he genuinely thought it had been stolen?'

Grace looked across to Harry, who hadn't taken his eyes from the road but if he had glanced across, he would have seen her raise her eyebrows inquiringly, it was the sort of look that said, '*seriously?*'

But instead of scoffing at his question, she found herself asking, 'What do you think?'

'I know you would like to think he did it, but that was a seriously shitty hiding place for a "reportedly",' he air quoted the word with one hand, 'stolen necklace. In a drawer in a hallway cupboard, where anyone could have stumbled across it. Surely if he had masterminded this entire plan, wouldn't he have done a better job of concealing said item?'

Grace thought this through for a moment, then sighed. She hated to admit it but Harry had a point. It was the most peculiar of places for it to have been stowed. But what other reason was there for it to be in the cupboard in the first place?

'Honestly, Harry, I don't know what to think anymore.' Harry remained silent, understanding there was more that Grace wanted to say, needed to get off of her chest. 'Initially the whole investigation was a bit of a minefield, a crime without any evidence and with an awful lot of potential players. But once we'd narrowed it down, I genuinely thought Martin Grey was responsible. There was just something about him, something that he wasn't being honest about. Only, his death put a bit of a spanner in the works.' She didn't mean to sound careless, crass even, but Grace couldn't explain it any other way. 'I knew the story about the necklace was absolute horseshit, and what annoyed me the most was, I was the one who gave him the idea, asking if anything had been taken. Only now I can't get any answers from him, I can't pull him up on his lies.'

For a moment Grace let her attention drift. She looked at the long, sweeping driveways of the large houses they passed, with their high hedges keeping everyone at bay. What must all these people do for a living to afford such privacy, such space, she wondered absent-mindedly.

'Do you know what bothers me the most though, I will never be able to say without any shadow of a doubt that he did it, that he was guilty, because I just don't know for sure.' There it was, the truth.

After a long pause, Harry finally asked, 'And you don't think it was one of the others, Joshua or Christopher Maddison?'

'If it was, they've covered their tracks. Who do you think did it?' Grace found herself asking. Suddenly she wanted nothing more than to hear Harry's theories, suspecting that they differed from her own. She wanted him to be honest, to give her some perspective on things perhaps, because having found the necklace seemed to have only muddied the waters for Grace further, rather than clearing them.

She thought she would have been elated, that any lingering doubts would have dissipated but they were still there in the pit of her stomach, telling her that something just didn't feel right, that somewhere along the lines, she had missed something.

Harry took a minute before he finally said, 'Don't ask me

why, but I don't believe Martin did it. I am not basing this on anything other than gut feeling, but he just didn't seem the type. Also, the placement of the necklace was bizarre. I think he told us what he truly believed, that it had been stolen.'

Grace nodded, having already suspected that that was what Harry was going to say.

'You might just be right,' she said, eyes trained on the outside world once more.

40

SUSAN

THE PARTY

Susan needn't have worried.

Her guests had started to arrive on time. Climbing carefully out of cars and taxis in suits and dresses, carrying cards and the occasional gift.

To ensure no one walked through the house, that Martin remained appeased, an elaborate path of fairy lights had been strung on vine-covered poles to guide the guests on a magical walk around the grounds, before delivering them at the revelry to the rear of the house.

Despite the sun having not set, the twinkling lights being somewhat overshadowed by the brightness of the evening, the whole entrance process had still set a tone, one which had everyone buzzing with excitement.

Susan had been watching, covertly, from the upstairs windows of the house. Darting from room to room, she was eager to witness their expressions as they traversed the maze.

The whole idea had been Susan's, inspired by the London restaurant she had visited with Rachel.

Once the guests found themselves in the garden, the low

hum of music greeting them, they were swiftly handed the first of many cocktails.

Susan was desperate to be down there but she'd got the idea into her head that she should make an entrance, be fashionably late to her own party.

Twenty minutes, she'd said to herself. Not short enough that it wasn't a noticeable delay but not so long that her guests would start to question her whereabouts.

Easier said than done, she'd quickly realised.

Susan spotted Rachel as she exited a taxi, wearing a fitted black dress. Susan could tell from her vantage point that she'd gone heavy with the smoky eyes, it had always been Rachel's signature look for any night out and tonight proved to be no different. What she hadn't expected to see, however, was Christopher climbing out after her.

A frown creased Susan's brow and she pressed her lips together.

Susan wasn't entirely sure what to make of that. Obviously it was cheaper for them to share a lift, that she understood, but they would have had to arrange it, would have been talking independently of Susan and neither of them had ever suggested they were in contact with one another.

Why would they keep it a secret?

Thoughts, unclear and fragmented, swirled through her mind. Was there something going on? If there was, should she be annoyed or bothered or even happy?

Still, she honestly wasn't sure how she felt about the idea, this was like being thrown a curveball that no one had told you to anticipate, let alone expect you to catch.

But perhaps she was jumping the gun somewhat, they had only taken a taxi together, that didn't necessarily mean there was anything else going on. Did it?

Inviting Christopher in itself had been a difficult decision.

Susan knew how Martin felt about her ex, understood the animosity which sadly lingered between previous and current flames. However, Christopher would always be Joshua's father and therefore a part of Susan's life. And besides, she wasn't expecting Martin to make an appearance tonight, so what did it really matter if Christopher was there or not?

Susan enjoyed being around Christopher, he was funny and charming and beneath his hard exterior, he was a very caring man. It was just a shame that they could never make things work between them. Not that Susan ever repeated those thoughts aloud to anyone else, she knew they would read into them, knew they would think there was some remaining spark left burning in her heart for Christopher.

Obviously they had both moved on in the years since separating. Susan with Martin and Christopher, well, perhaps he was with Rachel.

The thought stung that time, like her skin had been pierced.

Another car pulled up, this time a couple of her old work colleagues climbed out, pulling Susan's thoughts back to the party, to the many guests still to arrive. She put her thoughts of Christopher and Rachel into a tiny box in the back of her mind. She would reopen it tomorrow, think about it then.

In between further glances outside, Susan repeatedly checked her appearance, lightly touching her hair, straightening out her already straight dress. She was nervous and exhilarated in equal measures.

This was more than simply a birthday party to Susan, it was the coming together of all her expectations, of all the dreams she'd had when they'd purchased this house. All the celebrations that had never happened, rolled up into one giant event.

She didn't want to dwell on the fact she would be celebrating solo, didn't want to allow Martin to consume any more of her thoughts for the entirety of the evening. It had been his choice not to engage, not to get on board with the idea, to not get on with her.

Stop it, she chided internally. She pressed her feet into the awaiting shoes and wandered over to the mirror, appraising herself, head tilted to the side, once more.

A light frown creased her brow. Something was missing.

Pulling open the top drawer from her chest of drawers, Susan trailed her fingers over the assortment of boxes before stopping on one of the larger ones, a square black box. She wrapped her fingers around it and took it out, closing the drawer after her.

She really needed to find a better place to keep her jewellery, her valuables. A safe perhaps or some sort of lockable box, after all, several of her pieces were rather expensive, but then she liked to have them to hand.

Placing the case on top of her vanity table, Susan flipped open the lid to reveal a necklace, a stunning string of emeralds and diamonds cushioned on a velvet pillow.

Susan laid her fingers on the larger emerald at its centre, a wry smile finding its way to her lips. It had been such a lot of money to part with and for something so unnecessary, something purely decorative. She had debated it for ages but had finally relented, telling herself she might never be in the same financial position again. She didn't often treat herself, not like then and not like today.

It was fitting that she wore it, she decided, and carefully clasped it around her neck.

The piece was surprisingly heavy. She had only dared to wear it once before and had to admit she'd forgotten how considerable it felt suspended around her neck.

Another glance in the mirror. It was pretty. Ostentatious. Over the top. But pretty.

With a final check of the time, Susan felt satisfied she had waited long enough to make her entrance.

Susan sucked in a deep breath, rolled her shoulders back and strode purposefully out of the bedroom.

Despite the joyful sounds filtering in from outside, the soul of the house was still and silent.

As Susan began to descend the stairs, the heels of her stilettos clicking noisily, a shiver ran down her arms, her hairs standing on end.

It was as if someone was watching her, their eyes boring into her.

Pausing, she cast a sweeping glance behind her, expecting to see Martin glaring at her from the door to his study. It wouldn't have surprised her in the least but he wasn't there. The house, as planned, was deserted, which only unsettled her more.

Susan gripped the banister and with a sudden haste she moved down the remaining steps, eager to be outside surrounded by people and noise and fun.

She was striding across the stone-tiled floor, heading for the kitchen when a young lady exited the corridor ahead of her, almost bumping straight into Susan.

Susan's hands flew up to stop the figure as a gasp escaped her mouth.

'Oh God, I am so sorry,' the unfamiliar woman wearing a white shirt and black trousers said, looking flustered. A member of the catering team, Susan realised.

'That's okay, can I help you? The house is supposed to be out of bounds this evening.'

'Yes, sorry. I was looking for the toilet.'

Susan smiled warmly. 'It's just there,' she offered, pointing to a closed door back along the corridor the woman had just come from.

'Oh, thanks. I didn't see it,' she responded with an absent shake of her head, already turning on her heels.

Susan lingered for a second, allowing the woman to locate the bathroom. It was in that heartbeat, her unease already evaporating, that Susan caught sight of her reflection in the hallway mirror.

'No, it's too much,' she said quietly to herself and instantly unclipped the necklace hanging around her neck.

She didn't want her guests to think she was showing off, that she was flaunting her wealth further. The party was already doing that for her.

Susan glanced around for somewhere to stow it, not wanting to traipse all the way back upstairs. Her gaze landed on the row of indiscernible cupboards.

Perfect.

No one ever realised there were cupboards here, plus everyone except the catering staff were outside, she reasoned as she clicked open a door, pulled out a drawer and dropped the necklace into it.

It would be safe there until later.

Closing both drawer and cupboard, Susan slid her hands down her dress for a final time and continued on out to the party, to celebrate with her guests.

The dinner, a buffet of delicious meats and breads, olives and pastries, had been exquisite, everyone had agreed and now with a few of the tables repositioned, the party was in full swing.

Much to Susan's surprise and if she was being truthful, dismay, Martin had wandered in. She hadn't known when exactly, she had just looked up to see him propping up the bar, a glass in his hand. Her heart had practically jumped into her throat at the sight of him.

He was wearing his everyday trousers and a shirt which was noticeably wrinkled from having been worn, but at least he had bothered to change out of his slippers, and replaced them with a pair of loafers.

She had been surreptitiously watching him, looking for any signs he may be about to cause a scene, but there had been none, he had simply sat there, drinking.

Susan watched closely as she spied one of Martin's old acquaintances approaching him, she'd even readied herself to intervene, but Martin had greeted him with a handshake, had chatted animatedly, smiling even as they talked for a few minutes. It was almost like seeing a glimpse of the Martin she'd once known. But when his companion drifted away, Susan watched as Martin's smile dropped, his features resuming their normal glumness.

It was sad to see.

Despite her initial cynicism, there was nothing in his behaviour to suggest he had an ulterior motive for attending, he had obviously been lured out of the study by the prospect of a drink, Susan reasoned, relaxing a little.

'I got you some champagne,' Rachel said loudly, thrusting a glass into Susan's hand.

'Thank you.'

'Everything all right?' She indicated with her head in Martin's direction.

'Yes,' Susan replied, not wanting to say any more.

Rachel put the straw from her drink to her painted red lips and drew in a large mouthful. 'It's a great turnout.'

'I know, I am so pleased.' From the periphery of her vision she saw Christopher, watched as he strode confidently towards the bar, the bar which Martin had been occupying as though he was one of the fittings. She saw Christopher offer Martin a tight smile, and said something she couldn't hear.

Susan sucked in a breath in anticipation of Martin's reproach, because she knew it was coming, expected nothing else from him.

Martin rose from his stool and without so much as a word, strode past Christopher. The only sign he'd seen Christopher was the look of disdain twisting his features, the one that made it look as though he'd had to step over something rather unpleasant on the pavement.

Susan sighed, disappointed but not surprised.

She would have to apologise to Christopher later.

Rachel leant into Susan then, her voice just loud enough to be heard over the din of the party. 'I have something I need to tell you.'

There was something in her tone that had Susan leaning back to look at Rachel's face.

Was that guilt shining in her eyes or was it something else entirely, triumph or excitement perhaps?

Susan knew in that heartbeat what it was that Rachel was going to say; a sickening feeling washing over her.

'I've been seeing Christopher. We're dating.'

When Susan had fleetingly considered the possibility earlier, she hadn't been sure how she would feel about the prospect of her best friend and her ex-husband dating.

But her feelings were clear, overwhelmingly so.

She was furious, every fibre of her body was shaking.

Her face twisted in anger.

How could Rachel, knowing all she knew about Susan and Christopher's tangled past? And how could Christopher, knowing this was her best friend? And why tell her now, tonight of all nights?

Susan didn't know who she hated more right now, who to blame.

Rachel, perhaps realising her mistake, that Susan wasn't about to congratulate her on her new relationship, took a step back, her free hand rising up as if to put a barrier between them.

Only, before Susan could form a coherent response, could demand to know what the hell they were playing at, Joshua stepped in between them, completely oblivious to the unfolding situation.

'Mum,' he said, attempting to hijack Susan's attention. And as he was standing right in front of her, directly in her eyeline, she had little choice but to acknowledge him.

'Josh,' she began, as calmly as she could muster. She wanted to delay whatever it was that her son wanted, she wasn't finished with Rachel.

A thousand questions had already lined themselves up in her mind, each one needing to be answered. When did it start? How did it start? Who made the first move? And why? Why Rachel and why Christopher?

Susan tried to look past Joshua but he leant to the side, blocking her view.

'Mum, can I talk to you for a minute?' He lifted up a blue folder which was gripped in his hand.

'I can see that now's not a good time.' Rachel practically threw the words at Susan, from behind the safety of Joshua, before using his interruption as her opportunity to retreat.

'Rachel,' Susan called out, but she was already halfway across the marquee. 'We'll talk about this later,' she said, throwing the words after her friend. Her best friend. Who was now dating her ex.

'Mum?'

Susan turned her attention back to her son. 'Yes. Joshua?' She knew there was a bite to her words, her body reeling from

Rachel's revelation, but she couldn't help it. The pain, the hurt, was too fresh to get it under wraps, to get control of it.

'I've put together everything you requested,' he said, unfazed by her tone, and held out the file for Susan to take.

Susan stared at it momentarily, confused. Then as realisation dawned on her, she looked up at her son, disbelief etched on her face.

With as much diplomacy as Susan could muster, which admittedly wasn't as much as was typically needed with Joshua, she laid her hand on the file, which was still in Joshua's hand, and lowered it down to his side. 'That is great, Joshua, but if you hadn't noticed, there is a party going on around you. I can't wait to see what you've put together but now is not the time.'

Joshua looked temporarily bewildered and then anger swam across his features. 'But you said.'

Susan's temper flared to match that displayed by her son. 'I know what I said and I will look at it. Tomorrow.'

She'd barely finished her sentence before Joshua was storming away, leaving Susan in his wake.

What was it with all the men in her life? Correction, all the people in her life?

Why are they all trying to ruin tonight for me?

Unwanted tears had sprung to Susan's eyes. She would not cry at her own party, she told herself, blinking them away before they had the chance to fall.

Susan threw a sweeping glance around the tent, thankfully no one had noticed the momentary hiccup, the tense atmosphere surrounding her. Everyone seemed to still be in the throes of celebrating, thank God. And that was exactly what Susan wanted, she wanted to recapture the lightness she had been feeling earlier, the joy. She wanted to celebrate.

She forced a smile on her face, sipped her drink and then approached the guest nearest to her in the hope of being distracted by some mindless conversation until she could really relax.

It was an acquaintance, Charles Schroder, chairman of a small business committee who she found herself standing next to, someone Susan recognised to be quite influential in the local community, hence his invitation.

After almost ten minutes of chatting, Susan politely excused herself from Charles's company. Despite a slight slur to his words, he had talked concisely and animatedly about the importance of supporting small businesses for the entirety of their conversation. Boring as it was, it had done the job, allowing Susan's anger and frustration and hurt to recede from the forefront of her mind.

She undertook a circuit of the marquee, making small talk with as many of her guests as she could until her gaze eventually landed on her sister.

Jennifer was wearing a plain cream dress which stopped just above her knees, and sandals in a matching colour. She had also brushed a little bit of make-up across her eyelids and cheeks. She looked bored, despite having been seated with her colleagues, people Susan genuinely thought Jennifer would be comfortable with, that she liked. Jennifer's back was turned to the cluster of women, a formidable barrier that no one seemed to want to bridge, her chin resting in her cupped hand on the table. Susan didn't let that faze her, Jennifer often looked like that, as though she was fed up with life.

Susan still hadn't told Jennifer about the bookshop, about her wonderfully exciting plans to grow the business. Susan had hoped to make an announcement tonight, but not until she'd told Jennifer first.

With her happiness restored somewhat, Susan was confident her news would at the very least raise a smile.

It would, after all, mean that Jennifer would pretty much be running the Storrington branch on her own, which she knew Jennifer would relish.

Susan grinned, she still couldn't believe it was happening herself. Everything had come together so neatly, the timings just perfect. She was going to be the proud owner of a chain of bookshops.

A warmth washed through her, helped along, she knew, by the several cocktails she'd already devoured.

Now. She would tell her now.

Susan began navigating her way around the dance floor, weaving around the many guests. She stopped frequently to chat or when someone spun her around and offered to get her another drink. She was making slow progress, but she'd get to Jennifer eventually.

She had just been handed another cocktail, an orange, fizzy-looking drink with a raspberry floating in its centre. An old friend of Susan's, George, had thrust it into her hand before asking if she wanted to dance.

How could she decline? So, with a nod of her head, they stepped onto the dance floor, just as the previous song faded out. They waited, along with everyone else for the DJ to play the next one when a thundering voice shattered the fun, fractured the joyful atmosphere.

Susan, along with all the other guests, looked around, unsure where it had originated from.

A second voice, pitched slightly higher, rang out then. It was Joshua's voice, she knew instantly, and the other one was Martin's.

Excusing herself as quickly as she could, Susan threw a look to the DJ, who understood the pleading in her eyes. A loud, booming track started up whilst she sought to find the source of the shouting.

Susan found herself exiting the marquee, a rush of cool summer air greeting her.

Perhaps because she was listening for it, or maybe because it was so loud, Susan could still hear their voices over the music, although she couldn't decipher what was being shouted.

Automatically, her eyes scanned the house, coming to stop at the open upstairs window, the only room with a light on. Martin's study.

She couldn't see either her husband or her son but she knew without a shadow of a doubt that that was where she would find them both.

41

GRACE

The search had yielded some positive results. Grace, at the very least, had been able to quash the theft allegations made by Martin Grey.

The necklace had gone straight to forensics and Grace had called to request that it was pushed through as quickly as possible.

There was little else she could do but wait now.

The whole investigation, the two investigations, she corrected herself, had seemed to stall. They had chased down each and every lead, exhausted every possible avenue, the search on the Greys' house being the last big puzzle piece to put into this abstract, annoying picture and Grace was still no wiser, still hadn't figured out who had done it, still couldn't work out what she was looking at.

Sitting at her desk, the office all but empty as everyone had drifted home for the evening, she realised how tired she was, how her shoulders slumped forward from the weight of the responsibility, from the guilt at having not solved the case.

Grace was sifting through her emails when her inbox pinged, signalling a new message.

She clicked on it.

Martin's autopsy report.

With lips pursed, Grace read through the document, twice. Martin Grey had had a significant amount of alcohol in his system. There had been nothing else of significance, no prescription drugs, no illegal drugs, just the alcohol.

Grace turned away from the desk in her seat and leant back, head resting on the back of the chair. There was a window behind her desk, which faced out onto the car park. It was an uninspiring view, but Grace wasn't looking at the scenery.

She was deep in thought.

Martin Grey had obviously been drunk. What the autopsy couldn't tell her and what she now realised she would never know was whether Martin's accident was exactly that, an accident, or whether it was suicide.

She would never know his last thoughts, what had happened to make that car drive off of the road. Grace knew there had been a bend, one which could have caught Martin out, what with his reaction times having been impaired by the alcohol. On the other hand, it was also likely that he knew the local roads like the back of his hand and as the corner approached, he chose not to turn the steering wheel, chose to let the car careen across the road.

It had been evident from the tyre tracks that he'd braked, attempted to swerve, but it had happened very late. Panic and fear were natural emotions even when the victim had chosen to end their own life, the tyre tracks could have been the result of one of those very emotions overwhelming Martin, or it could have been a desperate attempt to avoid the inevitable.

Grace could only guess at Martin's state of mind beforehand, and she found that she didn't want to presume either way. But what she could say for sure was that his death was not suspicious in any way.

Grace couldn't help it but her thoughts turned to her mother then. Martin's actions had in one way or another ended his own life, whereas her mother had fought tirelessly to keep living hers but had been beaten, had been defeated.

The unfairness of it all never escaped Grace when she came across these sorts of situations. She wished her mother's fate could have been different.

A tear ran down her cheek. She wiped it away with the back of her hand.

She knew now was not the time for tears, she would store them away for later, when she was at home, alone, when they could fall freely as she allowed her loss to engulf her.

Swinging her chair back around to face the desk, she closed the still-open email.

For a moment her fingers hovered over the keys of her computer, it was in that pause that she saw Amy's email, the one with the sound recording of the anonymous call attached.

This is where it had all started, she thought to herself, why it all started. Had this person not come forward, had they not picked up that phone, Susan Grey's fall would have been forever deemed as an accident, whatever the end result of her injuries.

Grace wouldn't have been assigned the case, wouldn't have been sitting here feeling like a failure, like she'd wasted her opportunity to redeem her reputation, to catch her criminal.

Was it all right to be royally pissed off with someone Grace didn't know, with the anonymous caller for being anonymous? If only they'd provided their name, or given her something more to go on, something to build a case around.

Grace hit the play button, her head coming to rest in her hands, her eyes closing as the call handler's voice crackled through the computer speaker asking what the emergency was.

It was as the male responded that a note of recognition

filtered through Grace's mind, her head whipping up, her eyes opening wide.

She turned the volume up to max.

She knew that voice, had heard it once before.

And she knew where.

She carried on listening, before replaying the recording again for good measure, a smile finding its way to her lips.

Yes. Grace was certain she knew who her anonymous caller was.

Switching her computer off, Grace was striding with confidence along the station's corridor, out to the car park and to her car.

She fired a quick message off to Harry, letting him know that she had a lead.

She knew the caller and she suspected she also knew who her criminal was, snippets of a previous conversation barrelling their way into her mind.

She couldn't believe she'd missed it.

The clues had been there, she just hadn't been able to see them, to piece it all together, it had been like a picture without paint, a flower without a scent, but now she had it all.

She got in her car, started her engine and drove.

42

SUSAN

BEFORE SHE FELL

Susan strode through the house as quickly as was possible in her ridiculous heels, each step echoing furiously on the cold, hard floor.

What the hell do they think they're playing at? Don't they know that everyone can hear them?

Anger emanated from the swing of her arms and the tilt of her head.

No one tried to talk to her as she left the party and no one tried to stop her, but she could feel the stares from her guests, the worried glances between her and the source of the noise.

Susan ignored them.

The house itself was dark, the only light, a glow of colour, was coming from the party outside. Not that Susan needed light to see, she could have navigated her house and all its furniture with her eyes closed.

Her foot had just landed on the first step of the grand staircase, when a familiar voice, a slightly panicked voice, called out her name.

She continued her ascent, not wanting to stop, her dress tail held aloft in one hand and the cocktail glass in her other.

'Susan,' the breathless voice said again, this time from right behind her, a large hand coming up to grab hold of her arm firmly. 'Didn't you hear me calling you?'

Susan stopped, half-turning around as much as the step would allow, to look at Christopher.

He looked terrified.

Looking at him now, she would have said he'd seen a ghost, if she didn't know any better that was. But she did. Christopher was clearly afraid of her reaction to his new budding relationship with her best friend.

'I don't have time for this, Chris.' Without waiting for a response, she began to turn away, Joshua's angry shouts resonating through the upstairs of the house. Only, Christopher still had a tight grip on her arm.

'Please just let me explain first.'

'What is there to explain?' She purposely looked at the spot on her arm where Christopher's fingers encircled her skin, then up at him, her eyebrows raised.

He released her slowly. 'Sorry.'

Susan huffed out a laugh. 'You're sorry?'

'Rachel had no right to tell you and especially not tonight of all nights, but it isn't what you think.'

Another shout, this time from Martin, had Susan looking back up the stairs. 'So you haven't been dating my best friend behind my back?' Susan's voice was dripping with sarcasm and she knew she was on the cusp of a shout.

Christopher nervously rubbed at the back of his neck. He looked as though he was internally debating his response, but Susan didn't have time to wait for him to decide how to lie to her further. Martin and Joshua could very well be killing each other up there for all Susan knew.

'Yes, I have been out with Rachel a couple of times, but it isn't serious. I don't want anything serious.'

'Christopher, it is none of my business who you choose to spend your time with, honestly it isn't. But I would have appreciated it if either one of you had had the decency to tell me sooner and perhaps not at my birthday party. Look, I have more pressing things to deal with right now.'

Susan turned and mounted the next step when Christopher's hand was on her again, this time gripping her shoulder. He was so close she could smell his aftershave, it was the same one he'd worn when they were younger. It was a smell which was woven into the fabric of so many of her memories, good and bad.

'Don't walk away from me.' Christopher's voice was hard, but not threatening. Susan had never felt afraid of Christopher.

'Oh, for God's sake, what else is there to say? What do you want me to say?' She was facing him once more, exasperation evident in her face. She couldn't bear to hear any more, didn't want to know any of the details. She especially didn't want to be having this conversation, or rather, this argument right at this very moment, when her guests were probably already talking about the fight happening in the study.

'I want you to say that you're angry with me, that you're hurt, that you give a shit.'

Whatever Susan had been anticipating, it certainly wasn't that. Her mouth, which had been poised ready to throw out a retort, clamped shut in her confusion.

Christopher's hand moved from Susan's shoulder to her neck, his fingers gently resting there.

'What?' Susan finally offered.

Christopher brought his face level with Susan's. 'Susan, I have never stopped loving you. Despite my actions, despite my self-destructive nature, I have always loved you and I think that if you're honest with yourself you've always known that. Rachel was company, that's all, but it will never be anything more, will never mean anything more than that because she isn't you.'

Christopher started to lean into Susan and for a moment Susan thought he might kiss her. She froze. She didn't know how she felt. She knew that she didn't want to lean away, that there was something comforting, reassuring about his closeness.

'I know I've hurt you over the years, you and Joshua,' Christopher continued. 'I haven't always been the best version of myself, the version you both deserved. But I could be, I know I could, if you'd just leave *him*.' He spat out the last word. Him, meaning Martin. 'You know you don't love him, not like you loved me, I can see there's no passion there, no fire. Martin's no good for you, Susan.'

At the thought of Martin, Susan pushed away from Christopher. No, this was all wrong. Christopher knew nothing about her marriage, her relationship with her husband. It may not be in a very good place but she wasn't going to do this, wouldn't go down this road. Adultery was a choice and one she wouldn't choose, perhaps if she had been single, perhaps if her marriage was over, things would be different.

'How dare you! What we had ended years ago because of you, not me, because you refused to grow up, to take responsibility for your own actions. At least Martin has been there for me, not that my marriage is any of your goddamn business.' She pulled herself free of Christopher. 'I can't do whatever this is, now. I have to go and sort that out,' Susan said, indicating upstairs as more shouts rang out. She took the next step.

'Is that it, is that all you're going to say?' Christopher growled but he didn't move to follow her.

'For now, yes,' Susan scoffed and stormed up the remaining stairs utterly dumbfounded by Christopher's nerve.

He had been caught out and yet had somehow managed to

turn it around, to make Susan feel like she was the reason for his actions. She was shaking her head in dismay as she reached the closed door of the study.

What the hell was going on tonight? This was supposed to be a celebration, a joyous occasion, but Susan felt weighed down by everyone else's problems and she wasn't even done yet.

Sucking in a deep breath, she pushed open the door with more force than was probably called for as it swung back and collided with the wall with a thud. 'What the hell is going on in here?' she demanded.

Martin was furthest away. He was standing behind his desk, both his palms pressed flat against its top, a look of fury burning in his eyes. Joshua, standing closest to the door, had his back to Susan. She couldn't see his face but from his stance, his rigid back and balled-up fists, it was evident that he too was royally pissed off.

Both men looked at her yet neither spoke.

'I said what the hell is going on in here?' Susan repeated, moving further into the room.

She looked between them both, waiting. Her heart was racing furiously. How could these two people who she cared so much about, hate each other so deeply?

From the corner of her vision, she saw as Martin straightened up, the rage that had been obvious on his face only moments ago had been smoothed out. 'I think we are all done here, wouldn't you agree, Joshua?'

Before Joshua could throw out some sarcastic retort, Susan put her hands up.

'That does not answer my question. Everyone outside can hear your slanging match, so thanks for spoiling my night. Now what are you arguing about? Joshua?'

As expected, Joshua was all too happy to recount the cause of their disagreement. 'He told me that my business venture is a joke and would end up being a money pit. He also said that you wouldn't be investing, unless it was over his dead body.'

It was only now that Susan realised her son was no longer in possession of the blue file, it was open on the desk in front of Martin.

'Is that true?' She was looking at Martin now.

'More or less. Obviously Joshua left out a few details, a few names that he called you and a few worse ones that he called me. But yes, in a nutshell, I told him that this whisky business would no doubt fold within a couple of months. That he didn't have the staying power or determination to make it work and that I didn't want him to drag you down with him.'

Susan nodded as she absorbed Martin's words. 'I see.'

'Do you though, Susan?' Martin responded glumly. 'I've said it all before but you don't seem to listen or learn. He thinks that you will invest in whatever half-thought-up idea he has just because you're his mother. And what makes this worse is that he is right. You may as well just burn our money in the fire.'

'You self-righteous arsehole,' Joshua shouted.

'Joshua. Enough.' Susan was looking at her son before she turned back to Martin. How had it come to this? The man standing before her wasn't the man she'd married, in truth she didn't recognise him at all. Yes, she had wanted to see him passionate, to see him all fired up about a cause but this wasn't passion, this was loathing and spitefulness. This was the opposite of what she wanted.

'I have already spoken to Joshua about his business and that is for me and him to discuss further, not you.'

'Well I beg to differ. I don't want you flushing any more of our money down the toilet.'

Susan knew that it was the drink talking now. The money that Susan invested was hers and hers alone. They had joint finances but they also each had an independent pot of money to do with as they wished and if she wanted to support her son then that was her damned choice.

'I am sorry, Martin, but what I choose to do with my money is none of your concern. But whilst we are on the matter, perhaps you should think about your lack of contribution to our finances before you complain about where money is being spent.' She knew it was a low blow but she was pissed off too.

'Mum.' She could hear the smugness in Joshua's voice.

'No, Joshua, I am just as disappointed in you. You knew that this was my birthday party and yet you've tried to sabotage it, because you never seem to be able to see beyond your own selfish needs and wants. Did you really think I was going to abandon the evening to sit down and talk shop with you? No, and nor would anybody else.'

She saw the set of Joshua's jaw before he wordlessly moved to the desk, swiped up the file and pushed past her as he headed for the door.

'I don't believe how unsupportive you're being. It's like you don't even give a shit about me sometimes,' Joshua spat as he walked out, slamming the door behind him.

Susan's head dropped, her chin practically resting on her chest. *What have I done to deserve this?*

'See what I mean–' Martin began but Susan's hand shot up, palm visible in a 'stop' motion. She didn't look at him as she said, 'You're no better than he is.'

Tears were burning in her eyes. She clenched her jaw tightly together as a distraction, she really didn't want to cry.

What to do now? Susan wasn't sure but she knew that she didn't want to remain in this room with Martin any longer. In fact, she realised, she didn't actually want to be locked in a marriage with him either. The reality hit her hard. She had been fighting for so long, trying to make it work but she was the only one. And she was so very tired of it all. This wasn't a marriage but a battle of wills, only she didn't want to fight.

The thought strangely wasn't as heartbreaking as it should have been. Perhaps deep down she'd known for some time.

Susan moved to the door. Martin, unlike Christopher, didn't try to stop her. As she pulled it open she looked back over her shoulder and said, 'I want a divorce.'

She didn't wait to see her words register, she simply moved out onto the landing and closed the door behind her.

43

GRACE

Grace pulled up at the address, the house looking exactly the same as it had previously.

She was pleased to see that despite the hour, several lights were still on, meaning someone was awake. She would have woken them up regardless, but at least her visit was less intrusive this way.

Grace was just about to get out of her vehicle when her mobile rang, it was Harry.

'Hello.'

'Do you need backup?' There was obvious concern in his voice.

'No, I think I will be fine,' Grace replied. 'I am just planning on having my suspicions either confirmed or denied. But if I haven't called you in twenty minutes then send support.'

'Text me the address.' He didn't sound thrilled, Grace knew, but she didn't want to wait for him to join her. 'Twenty minutes.'

Grace ended the call before swiftly firing off a message containing her current location.

She slid the phone into her pocket, grabbed the file she'd brought with her and climbed out of her car.

There was a knot of anticipation in her gut. How had she let this individual, this suspect, elude her for so long, it all seemed so obvious now.

'Don't get ahead of yourself,' she whispered as she strode down the path.

Grace didn't hesitate when she rapped her knuckles firmly against the door.

There was an instant commotion, a cacophony of noise from within the property before a figure appeared.

'Who is it?'

'Detective Roth, I just have another couple of questions regarding our investigation.'

There was a noticeable pause from behind the door. Grace was unsurprised, they probably hadn't expected to see Grace again. Eventually it was unlocked, the familiar face of Lisa Hatton, the waitress from Susan Grey's party appearing.

'It's a bit late, isn't it? I was just about to go to bed,' Lisa commented without malice.

'Yes, my apologies, but I wonder if you have a couple of minutes to spare? It is important,' Grace found herself adding.

Doubt flashed across Lisa's face. Grace didn't blame her, she had clearly seen the worst side of the police previously, admittedly due to her own actions, but it didn't mean that they couldn't forge a new understanding.

Grace waited patiently, calmly, despite her insides being a bundle of nervous energy.

'Okay, but only for a few minutes,' Lisa said, relenting.

'Thank you.'

Grace was surprised to find Lisa alone. The dogs were shut up in the kitchen already and apart from the occasional whine or half-hearted bark they were rather sedate.

Lisa perched on the armrest of the chair as she had done previously. Following suit, Grace sat on the edge of the sofa, in exactly the same spot as the last time she was here. She placed the file next to her.

'No Jonny tonight?' Grace questioned. She had hoped to talk to them both, but she wasn't too concerned, Lisa was the person she really needed to see.

'He's at his mum's.'

Grace nodded. Then, not wanting to wait another moment said, 'You saw what happened that night, didn't you? You saw Susan Grey's fall.'

Lisa's eyes widened, and the colour seemed to drain from her face instantly. Grace watched as she carefully lowered herself onto the seat of the chair.

She began to shake her head, so Grace cut in, 'Don't worry, Lisa, you're not in any sort of trouble. Quite the opposite in fact. You may be able to help me solve this case, to put away the bad guy.'

Grace wasn't sure if her words offered any sort of reassurance as Lisa looked genuinely petrified.

Lisa, wearing pyjamas and a dressing gown, pulled the gown tightly across her chest and held it there as though it was a safety blanket wrapped around her.

'It was Jonny who called the police, wasn't it? Made the anonymous tip-off for you? He has a rather distinct voice once you've heard it,' Grace added, not wanting to leave Lisa with any room for denial.

Lisa bobbed her head just once. Yes.

Yes indeed, Grace thought with a rush of excitement.

'But he wasn't there that night, at the party. You were though, you've already admitted that to me. You saw what happened, didn't you?'

'Yes,' Lisa croaked nervously.

'Can you tell me? What you saw that night, what you remember?' Grace knew that she had edged further forward in her seat, her weight now barely supported by the chair.

'I'm not really sure,' Lisa replied, but Grace could tell she remembered enough to help her catch her would-be killer.

With a sympathetic smile Grace said, 'It's okay, take your time. Just tell me what you remember. Why were you in the house, let's start there.'

Lisa pouted, pinching her lips tightly together before she spoke. 'I was being nosy. I mean, I've never been in such a huge house before and I wanted to have a look around. I was on a break. We were meant to stay in the kitchen but I went to the loo, and when I came out and saw that no one was around, I just thought, why not? I wasn't going to steal anything, I already told you I'm done with all that.'

Grace held her hands up to placate Lisa. 'I never suggested that you were. It is a rather spectacular property. But it was dark, wasn't it?'

'Sort of. The lights were all off, but there's that big window, you know the one?' Grace nodded. Lisa meant the floor-to-ceiling window at the top of the stairs. 'There was light coming in through there, from the party, and there was some from the kitchen too. So you could see a bit, enough to know where the furniture was, you know?'

Grace nodded. 'So you were looking around?'

'Yeah, I'd been into the front room or the lounge, I don't know what you'd call it, opposite the corridor to the kitchen. I'd been in there maybe two minutes, just looking and I thought I'd best get back before I got in trouble. It's a good job and I like the woman I work for. I was about to leave the room, when I heard footsteps. I peeked out of the door and saw Susan on the landing.'

'Did you know it was Susan then?'

'Yeah, she was wearing a very distinctive silver dress. You couldn't miss her even in the dark. Also, it was her house.' She shrugged.

'Right, so you saw Susan from the door to the lounge, then what happened?'

Lisa looked apprehensive, uncomfortable even. 'I don't know exactly, I was trying to stay hidden. As I said, I didn't want to lose my job and with my history they would have thought the worst.'

'What did you see?' Grace encouraged.

'I saw another figure appear at the top of the stairs, but Susan was already walking down, she didn't know that they were there. I did think it was weird that they didn't say anything, you know, so that Susan would turn around. But I was worried that Susan would see me, so I ducked out of sight, hid behind the door. That's when I heard her. Susan's cries and shouts as she fell. When I looked back out, she was lying at the bottom of the stairs. She wasn't moving and I thought she was dead.'

'I am sorry you saw that. Did you happen to notice where the other person went, what they were doing?'

Lisa finally released her dressing gown and wiped her hands down her cheeks as though wiping away the memory. 'I saw them dart for a room upstairs, on the left side.' She indicated with a hand.

'So they didn't run down the stairs after Susan, didn't try to help her?'

'No.'

'And what did you do?' Grace asked carefully, without accusation.

'I carried on hiding, like a coward. It was only a minute, I promise, until the other girl found her. I nearly went out, I wanted to, but I knew what people would say, what they would think if I had been there. So I waited until there was enough of a commotion that I was able to slip out of the room. Then I joined the crowd and tried to help.'

Lisa looked as though she wanted to apologise, but she didn't.

'Thank you for your honesty, Lisa.' Grace reached to her side and from within the file, she pulled out a photo. 'Do you recognise this individual?'

Lisa looked at the picture and then at Grace. 'That's who I saw, the woman on the stairs. But if you knew it was her...?'

'I didn't up until just now. Once I knew that Jonny had made the call, I thought about our last meeting. It was something you said to me that got me thinking. You said, *"you've got the wrong woman,"* and at the time I didn't think anything of it but really it was a strange thing to say. Then it all fell into place. You said that because you knew.'

Lisa nodded.

Grace couldn't help the smile that had spread across her face. 'You have been exceedingly helpful.'

Grace rose to her feet and having said her goodbyes left Lisa alone. Once outside she called Harry to tell him that she was safe and that she knew who was responsible for Susan's fall.

'Fancy making an arrest?' she questioned excitedly. She didn't need to wait for his response, Grace could hear that Harry was already in his car.

44

GRACE

Grace waited impatiently in her car, outside of the suspect's address.

She knew she had enough to make the arrest, enough to get a conviction even. She had her eyewitness at last.

Harry turned up two minutes after Grace, pulling in right behind her vehicle.

Grace, full of anticipation, sprung from her car like a jack-in-the-box and was at his door before he'd even turned his engine off.

'Are you sure about this?' Harry asked as a way of a greeting. The corner of his mouth was quirked up to the side a fraction, he was trying to hide a smile. He could see that Grace was confident, he knew that they had enough too.

'As sure as I can be. Shall we?'

Silently they approached the door, despite the property being a flat, it had its own front door, which was better, Grace decided.

Grace pulled the cuffs from her pocket and held them tightly in her left hand.

With a final glance at Harry, who was stony-faced now, she

knocked on the door loudly. Three short sharp taps. If you were awake, you'd hear it.

Almost instantly a light was switched on.

She was awake.

It took another minute before they heard the unmistakable sound of a key being turned in the lock.

The door swung inwards.

'Jennifer Russell, I am arresting you on suspicion of the attempted murder of Susan Grey.'

45

———

MARTIN

BEFORE HE DIED

Martin remained in the kitchen, his eyes still darting from window to window. What was he expecting to see? He didn't know. He was convinced someone was out there, that she was out there, lurking behind a tree, spying on him, watching him.

He was sweating. His shirt felt uncomfortable. He was hot and cold at the same time.

The phone, with its taunting ring, had eventually stopped. She had called, time and time again. He never answered of course, aware that she wasn't calling out of the kindness of her heart but rather to threaten him, to extort him.

She obviously wasn't going to go away, the situation wasn't going to disappear on its own, he realised, but then that meant he needed to take action. Only, he wasn't a man of action but rather of thoughts and words.

He was morally culpable for his behaviour, for his heinous act, he knew, but perhaps if Susan had realised how less and less valuable he'd felt since his redundancy, how his loss of work had stripped him of his confidence, his self-worth, she might at the very least understand even if she couldn't forgive him.

He had been chucked on the scrap heap, labelled as old. They had believed him to be past his best. Out with the old and all of that. Of course, they had dressed it up neater than that, redundancy due to the strain the pandemic had had on the economy, on the company. But he had been one of only two to suffer that fate, everyone else had remained.

Martin paced as he ruminated on the past and on the present.

Susan's life here had continued to flourish whilst his had ultimately failed. He had been hiding, or was that drowning, his inadequacy in his drink, floundering with no sense of purpose.

It wasn't her fault what I did but perhaps it wouldn't have happened if she'd understood, if I'd told her the truth.

The truth.

That word sparked a tiny flame within Martin. The idea had never truly occurred to him, he had resented her for not understanding, but how could she if he'd never voiced his feeling, never explicitly said?

It was like someone switching the light on in an otherwise dark room. Martin instantly knew what he needed to do.

He hadn't wanted to wait until morning in case the sudden clarity he'd been experiencing dissolved.

Martin was driving with urgency, his foot resting a little firmer on the accelerator than usual. Having driven these roads for years, he felt at ease navigating his way through the twisty lanes of West Sussex.

His mind was preoccupied by the words he needed to say, the truths he needed to share with Susan. But most of all, the apology he needed to make. He had let them become estranged, he was jealous of her new-found life, her success, and rather than celebrating with her he had become distant and broody.

He knew she hadn't meant it when she'd said she wanted a divorce, she was angry, and who could blame her.

His mind drifted back to that night, to her parting words.

He hadn't seen it coming, hadn't realised how far apart they had slipped.

When she'd left, he was in shock not to mention furious. He remembered pulling the whisky bottle out of the drawer in his desk, his emergency bottle, a rather expensive Macallan single malt. He'd poured himself a double measure.

Martin slowed as he neared a junction. He indicated left. With no other cars on the road, he pulled out, increasing his speed once more. His resting leg bounced up and down incessantly with nothing else to do.

Beneath the canopy of the tree-lined road, the dim evening light became even more scarce. He turned on the headlights.

His mind floated back once more. He recalled downing his drink in one before refilling the tumbler instantly, the whisky bottle having remained gripped in his hand.

She wasn't going to leave him, he had told himself, she wouldn't. He had wanted to chase after her but he hadn't known what to say, his thoughts so tangled and twisted at the time.

That was when the door had opened.

He had honestly expected it to be Susan, for her to walk in and apologise for what she'd just thrown at him in the heat of the moment. But it wasn't.

He shivered at the memory.

Taking the next corner with more speed than Martin had realised he was doing, he drifted across the lane divider. He yanked the steering wheel, the tyres groaning, as he grappled to correct his mistake.

'Shit,' he breathed, shaking his head. Had there been an oncoming vehicle, that would have been a head-on collision.

With forced concentration, Martin watched the road ahead. Taking each corner a little more carefully. His knuckles turned white from the grip he held on the steering wheel.

But he couldn't stop the memory from unfolding, it was like a flower blooming beneath the summer sun.

The image of Jennifer as she'd peered nervously around the door, her eyes searching the room until they'd landed on him, took him back to that night once more.

She had smiled softly. 'Is everything okay?' she'd asked, moving into the room.

Martin had always made an effort with Jennifer, chatting to her at family gatherings, although they had been few and far between these past few years. They would find common ground talking about books and the news.

Beyond that she was something of an enigma. Older than Susan, but in some ways she was so much younger. She hadn't lived any sort of life, didn't seem to have any ambitions. But who was he to talk?

'I honestly don't know,' he had said, swigging at his whisky.

'Is there anything that I can do?'

Unbeknownst to Martin, Jennifer had moved closer, until she was standing barely an arm's length away from him.

Had she heard Susan's words, her threat of separation? If she had, she wasn't letting on.

Martin had shaken his head to dispel the thought. Picking up the whisky bottle, he held it aloft, in offering to Jennifer.

Surprisingly, she nodded. He'd eyed her suspiciously, but had poured her one anyway, before topping up his own glass. Why drown his sorrows alone?

He pushed the glass across to her, before turning around and leaning against the edge of the desk.

Taking the glass, Jennifer stood next to him, mimicking his stance.

'You know, Susan can be a bitch when she wants.'

Martin spluttered loudly. He had never heard Jennifer swear before, let alone in reference to Susan. He coughed, which turned into a half laugh.

Jennifer had, with her off-the-cuff comment, lightened the mood a fraction.

Perhaps noticing the shift in mood, Jennifer had smiled at Martin then. 'Honestly, you must have the patience of a saint to put up with her.'

'She certainly does have her moments.'

With the music from the party filling the space around them, they fell into a companionable silence for a breath, both sipping at their drinks, before Jennifer turned slightly towards Martin. He had looked up, aware of her eyes on him.

'She doesn't deserve you, you know? You could do so much better.'

It was as though she had been reading his thoughts. He had been thinking about how much he had given Susan over the years, all his love, his time, his energy. How he had put up with Joshua and his selfish ways for years, how he had supported Susan when she was selling her business, had stroked her hair when she'd cried from being stressed and exhausted. And what thanks had he got in return, the threat of a divorce. Not that Martin truly believed she had meant it. 'You might be right,' he'd finally agreed.

He hadn't seen it coming, or perhaps he had. Maybe she had leant in first or was it him? He couldn't remember now. He would like to think that it was Jennifer, that she had been the instigator, but in truth he wasn't sure.

Either way, they had kissed. It had been full of desire and passion and an electricity he hadn't experienced for years. Was it the thought of getting caught, or that it was Susan's sister, or was it something simpler, the knowing that someone wanted him, even if he hadn't exactly felt the same? He didn't know and in that moment he didn't care.

Martin's hands had been roaming freely, the whisky on her breath drawing him in. In his mind though he was imagining Susan, Susan from when they'd first met.

Jennifer's hands had clumsily slid down to his trousers, she had struggled with his belt, then the zip. As her fingers grazed the bare flesh of his stomach, slipped under the waistband of his boxers, a shock of reality sparked through him, it was as if he'd been struck by lightning.

He pushed Jennifer away instantly, realising the mistake he was making. This wasn't the answer, this wasn't what he wanted. Despite it all he still loved his wife, even if she didn't love him. And Jennifer could never compete with that, with her.

He knew that his face was twisted in disgust, disgust at himself for his actions, for this heinous transgression, at the immense mistake he knew he had just made. And Jennifer stood there, watching all of those emotions, those thoughts, flash across his face.

She had taken a step back, away from him. Hurt, anger, hatred burning in her eyes.

'Am I not good enough for you, not attractive enough or is it that I'm not rich enough?' she had spat at him, venom lacing each and every word. 'Do you think you can use me then throw me away like a piece of rubbish? You can't. Susan will never forgive you for this, I'll make sure of it.'

For the first time in a long time he had felt sober. The reality of what he'd done, shocking him awake. Martin had wanted to say something, to apologise maybe or to grovel, to beg Jennifer to forget that it had ever happened, to explain how low he had been and how out of character that had been for him. Only before any words had made it to his lips, Jennifer strode out of the office, pulling the door shut behind her.

He was so full of guilt, not only because of what he'd done but also because he hadn't heard Susan fall only minutes later. And why? Because he had been curled up in the corner of the room, a grown man, sobbing. Because he'd believed that he had just managed to put the final nail in the coffin that was his marriage, that there would be no convincing Susan to give him another chance, to forgive him. Because he was a broken man.

Martin was suddenly aware of his speed, the speedometer which had crept up and up. He gently eased his foot slightly off the pedal, aware that the last thing he needed was to be stopped for any reason. He was sure he wouldn't be over the limit but he had admittedly had a drink.

Not much further and he would be out of the country back roads and onto the main road, after that it was a mere twenty minutes.

He would tell Susan everything, would come clean. The nurses had assured him that she could hear his words. Jennifer would have nothing to hold over him then and he could tell the police the whole story. At the very least they would then be able to eliminate him from their investigation.

What would Susan think? What would she do? He wasn't entirely sure, that was a bridge they would have to address once she recovered, but he couldn't live with this secret any longer.

Driving around the next bend, Martin was instantly blinded by the beaming lights of an oncoming car. He attempted to shield his eyes, to block the brightness assaulting his vision. He released the steering wheel with one hand and threw it up in front of his face. 'Fucking hell.'

Just as quickly as it had happened, the offending vehicle with its full beams still in place, faded, driving on utterly oblivious of the effect they'd had on Martin.

In the rear-view mirror he watched the car as it gradually disappeared around a bend.

Too preoccupied by the selfishness of others, of the carelessness with which that particular individual was navigating these narrow lanes, Martin didn't notice the sharp turning creeping up on him.

He didn't have both hands in place on the wheel to divert the car back on course.

He also didn't have the lightning-fast reactions needed, the alcohol having dulled his senses, to steer the car safely past the hundred-year-old tree, rooted proudly on the verge beside the road.

Martin's eyes widened in horror as the tree advanced upon him.

The car, fixed in its direction, collided head-on.

A scream burst from Martin's mouth as he brought both hands up to protect his face.

The bonnet crumpled as easily as a piece of paper in an ear-piercing screech of metal as the tree held fast.

The windscreen shattered, raining shards of glass all around.

The car continued to fracture, continued to wrap itself around the tree's trunk. Martin, unable to move, surrendered himself as he thought only of Susan.

46

JENNIFER

Jennifer had been lying in bed, awake. She hadn't been stupid enough to think that what she had done would go unpunished.

She had laid awake in bed every night since the party, wracked with such mixed emotions, sometimes she felt guilty, albeit fleetingly, whilst other times she felt justified. Yet every morning when she rose, sleep-deprived and groggy, when she commenced her day, which was exactly the same as the day before, those feelings would dissolve until she was left with only rage and fury. Even knowing that Martin had died, Jennifer couldn't force herself to feel anything else, any remorse, her heart so black and angry.

They were all culpable for their own actions, Martin as much as anyone and yet things could have been so different.

Only tonight, instead of the silence which gave volume to her own whirling mind, there was a confident, firm knock at her door.

Jennifer had been waiting for it, had known that at some point, at some unsuspecting hour, they would come for her, they would work it all out.

And it would appear that tonight was to be that night.

She rose from her bed and draped her thickest dressing gown around her, suddenly cold.

Slowly, she padded out of the bedroom and towards the front door, her mind preoccupied with the events of Susan's party. For her, the night that changed everything whilst also changing absolutely nothing.

For so long, Jennifer's feelings for Martin had grown, blooming from a tiny seed, until they had stretched, rooted themselves into every part of her. She had believed that he was different, that he could see in her what everyone else chose to overlook; a strong, independent woman.

She wasn't stupid enough to think that he thought her to be attractive, she did, however, hope that he saw past her physical appearance, looked at what was hidden beneath. Her warmth, her love of literature, her sense of humour.

He would seek her out at gatherings, stand and talk to her like a human being. When she had called Susan at home, he would always ask how she was if ever he answered the phone, would take the time to listen to her. Jennifer suspected that he might just feel the same about her.

But then Martin had dismissed her, like every other man she had ever met. Only this had been so much worse, she had been vulnerable and alight with possibilities when they'd kissed. That was until he shoved her away, had looked down his nose at her with such disgust and shock that her heart had broken, that her cheeks had flushed with embarrassment and her eyes had started to fill with tears.

Jennifer hadn't planned to make a move on Martin but then there was a chain of events which seemed to change all of that.

She had gone in search of Susan, her guests were asking questions and with the house out of bounds, it seemed as though she was the person to find her. Also, Jennifer didn't mind admitting that she wanted to know what was going on for herself.

Jennifer had noted Christopher departing through the kitchen doors as she made her way to the house. He didn't see her. People often didn't.

She had followed the voices until she'd found herself upstairs on the landing outside the study. She should have gone in, should have made her presence known to them, but she didn't. Jennifer had instead remained outside, standing to the side of the door which was ajar, shrouded in the darkness of the corridor. She hid and she listened.

She had heard every hurtful word that they threw at each other.

Joshua had left first, storming off like the petulant child that he was. Jennifer had never really liked him. He was the complete opposite of her, he was vain and superficial, rash and hasty. She always sent him birthday and Christmas cards of course, but she had never spent more than a few minutes with him alone, even when he was little, had never seemed to bond with him.

Then she'd heard Susan's cutting words, the way she'd cast Martin aside, the exact same way that Jennifer had been cast aside by others, the way Susan was about to cast her away when she sold the shop, before she too stormed out of the room, leaving Martin alone.

Neither Joshua nor Susan saw her, she was very good at being invisible. The blackness of the house helped, of course.

Fuelled with a confidence Jennifer only experienced when she'd consumed any alcohol, which admittedly was exceedingly rare, and with a self-assuredness that Martin understood her, that he needed her now, she went in.

And that was where it all went so right before it all went so wrong.

Jennifer truly believed that Susan didn't deserve Martin, he was a more gentle soul than she was. Susan should have remained with Christopher, it was clear to everyone except Susan that they were supposed to be together. Martin, however, needed someone more reserved, someone who, like him, was quiet and thoughtful, someone like Jennifer.

After a few minutes, she had managed to raise a smile from him and he hadn't disagreed when she'd suggested that he could do better than her sister. And it was in that moment that Jennifer thought that he might have some feelings for her, perhaps not as strong as Jennifer's but feelings nonetheless.

She had leant in and kissed him.

And after a moment he had kissed her back.

For thirty seconds, it had been everything she had hoped it would be, hot and passionate and all-consuming, everything the books made it out to be. Only, it had been short-lived. Martin had drawn back from her sharply, as though he had been shot. Jennifer unexpectedly found herself looking at the contorted face of a man she didn't recognise, a man full of fear and disgust.

He was looking at her as though she was a monster, a hideous freak of a creature.

All those feelings of love and admiration she'd quietly nurtured blackened instantly, enveloped into the rage and anger which had built up within her over the years, an inky mass of hate for every look, every comment, every time she was ignored. And instead of quelling it, instead of pushing it down like she had done so many times in the past, she let some of it out.

Her words had stung, she realised, but that wasn't enough, wasn't nearly enough. So she'd threatened him. She wanted Martin to be afraid, to be tortured for a time, for how he'd rejected her and humiliated her. She wanted him to feel just a fraction of what she felt.

Before he could beg her to rescind the threat, she had fled, only she couldn't go back to the party, not when her tears had started to flow freely. Rather than heading for the stairs, she turned to the left, pushing into one of the many spare bedrooms that this house had.

She had wanted to collect herself. She never liked anyone to see her cry, to see her weak.

She had been furious, pacing the room like a caged bear. Why hadn't he wanted her? What was it about Susan that had men falling over themselves? A thousand dark thoughts consumed her, the oily hatred boiling to the surface.

No, she'd had more that she needed to say to Martin. She didn't want him to be able to walk away from this scot-free, not when she wouldn't. She would be forever changed.

She had pulled open the door, ready to confront Martin further, when she had caught sight of her sister, her glittering dress sparkling brightly despite the dark.

Even that, the way her dress lit up the space, irritated Jennifer. Did nothing ever go wrong for Susan?

Edging forward silently, Jennifer had watched her sister as she'd paused at the grand window, looking out to the party, her party, all the people who had made an effort for her. It was as if nothing was amiss, as if she hadn't just ended a marriage, and ruined her sister's life in the process.

Yes, it was Susan's fault, Jennifer had realised in that moment.

If she had never thrown that word, divorce, at Martin, Jennifer would have never acted on her feelings, feelings which had made her feel stupid and unattractive and hurt.

It was *all* Susan's fault.

She was going to sell the business, leave Jennifer without a job, an income, she was going to take away the only thing in her life that she loved. She had it all and it was never enough for

Susan. She was going to discard Jennifer, the way she had discarded Martin and before that, Christopher.

It was as Susan began her descent, having once again failed to notice Jennifer lingering in the shadows, that Jennifer's rage bubbled over the edge, a volcano of emotions erupting with such fury that there was no possibility of containing it.

Jennifer had rushed forward, her sandals barely registering on the floor, only Susan had heard her, had begun to turn.

Jennifer couldn't see for her rage, however, couldn't stop herself. She had charged towards her sister, hands raised. She'd wanted Susan to suffer the way she had been suffering.

As she was upon Susan, Jennifer channelled all those pent-up feelings, all the reaching tendrils of hurt and shoved Susan with as much force as she could muster. More even.

Susan tumbled, falling down the stairs. Her body hit each and every step, her glass shattering, orange liquid splashing everywhere, a shoe flying off.

Susan screamed. She cried out.

All the while Jennifer stood motionless, only her chest heaved up and down.

She had felt strangely detached, as though it was something she was watching on the television, something someone else had done. She had disassociated herself with the incident, with the twisted and broken body lying at the base of the stairs.

Jennifer knew that she should've felt remorse, guilt-stricken even, knew that she should've run down those same stairs to help her sister, but she hadn't, all of those normal, expected emotions having abandoned her.

Instead, she felt satisfied, powerful even.

It was only her fear of being caught that made her move. Collecting herself, she darted away from the scene before she was spotted. She hadn't consciously known where she was going and yet she headed straight for the back stairs. A staircase disguised as nothing more than a section of panelled wall, a little like the cupboards downstairs. It was only visible if you knew it was there. Susan hadn't ever liked this feature, claiming they were too dangerous to use, but she had told Jennifer about them, showing her once. And Jennifer had remembered.

This exit had all but been forgotten about in favour of the ostentatious grand staircase. She'd made the narrow descent, originally designed for servants to use, spiderwebs and dust lining the walls, before she peered out into the empty utility room. The door obscured by shelving opened inwards.

As she moved into the kitchen, no one noticed her. No one even looked up as she strode outside.

No one had even noticed that she'd disappeared for a time.

Perhaps being invisible had its perks, she had thought to herself as she took her seat in the marquee and picked up her drink.

Only she clearly hadn't been as invisible as she'd believed.

Detective Roth was standing at Jennifer's front door, handcuffs held aloft in her hand and a look of knowing on her face.

Jennifer didn't know how she knew, but she did.

She hadn't gotten away with it, Jennifer realised in that moment. And she also realised that she was okay with that. She didn't want to be unseen any longer, she wanted everyone to know what she'd done and why.

She wanted everyone to see her.

47

GRACE

FIVE DAYS AFTER JENNIFER'S ARREST

Grace was at her desk, scanning through her final report.

She was relieved to be able to add that as of this morning when she had called the hospital for an update, Susan was awake.

It was obviously very early days in her recovery but the nurse had been positive, reporting that Susan had said a few words and seemed to have retained most if not all of her memories, although time would tell.

Grace would, in due course, interview Susan, but she would wait until Susan was further along the road to recovery. After all, there was no rush.

Grace had also found herself delighted and not at all surprised when she had been informed that Christopher Maddison had remained a permanent presence beside Susan's bed for the past several days. The nurse had even suggested that this may have been the connection, the motivator that Susan had needed.

As far as Grace was aware, no one had informed Susan that it had been her own sister, Jennifer, who had been the perpetrator of this hateful crime.

And if Grace was being honest, she was still struggling to comprehend that fact herself. But then this job continued to find ways of surprising Grace.

Grace shook her head lightly as she recalled Jennifer's interview.

Jennifer hadn't held back, she had told Grace and Harry everything they had wanted to know, obviously against the advice of her concerned and rather frustrated-looking solicitor. It was almost as though she was proud of herself, of her actions.

And then there was the staircase, the servants' one. That had been an utter shock to them both. Grace had had to admit that no one on her team had noticed a second stairway during their search, but that was the point, wasn't it? That it wasn't seen.

Grace and Harry had revisited the house, of course. And sure enough, there it was in plain sight, or not. A second staircase. The perfect exit for their assailant.

Still, they had their woman. A sad, sour woman at that.

Grace had been advised by the CPS that the case would likely be tried as grievous bodily harm, rather than attempted murder as they couldn't prove intent. Despite revelling in the incident, Jennifer had never admitted that she had planned to kill Susan, only that she had wanted to hurt her, to cause her some pain.

Grace was still hopeful though that owing to Jennifer's lack of remorse, a judge might just serve her a lengthier sentence.

Still, she had actually solved it, the case that wasn't even a case, the case without any evidence, any forensics.

And in doing so Grace believed that had cemented her place in the team, not to mention restoring her confidence.

Grace's phone, which was beside her on the desk, rang. She picked it up. 'Hi, Dad.'

'Hi, pumpkin. You sound happier.'

'Do I?'

'Yes you do. Did you find that proverbial needle?'

Grace smiled to herself. 'Yes I did.'

'I knew you would. Well done. Will you tell me about it on Sunday, at lunch?'

'Of course, Dad.' Grace's gaze drifted upwards then, towards Harry who was also finishing up his report. He had mentioned that he was at a loose end this weekend. 'Would it be all right if I brought a friend?'

Her dad didn't respond straight away and then in a rush of words replied, 'A friend. Yes of course, how lovely. In that case, I have just the recipe I want to try–'

'Dad,' Grace interrupted, 'don't do anything too weird, okay?'

'I don't know what you mean,' her dad responded. Grace could hear the smile in his voice. 'I will see you and your friend on Sunday.'

'Bye, Dad.'

Grace replaced her phone and was just about to shout across to Harry when DCI Potter strode into the room holding a file.

She had a look of concern etched into her face.

'Roth. Amberidge. I need you both on this one immediately. We have just received a report of a kidnapping, a fourteen-year-old girl is missing and she is the daughter of some very influential people.'

Grace's heart thumped loudly in her chest and she stood up and grasped hold of the file in DCI Potter's outstretched hand.

THE END

ACKNOWLEDGEMENTS

Thank you to all the readers out there, you have made my hope of being an author a reality.

I also want to say a massive thank you to Betsy Reavley and the fantastic team at Bloodhound Books for once again seeing the potential in my manuscript.

To Shirley Khan, my editor, thank you for your guidance and support.

To Kelly Nicholson, my wonderful, supportive friend. You don't know how much I appreciate your kind words, your encouragement and your enthusiasm for my books.

But, as always, my biggest thanks goes to my family, to my husband, Dean and my two boys, Heath and Eden. Thank you for your never-ending support, your love and your proof-reading skills.